Italian Literature and Thought Series

*The Italian Literature and Thought Series makes available in English repre-
sentative works of Italian culture. Although the series focuses on the modern
and contemporary periods, it does not neglect the humanistic roots of Italian
thought. The series includes monographs, anthologies, and critically updated
republications of canonical works, as well as works of general interest.*

Italian Tales

An Anthology of Contemporary Italian Fiction

Edited by Massimo Riva

YALE UNIVERSITY PRESS   NEW HAVEN & LONDON

Designed by Rebecca Gibb. Set in Janson type by Integrated Publishing Solutions.
Printed in the United States of America.

Library of Congress Cataloging-in-Publication Data
Italian tales : an anthology of contemporary Italian fiction / edited by Massimo Riva.
p. cm.—(Italian literature and thought series)
Includes bibligraphical references.
ISBN 0-300-09530-9
1. Short stories, Italian—Translations into English.   2. Italian fiction—21st
century—Translations into English.   I. Riva, Massimo.   II. Series.
PQ4257.E5I84   2004
853'.0108092—dc22
2004042281

A catalogue record for this book is available from the British Library.
The paper in this book meets the guidelines for permanence and durability
of the Committee on Production Guidelines for Book Longevity
of the Council on Library Resources.

10 9 8 7 6 5 4 3 2 1

Contents

Acknowledgments

~~~~~~~~~~

An ANTHOLOGY is a collective enterprise, as I came to realize over the years I worked on this project. Among the people I would like to publicly acknowledge for their contribution to one aspect or another of the final product: my longtime colleague in the Italian Department at Brown University and fine translator Anthony Oldcorn, especially for the two pieces he translated and generously contributed to this work; various editors at Yale University Press, including in particular Jonathan Brent and John Kulka; the director of the Yale Italian Series (and one of the writers included here), Paolo Valesio; my manuscript editor, Eliza Childs; and the anonymous readers who provided critical insight and helpful suggestions. Finally, thanks to Brown University for providing financial support. My debt to my wife, Lesley, my in-house editor and the real coauthor of all my work, goes beyond gratitude.

Introduction

Mapping Contemporary Italian Fiction

Language, Identity, and Translation

This anthology is both a sort of literary map and a travelogue meant to guide the American reader through the changing territory of contemporary Italian fiction. The world we live in is reorienting itself, redrawing its coordinates and boundaries, be they natural, social, or imaginary. The metaphor of the writer as a cartographer of a virtual dimension—parallel in space and time to the one we all inhabit—is thus particularly apt in describing the work of writing fiction at the end of a millennium that, in the words of Italo Calvino, "has seen the birth and development of the modern languages of the West, and of the literatures that have explored the expressive, cognitive and imaginative possibilities of these languages."[1]

Despite their wide range of styles and inflections, the eighteen writers collected here all share a fairly standardized Italian idiom, which is remarkable given that in the 1860s, at the time of political unification, roughly 75 percent of the population did not write or speak Italian. A century and a half later and after the advent of radio, cinema, and television, linguistic unification is an acquired fact for Italy, the realization of a goal set by its literary elites as far back as Dante Alighieri's *De Vulgari Eloquentia* in 1303–4. Yet, while spoken Italian is undoubtedly replacing local dialects, Italians still alternate between the "national" Italian language and their native dialects when talking to family and friends (and to a lesser degree, strangers).[2] For centuries Italian was primarily a written language, the expression of a cultural elite. This is no longer true. But as critic Lino Pertile has observed, "The written word had not managed to establish itself as an integral part of Italian popular culture before it was overtaken and replaced by audio-visual communication."[3] As a result, Italian authors still write for a relatively small minority of Italian readers, and their writing is increasingly affected by the context of a mass-mediated culture.[4]

From this and many other points of view, the year 1976 represents a watershed in recent Italian history. That year saw the official deregulation of the Italian airwaves, which, as film scholar Millicent Marcus writes, "sent Italy on a televisual binge," preparing the way for the political ascent of media tycoon Silvio Berlusconi.[5] The audiovisual revolution also helped perpetuate the old dilemma of cultural elitism, as literary Italian now had to protect its domain against the invasive "national-popular" language of television.[6] Reconciling the (spoken) dialect and the (written) language may no longer be the Italian writer's major stylistic preoccupation, as it was, with markedly different results, for the generations of Giovanni Verga (1840–1922), Carlo Emilio Gadda (1893–1973), or Pier Paolo Pasolini (1922–75).[7] Yet such remarkable recent works as the Neapolitan author Erri De Luca's *Montedidio* (an excerpt is included here) show that the expressive tension between regional dialect and national language still runs high, particularly (but by no means exclusively) for southern Italian writers.[8]

This internal dilemma of a split linguistic and literary identity must be seen today within a larger context. If Alessandro Manzoni (1785–1873), the author of the most influential nineteenth-century Italian novel *I promessi sposi* (*The Betrothed*), were to return today to the Ponte Vecchio in Florence "to wash his linguistic rags in the Arno river" (i.e., the Florentine vernacular), he would hear a cacophony of pidgin Italian, American English, German, Spanish, and Japanese. More than ever before in its long history, Italy is a popular destination—if only in the guise of that "virtual" country portrayed in such recent examples of cultural grand tourism as the books of Frances Mayes (*Under the Tuscan Sun* and *Bella Tuscany*). To be sure, the Florentine parlance may still be heard in the streets, spoken by artisans or merchants catering to foreigners buying leather goods, jewelry, scarves, shoes, or souvenirs, but its sound is often mixed with the African languages or dialects spoken by immigrant street peddlers. And as immigrant communities take root within Italy, a new "migration literature" is emerging.[9] This, in short, is Italy in the age of globalization; this is the context in which the storytellers collected here are writing.

Italian writers and their readers (especially those belonging to younger generations) may increasingly be Italian (and not Sicilian or Neapolitan) native speakers, but like most of their contemporaries, they are also awash in the lingua franca of a global media culture. True, local idioms are increasingly contaminated (some would say outright polluted) by linguistic imports and hybrids of all sorts. Yet they are also paradoxically energized by such global "sampling."[10] Such phenomena, however, go well beyond traditional literary confines: an appropriate example is a recent anthology of Italian rap, *Potere alla parola* (*Power to the Word*) introduced by the popular rapper Jovanotti with an essay entitled "La musica della razza urbane" (The Music of the Urban Race).[11] According to Jovanotti, rap as an import effectively provides a bridge between local dialect culture (most of the texts included are in dialects from various regions of the Italian peninsula) and transnational urban rhythms.

Another striking consequence of globalization is the demographic recentering of the world literary map. Paradoxically, at a time when Italian is finally becoming the linguistic medium of a "national" culture, rather than just the sum of regional subcultures, this historical "modern" language of the West is spoken, written, and read by a very small minority on a global scale. The contemporary Italian writer belongs to an endangered species. (For the past ten years, deaths have outnumbered births in the Italian population.) This amounts to an erosion of the very idea of a "national" literature. On the one hand, it is easy to agree with the general assessment that "Contemporary Italian literature is not only Italian but also international as far as its geographical referents are concerned, as befits an increasingly homogenized but still multicultural world."[12] On the other, the Italian writer is in a position far different from that of a writer belonging to the Hispanic or French, let alone English, linguistic worlds (to speak only of those languages that traditionally represent Western culture). Although there are many communities of Italians living abroad, Italian literature does not have the postcolonial range and reach of these languages. On the contrary, Italy may increasingly become a community of immigrants and transients—students, pilgrims, and tourists (a trend accelerated by the process of European unification)—and the future of Italian writing may indeed reside in a creative encounter between "native" and immigrant talents.

Inhabiting the new global, Babel-like milieu thus renews an old dilemma for Italian writers: the question of a national identity that, as a late acquisition in Italian history, was often transformed (by writers) into an exquisitely literary issue—the issue of a place, a country that needed to be invented in words.[13] And yet, not only do so-called national literatures continue to exist as long as their languages are spoken, written, and read by a community (no matter how small or geographically dispersed), but, paradoxically, they also exist only as long as there is a global background against which to appreciate their differences.

In this context, local idioms come necessarily to rely ever more upon translation. Translation into a foreign language—English most prominently, as a "global" language—is proof of the (literary) existence of contemporary Italy, just as works written in (Tuscan) Italian provided proof of a national identity before the country's political unification.

The End of History (and the Novel)

Most of the pieces collected here were written or published during a time of dramatic change in the Italian (and European) social and political landscape. From the leaden years of terrorism (1970s) to the "golden" years of economic affluence and political corruption (1980s), up to the "deconstruction" of the 1990s,[14] Italy has been a nation in turmoil, a place where rapid and dramatic modernization could not entirely loosen the grip of a stubbornly persistent past.[15]

Against this historical backdrop, the 1980s, in particular, gave rise to an explosion of published fiction and the emergence of prominent new writers, some of whom are included in this collection (Celati, Del Giudice, and Tabucchi, for example). Although I do not wish to suggest that fiction flourishes only in either connection or reaction to social, political, and environmental upheaval, postwar Italian culture has often followed precisely this trend.[16] In short, in the 1980s the collective dramas and ideologies of the Cold War were replaced by "a profound disillusionment with public life, radicalism and what used to be called History." A general retreat into individual private lives as "the only safe area for the novel to explore" is undoubtedly symptomatic of such a collective disillusionment.[17]

I would point again to the watershed in contemporary Italian culture, marked by the deregulation of the airwaves in the mid-1970s and further characterize it in a sentence (paraphrasing both Melville and Fukuyama): in the end (of history) is our beginning. The history supposedly coming to an end is the history of the modern novel, whose demise also marks the beginning of a new age of storytelling. Yet according to some critics, in the mid-1970s we also find the roots of a conservative narrative movement, a restoration of more traditional "narrative codes."[18] Of course, such ambivalent interplay between tradition and innovation (the continuous reinvention of tradition) has been a characteristic peculiar to Italian culture since the Renaissance. Most striking from this point of view is the revival of the historical novel in a contemporary context.

Consider, for example, a novel published in Italy in 1974 by the most important female writer of her generation. Even before its publication as a whole (excerpts had appeared in the high-circulation weekly *L'Espresso*), Elsa Morante's *La Storia* (*History: A Novel*, the word *storia* being translatable as both *history* and *story*) became the center of a controversy over "popular" or "populist" counterhistory. Morante's novel tells the story of a group of humble characters during World War II and can be read as an anti-epic: the indictment of *history* from the point of view of its powerless victims (women and children).[19] History, according to Morante, is "a scandal that lasted for ten thousand years"; and yet her novel effectively reaffirms the centrality of history and rebuffs the postmodernist ideology of the end of history (and the end of ideologies). As an example of fictional antihistory, *La Storia* was also the emblematic expression of a peculiarly Italian crisis: the crisis of the intimate link, in the Italian neorealist tradition, between the novel as a *genre* and its didactic or ideological public role.[20]

Another striking example of this crisis is the experimental novel *Petrolio* (*Petrol*) by Pier Paolo Pasolini, left unfinished at his untimely death in 1975 and posthumously (and controversially) published in 1990 in a "metaphilological" edition (translated from the Italian by Ann Goldstein). Pasolini's book, stylistically split like its protagonist and narrator (Carlo 1, an executive of ENI, the Italian national oil company, and Carlo 2, his sex-obsessed and unregenerate alter ego), part autobiographic narrative, part fictional chronicle, part metaliterary exercise, and part apocalyptic vision, marks the return to the novel of this acclaimed poet and filmmaker. Yet in its mixture of fiction and nonfiction, *Petrolio* is also symbolic (like *La Storia*) of both the crisis of the novel as public discourse and of its renewed fertility as a form of critical (narrative) realism.[21]

Pasolini's antinovel, had he lived to complete it, would have presumably reached the public at the same time as the best-selling novels by Italo Calvino (*If on a Winter's Night a Traveler*, 1979) and Umberto Eco (*The Name of the Rose*, 1980), two books well known to American readers and widely considered foremost examples of "postmodern" narrative. The Calvino and Eco brand of postmodernism is certainly better known abroad (in the United States at least) than Pasolini's posthumous narrative hodgepodge. Yet critical attention to Pasolini is significant and has come to symbolize the persistence of what we may call a southern (Mediterranean) perspective—a resistance to mass-mediated globalization in the name of what is left of marginal realities. Indeed, Pasolini and Calvino, with their opposite responses to the crisis of neorealism as an all-encompassing narrative code, have come to symbolize no less than two alternative conceptions of literature in recent Italian critical debates.[22] That Italian culture could produce *both* at the same time is symptomatic of its deep internal divide.

Within this rapid sketch, one could pose the hypothesis that the "renaissance" of fiction writing in the early 1980s—in the wake of the widespread success of Calvino's and Eco's postmodern novels—was actually an escapist turn in a culture like that of Italy, overburdened by both a reality and a history often stranger than fiction.[23] An even more direct connection could perhaps be drawn between the economic, social, and cultural context of the early 1980s and this so-called renaissance of fiction, fostered, as it was, by a powerful cultural industry. The end of the state monopoly on information in 1976 soon led, after all, to the creation of large conglomerates that controlled traditionally separate media and institutions, including "literary awards, daily newspapers, weekly and monthly magazines, radio stations, television networks and film production."[24] Thanks to this powerful cultural industry, a new and enlarged reading public came along right at the moment when "confidence in the large-scale ideological discourses for which the novel [from the nineteenth century up to neorealism] acted as vehicle [had] gone."[25] The distaste for the invasive stereotypes of mass media culture and the opportunity to reach a potentially larger readership may also help explain the paradoxical coexistence—within the same context and sometimes within the same author—of both traditional (even retro) narrative codes and innovative, experimental writing styles.

From this point of view, Calvino and Eco can provide, at least theoretically, the models against which to measure the work of a variety of lesser-known yet no less remarkable writers. In their unique ability to combine tradition and innovation, metanarrative experimentation, and linear storytelling, *If on a Winter's Night a Traveler* and *The Name of the Rose* best represent the end of one literary era and the beginning of another.[26] Particularly crucial to both works was the weakening of the "traditional rigid demarcations between 'high' and 'low,' 'cultivated' and 'popular' in Italian culture," as noted by critic Michael Caesar, the creative *montage* of various popular genres (detective story, feuilleton, etc.), and finally, the translation into narrative of "a language that was capable of speaking of culture as a whole . . . that of semiotics."[27] Not only were they written in a standard literary Italian which seemed to have definitively shed its most idiomatic features (while subtly parodying the contemporary contamination of a media-influenced idiom); not only did they present themselves as best-selling leaders of a transnational trend (that is, again, postmodernism); but they also presented themselves as two skeptical yet entertaining essays on the death and rebirth of the novel as an epistemological or cognitive enterprise.[28]

There is, however, a decisive difference between these two major postmodern authors: whereas Eco, after *The Name of the Rose*, clearly moved toward the intellectual parody of a traditional type of historical and "popular" novel (*Foucault's Pendulum*, *The Island of the Day Before*, and *Baudolino*), Calvino, after producing the parody and antimodel of *If on a Winter's Night*, moved decisively in the direction of decomposition and fragmentation, toward a new level of observation and engagement with the shifting surface of the world (*Mr. Palomar*)—at a "degree zero" of narrative realism.

At the crossroads between historical and semiotic narratives, fiction and nonfiction (or metafiction), stylistically stretched between a critical (often ironic) revisiting of the past and a keen (often ironic) observation of the present, between a return to traditional *genres* and the exploration of new forms and styles, the pieces collected here are rooted in the end of one of the great literary traditions of the West.

"New" Writers

In a book on the "new Italian narrative" published in the mid-1990s, critic Filippo La Porta characterized some of the writers who emerged in the early 1980s as "the cloven Calvino" (an allusion to *The Cloven Viscount*, one of Calvino's tales from the trilogy *Our Ancestors*, written in the 1950s).[29] This collection should prove that there is far more on the map of contemporary Italian fiction than a *cloven* (or cloned) Calvino or a best-selling Umberto Eco. As the best-known and most translated Italian novelists of their generation, Calvino and Eco themselves are not included here, so as to make room for their lesser-known yet no less worthy peers. Yet in making my selections, I have tried to resist novelty as a value in and of itself.[30] Rather, what I offer here is a sample of more established and seasoned literary practitioners, writers who have been active on the Italian literary scene for the past two or three decades (or longer): their work, in my opinion, represents some of the most enduring values in contemporary Italian writing. Obviously, no anthology can be truly objective or comprehensive. Choices and exclusions are always difficult and painful, and they are often dictated by circumstances that have little to do with one's actual critical preferences or tastes (the availability of good translations, above all). As vulnerable as any anthologist inevitably is to criticism, it is important that I clarify as precisely as possible the guiding principles of this book.

Not only do the eighteen authors collected here best reflect, in my opinion, the persistence of a literary tradition, with its fundamental stylistic values, they also exemplify the characteristic multiplicity and displacement of contemporary writing, what I would call its "nomadic" quality. In an era characterized by cultural diasporas of every kind, contemporary Italian writers are both at home and abroad in their own language, forced to renegotiate their own identity and find their own voices. I have divided the selected pieces into four sections ("Ruins with a View," "Memory Lanes," "Vanishing Points," "Views from Afar"). With each selection I have included a short sketch of its author. In keeping with the leitmotif of mapping, I have grouped seemingly dissimilar pieces under these titles according to subtle similarities in vision; in many of the following pieces the most intimate sense of place often becomes the most abstract view from afar, while even the most literary perspective has the intellectual, and emotional, intensity of the search for home. This "pathos of distance" is the essence of nomadic writing. If these writers have something in common, it is the way in which they all give expression to a shared contemporary condition: stranded in no-man's-land, suspended between the end of one literary tradition and the beginning of another, they all explore a new way of seeing, of exploring (and inhabiting) the world, with words. It seems appropriate, for instance, that a culture so sophisticated in matters of vision and representation as the Italian would, at the end of a century in which literature has been challenged by the explosion of other, apparently more powerful representational and visual technologies, produce narratives that focus on the paradoxes of representation and vision. And it seems equally appropriate that a culture traditionally characterized by a hyper sense of time and history, memory and identity, would, at the end of a century in which history has betrayed all expectations, produce narratives that focus on lost identities or a buried past. This characteristic ambivalence may also be inspired by the peculiar quality of contemporary Italian landscapes (and cityscapes), which, with their uneasy, multilayered coexistence of both the old and the new, the perennial and the perishable, the virtual and the real, foster in writers a sort of hyperenvironmental self-awareness and, at the same time, a highly fictional sense of reality.

Reading the vastly different pieces collected here may simply confirm that we are far from that communal, "anonymous voice of the age, stronger than individual inflections" that Italo Calvino spoke of in 1964 while retrospectively describing the postwar neorealist experience.[31] Indeed, the contemporary renaissance of fiction writing in Italy cannot be compared to the collective *moral* rebirth experienced by Calvino's generation. It does, however, bring to mind another image he used in the same 1964 preface to his first novel (*The Path to the Nest of Spiders*, 1949): a "cacophony of voices," all expressing, in different ways, a mystifying experience, a common fin de siècle ethos, the search for a new way of looking at and finding oneself in the world—through writing. The eighteen authors included here belong to a transitional period, between the old century and the new, the old Italy and the newly deconstructed Italy. And although they share a unified literary idiom, they betray their origins readily. One can detect the specific regional heritage that affects the pitch of their prose: the "baroque" Sicilian subtext of Bufalino, the Emilian koine of Celati, the Lombard intonation of Vassalli, the Neapolitan inflection of De Luca, all reflect the polyphonic quality of an Italian culture rooted in Europe and yet anchored deeply in the southern Mediterranean basin. For some, such as Anna Maria Ortese, a personal quest results in the creation of a pan-Mediterranean tongue original to the point of idiosyncrasy. Intentionally included here are also a few writers (Pasinetti, Ferrucci, and Valesio) who have lived abroad for much of their lives and thus write as modern transatlantic nomads between two languages, Italian and English (the two languages of their professions, since these writers have all been professors of Italian literature at American universities).

What finally emerges from this *contrappunto*, this polyphony of narrative styles and voices? Lightness, quickness, exactitude, visibility, and multiplicity—five of the six qualities or values that Italo Calvino would have liked to see preserved for the next millennium—are certainly more detectable on the map of contemporary Italian fiction than his last, lost sixth quality, consistency. (These are the titles of Calvino's *Six Memos for the Next Millennium. Consistency* was never written because of Calvino's premature death in 1985.) The fragmentary narratives collected here may represent only an approximation of those values; these writers after all are still contemporaries of Calvino (and Eco). They are not the entirely new generation

that will come of age in the new millennium, yet they are all witnesses (to the extent allowed by translation) to the great variety and
vitality of the written word in the late twentieth-century Italian
idiom, the culmination of seven centuries of expressive and cognitive explorations.

It might take an entirely new technology of writing, beyond the
boundaries of any local idiom, perhaps more reliant on images and
sounds than written words (or an unprecedented hybridization of all
three), to incarnate in its entirety Calvino's utopian prescriptions.
Or perhaps his "memos" will remain the musings of a late modern
master, the last of an entire generation. Yet Calvino's somewhat paradoxical legacy best sums up, in my view, the universal plight of his
fellow writers, faced with the uneasy task of finding, if not a center,
at least a point of balance in the whirlpool of stories that continues
to reflect our uniquely human condition.

NOTES

1. Italo Calvino, *Six Memos for the Next Millennium*, trans. W. Weaver (New
   York: Vintage, 1988), preface.
2. According to a survey conducted by the linguist Tullio De Mauro, in the
   early 1990s, only 38 percent of the Italian population speak solely Italian all
   the time; thirteen other languages are still spoken on the peninsula (by historical minorities, not including more recent immigrant communities); 60
   percent of the people speak one of roughly a dozen dialects and 14 percent
   speak only or mostly dialect. (These percentages have not significantly
   changed in the last decade.) Tullio De Mauro, "Lingua e dialetti," in *Stato
   dell'Italia*, ed. Paul Ginsborg (Milan: Saggiatore, 1994), 61–62. Even today,
   ten years after De Mauro's survey and a few years into the twenty-first century, according to a 2002 report of the ISTAT (Central Institute of Statis-

tics), only 44 percent of the population over age six (approximately 24 million) speak Italian at home. This percentage grows for relationships outside the family (48 percent speak Italian with friends and even more so with strangers, 72.7 percent). Of Italians aged six or older, 19.1 percent use mostly dialect within the family, but only 16 percent with friends, and a meager 6.8 percent with strangers. In other words, 92.3 percent of Italians (a full percentage point more than in 1995) speak mostly Italian, alternating it with dialect in at least one of the contexts mentioned (with family, friends, or strangers). Yet 56.1 percent (the same percentage as in 1995) speak exclusively or mostly dialect in at least one of these contexts (usually within the family). Even if dialect continues to hold on as the familial tongue, Italian is now firmly established as social vehicle.

3. Lino Pertile, "The Italian Novel Today: Politics, Language, Literature," intro. to *The New Italian Novel*, ed. Zygmunt G. Baranski and Lino Pertile (Edinburgh: Edinburgh University Press, 1993), 14.

4. Even the most optimistic recent statistical data do not support the thesis that Italy is closing the gap (within Europe) with more developed reading countries like Germany or France: in 1984, according to ISTAT, 46.4 percent of Italians had "at least minimal contact with a book," yet in 1995, according to a poll by Doxa/Sole 24 ore, Italian readers represent only 49.5 percent of the population. See Pierfrancesco Attanasio and Elisabetta Carfagna, "L'enigma dei lettori," in *Tirature 98: Autori, Editori, Pubblico* (Milan: Fondazione Mondadori, 1997), 172–78.

5. M. Marcus, *After Fellini: National Cinema in the Postmodern Age* (Baltimore: Johns Hopkins University Press, 2002), 4–5.

6. If, for example, before the advent of the mass media in the late 1950s, "neorealist" writers pitched language at a lower, accessible level in order to bridge the gap between the spoken and the written word, as Pertile writes, "the writers of the 1980s pitch it high to avoid the trap of uniformity and indistinctiveness set by the media." Yet while one can agree with Pertile that the average quality of contemporary Italian writing is high, one can only partially agree with his observation that today's consensus seems to be "for a *modern* language that does not reside anywhere in particular": in other words, a literary language without easily detectable vernacular or regional undertones. "The contemporary literary scene in Italy is rather exciting precisely because the writer no longer feels bound for a destination that has been fixed in advance by someone else. Now that the linguistic divide between writer

and reader has been all but bridged, the writer's allegiance and responsibility need only be to literature. This awareness is limiting but is also liberating" ("Italian Novel Today," 18).

7. A late nineteenth-century master of *verismo* (naturalism), the Sicilian Giovanni Verga emigrated to Milan but explored his origins with the eye (and the linguistic tools) of a cultural anthropologist. His major novels, *I Malavoglia* and *Mastro Don Gesualdo*, are family sagas set in the fishing community of Trezza, near his birthplace, Catania. Verga's characters speak an Italian "translated" from their Sicilian dialect. As the work of the twentieth-century masters Carlo Emilio Gadda and Pier Paolo Pasolini also exemplifies, experimentalism and realism are closely intertwined in Italian modernism (another example is literary and cinematic neorealism, a peculiarly Italian avant-garde phenomenon). Both Milan-born Gadda and Friuli-born Pasolini set their experiments with the novel in Rome, the capital of the republic, the ideal center of the nation, yet with opposite results: Roman dialect was for Gadda a vital expressive source, a vehicle for a corrosive critique of bureaucratic Italian jargon, symbol of a state artificially imposed (by Fascism) on the everyday life and culture of its citizens (*Quer pasticciaccio brutto de via Merulana*, published in 1957). In contrast, the same dialect spoken by the marginalized youth of the Roman *borgate* provided Pasolini with the vehicle for a serious, "ideologically correct" attempt to give voice to these characters marginalized by history and the rapid modernization of the 1950s and 1960s (*Ragazzi di vita*, 1955, or *Una vita violenta*, 1959). For a recent survey, see Anna Laura Lepschy, Giulio Lepschy, and Miriam Voghera, "Linguistic Variety in Italy," in *Italian Regionalism: History, Identity and Politics*, ed. Carl Levy Oxford (Washington, D.C.: Berg, 1996), 69–80.

8. An expressionistic pastiche of Italian and Sicilian, for example, is key to the most notable success of recent years on the literary scene: Andrea Camilleri's best-selling series of popular novels centered on the fictional character of a Sicilian detective, the *Commissario Montalbano*, now also a popular television series. It is no accident that before "coming out" as a writer, the Sicilian Camilleri had a long career in Rome as a screenplay author and producer for Italian national television. Camilleri's mysteries *The Terra-Cotta Dog*, *The Snack Thief*, *The Voice of the Violin*, and *The Shape of Water* are now available in a translation by Stephen Sartarelli, published by Penguin.

9. Graziella Parati, ed., *Mediterranean Crossroads: Migration Literature in Italy*

(Madison, N.J.: Fairleigh Dickinson University Press, and London: Associated University Presses, 1999).

10. Importing "extraliterary" languages (and genres) into the body of literature is in fact what specifically distinguishes postmodern writing according to some critics. See Bruno Pischedda, "Postmoderni di terza generazione," in *Tirature 98*.

11. Pierfrancesco Pacoda, ed., *Potere alla parola: Antologia del rap italiano* (Milan: Feltrinelli, 1996).

12. Gian Paolo Biasin, "Narratives of the Self and Society," in *The Cambridge Companion to Modern Italian Culture*, ed. Z. Baranski and R. West (Cambridge: Cambridge University Press, 2001), 170. For a stimulating articulation of the concept of a world literature in relation to the influence of the Western European novel, see Franco Moretti, "Conjectures on World Literature," *New Left Review* 1 (January–February 2000), readable online at: http://www.newleftreview.net/NLR23503.shtml. Moretti is also the general editor of an ambitious comparative encyclopedia of the novel and its multiple traditions—*Il romanzo* (Turin: G. Einaudi, 2001).

13. The issue of national identity is still the subject of lively debate in Italy, both in academic circles and in the media, reflecting the political changes of the post–Cold War era: the rebirth of micronationalisms and regionalisms (exemplified by the Leghe movements in the north of Italy) and the progress of European unification, which raised the question of a transnational, European identity.

14. Salvatore Sechi, ed., *Deconstructing Italy: Italy in the Nineties* (Berkeley: University of California Press, 1995).

15. The new, violent Mafia in the south and the fiscal protests bordering on a secessionist movement in the north (the "Leghe") appeared to pose a threat to the integrity of the Italian national state after the fall and dissolution of the Christian Democratic party, which had represented the center of balance and stability in the previous regime. Toward the end of the 1990s both of these threats decreased in intensity (although they have not disappeared), counterbalanced by the process of European unification.

16. The ruin and "rebirth" of the 1940s and early 1950s were the catalyst for the regenerative energies of neorealist prose and film narratives (a peculiarly Italian brand of modernism). The economic boom, the social movements, and the ideological passions of the 1960s were the backdrop for the return of the avant-garde (including experimental attempts in prose writing as

well). The chaotic 1970s (marked by class struggle and marred by the insurgence of political terrorism) saw an explosion in the translation and publication of political, historical, philosophical, and sociological pamphlets and essays, as well as the beginning of a gradual yet steady return to the "pleasures of prose." For a selective and retrospective survey, see the anthology *Il Piacere della letteratura: Prosa italiana dagli anni '70 a oggi*, ed. Angelo Guglielmi (Milan: Feltrinelli, 1981).

17. Pertile, "Italian Novel Today," 17.

18. The expression is used by the Marxist critic Romano Luperini, "Rinnovamento e restaurazione del codice narrativo nell'ultimo trentennio: Prelievi testuali da Malerba, Consolo, Volponi," *I tempi del rinnovamento*, Proceedings of the International Symposium of Lovanio, 1993 (Leuven and Rome: Bulzoni, 1995), vol. 1, 535.

19. On *La Storia* as "counterhistory," see Cristina Della Coletta, *Plotting the Past: Metamorphoses of Historical Narrative in Modern Italian Fiction* (West Lafayette, Ind.: Purdue University Press, 1996), chap. 3.

20. See, for this point of view, Ann Hallamore Caesar's concise "Post-War Italian Narrative: An Alternative Account," in *Italian Cultural Studies, an Introduction*, ed. David Forgacs and Robert Lumley (Oxford: Oxford University Press, 1996), 248–60.

21. Another notable example is the partly experimental novel *Corporale* by Paolo Volponi, published as *La Storia* in 1974. Volponi's book may have influenced Pasolini as well.

22. A recent book by the critic Carla Benedetti, in which she presented Pasolini and Italo Calvino as symbols of opposing conceptions of literature, stirred a controversy in the Italian press. In her book, Benedetti extols Pasolini in the name of a passionately "impure" literature while condemning Calvino as the representative of a (triumphant) postmodern paradigm, which celebrates the unholy marriage of literature and the cultural industry, in the name of the "death of literature" and the demise of the (traditional) novel. Carla Benedetti, *Pasolini contro Calvino: Per una letteratura impura* (Turin: Bollati-Boringhieri, 1998).

23. Of course, the semiotic narratives of Calvino and Eco were not the only narrative models circulating in Italy in the early 1980s. Separate treatment should be reserved for a number of translations from other languages whose influence on Italian writers is often easy to detect but difficult to assess in the global context of world literature (Jorge Luis Borges, Gabriel García

Márquez, Thomas Pynchon, Paul Auster, David Lodge, Salman Rushdie, Georges Perec, Günter Grass, Peter Handke, Fernando Pessoa, José Saramago, to give only a few recognizable examples). Vice versa, Calvino's and Eco's works certainly remain the most authoritative and provocative *Italian* contributions to the new international narrative scene that developed (and found its selected or mass consumers) between the 1980s and the 1990s.

24. Pertile, "Italian Novel Today," 9.

25. Hallamore Caesar, "Post-War Italian Narrative," 249.

26. On the postmodernism of Calvino and Eco from an Italian perspective, see: Remo Ceserani, *Raccontare il post-moderno* (Turin: Bollati-Boringhieri, 1997), 146ff.

27. Michael Caesar, "Contemporary Italy (since 1956)" in *The Cambridge History of Italian Literature*, ed. Peter Brand and Lino Pertile (Cambridge: Cambridge University Press, 1996), 599ff.

28. If, on the one hand, they officially celebrated the demise (or disguise) of the author, on the other they effectively re-established, with added critical value, the paradigm of authorship, perhaps their most influential consequence. It is no coincidence that the metaphor of the traveler, so prominent in the title of Calvino's "meta-novel of the Reader" (as *If on a Winter's Night a Traveler* has been defined), could be coupled with that of the narrator as a detective in Eco's medieval thriller. If Calvino's (double) reader is hopelessly searching for the end of the novels that he (she) begins reading anew, always looking for the missing end, Eco's monk-detective is in search of a secret map (in fact an ancient manuscript) that might have radically changed, had it been found, the entire course of (cultural and political) history. Both authors drag their readers into a new kind of narrative space typical of a posthistorical perspective: the circular and labyrinthine web of "unlimited semiosis." On Eco, see the essays collected in *Reading Eco: An Anthology*, ed. Rocco Capozzi (Bloomington: Indiana University Press, 1997).

29. Filippo La Porta, *La nuova narrativa italiana: Travestimenti e stili di fine secolo* (Turin: Bollati-Boringhieri, 1995), 11ff. In his essay, La Porta stresses how in these writers (and in others who manifest a somewhat more indirect influence) the Calvinian ethos, result of a coherent itinerary spanning at least three decades, is fragmented and translated into the various cultural passwords of a "postmodern condition." Its most remarkable stylistic qualities are, on the one hand, a new "existential minimalism" shared by many of these "new" authors and, on the other, an ingenious balance between the

short and the long narrative, fundamentally linked to Calvino's "constant use of meta-narrative awareness throughout his *oeuvre*" (Biasin, "Narratives of the Self and Society," 168).

30. Much has been written about the marketing of successive waves of "new" writers over the past few decades. Such marketing strategies have come to be a fundamental component of our contemporary cultural infrastructure, with its emphasis on ever-younger targets as both producers and consumers of new styles. Thanks to the new cultural-industrial apparatus, Italian publishers are now able to court a broader, more sophisticated segment of younger readers, the byproduct of more than a decade of open higher education (in the aftermath of 1968) and the subjects of a new type of cultural consumerism. Thus we find, well into the 1990s, the latest in a series of publishing trends: the so-called cannibals, young pulp writers who have grown up within the media culture (comic strips, movies, television) and wear it as a second (or even first) skin. Ironically, this perfectly packaged group of "restless" young writers is promoted, on the back cover of a recent collection, as the product of "a new literary sensibility, immune to fashions and traditional clichés." See, for example, the "splatter" anthologies *Cuore di pulp* (*Heart of Pulp* [n.p.: Stampa Alternativa, 1997]) and *Gioventù cannibale* (*Young Cannibals*), ed. Daniele Brolli (Turin: Einaudi, 1996), or the collection *Anticorpi* (*Antibodies*), also published by Einaudi in 1997. This trend can be traced back to 1986 and [gay writer] "Pier Vittorio Tondelli's initiative in instigating and editing *Under 25*, an anthology of . . . young authors, three volumes of which were published within two years: *Giovani Blues* (*Puberty Blues*), *Belli & Perversi* (*Beautiful and Perverse*) and *Paper Gang*" (Pertile, "Italian Novel Today," 3). Among the best representatives of the new "cannibals": Nicola Ammanniti, *Fango* (*Mud* [Turin: Einaudi, 1995]), *L'ultimo capodanno dell'umanità* (*The Last New Year's Eve of Humanity* [Turin: Einaudi, 1997]); Tiziano Scarpa, *Occhi sulla graticola* (*Eyes on the Grill* [Turin: Einaudi, 1996]). For a balanced critical assessment, see Mario Barenghi, "I cannibali e la sindrome di Peter Pan," in *Tirature 98*, 34–40. According to this critic, two main features distinguish the work of the young cannibals from that of their historical forefathers (such as nineteenth-century "scapigliati"): lower linguistic and stylistic registers, not necessarily "realistic" in their effects (given the precarious status of "reality" in multimedia society) and often mixing verbal and thematic brutality with a bent for sentimental pathos; and the emphasis on youth (adults are almost entirely absent from these

narrators' works). For criticism in English, see Stefania Lucamante, *Italian Pulp Fiction: The New Narrative of the Giovani Cannibali Writers* (Madison, N.J.: Fairleigh Dickinson University Press, 2004). But the "young cannibals" do not exhaust the variety of new writing that we find in Italy today. As militant critic Goffredo Fofi underlines in his introduction to *Luna Nuova: Scrittori dal Sud* (1997), a collection of stories by young southern writers, this collection precisely claims to go against the current of the fashionable debate about new and young authors, a debate focusing its attention exclusively on the tribes of "pulp-cannibals" or crude "minimalists."

31. In the preface to the 1964 edition of his first novel, originally published in 1949, *Il sentiero dei nidi di ragno* (*The Path to the Spider's Nest* [Turin: Einaudi, 1964]).

PROLOGUE

Consuming the View

Luigi Malerba

THIS COLLECTION opens with an ironic prologue. I selected this corrosive little story (*storietta*), originally published in a series for young readers, *Storiette tascabili* (*Little Pocket Stories*), from the rich repertoire of one of the most prolific writers of late twentieth-century Italy, Luigi Malerba (pen name of Luigi Banardi). It perfectly illustrates the leitmotif of this anthology: remapping the virtual place that Italy is today, so familiar and yet unfamiliar to its inhabitants and its visitors alike. And what better way to begin than from that most canonic of sites, the Eternal City? Deceptively naive, Malerba's story has the simple transparency of a morality tale (recalling the very origins of the Italian novella in the thirteenth century). Although it may not be entirely representative of this writer's exuberant oeuvre, it preserves at least a trace of the delirious nonsense crucial to Malerba's most experimental style. Malerba (b. 1927, Berceto, Parma) came to prominence in the early 1960s with *La*

scoperta dell'alfabeto (*The Discovery of the Alphabet*, 1963), a collection of stories, and three years later, with a major novel, *Il serpente*
(*The Serpent*, 1966), "the bewildered confession of a Roman stamp-
dealer who claims to have eaten his lover."[1] In tone, the "little story"
included here is somewhat reminiscent of Calvino's *Marcovaldo*, a
collection of stories, written in the 1950s and 1960s, that deals
ironically with the unsettling consequences of urbanization and
modernization.

NOTES

1. Michael Caesar, "Contemporary Italy (since 1956)," in *The Cambridge History of Italian Literature* (Cambridge: Cambridge University Press, 1996),
578. *The Serpent* is available in English in William Weaver's translation for
Farrar, Straus and Giroux, as is the subsequent *What Is This Buzzing? Do You
Hear It Too?* (*Salto mortale*, 1968). Over the years, Malerba has assembled an
exuberant corpus of works, wide-ranging in both style and subject. To mention a few titles: *Il protagonista* (*The Protagonist*, 1973); *Il Pataffio* (*A Pitaph*,
1978—an untranslatable pseudomedieval word that sounds like "epitaph"
yet means something like "a bizarre plot"); *Diario di un sognatore* (*Diary of a
Dreamer*, 1981); *Il pianeta azzurro* (*The Blue Planet*, 1986); *Il fuoco greco* (*Greek
Fire*, 1990); *Le pietre volanti* (*Flying Stones*, 1992); *Avventure* (*Adventures*,
1997); *Itaca per sempre* (*Ithaca Forever*, 1997); and *Interviste impossibili* (*Impossible Interviews*, 1997).

Consuming the View

by Luigi Malerba

THE SKY was clear and the air clean, yet from the telescopes on the Gianicolo hill the Roman panorama appeared hazy and out of focus. The first protests came from a group of Swiss tourists complaining that they had wasted their hundred lire on malfunctioning devices. The city sent out an expert technician who had the lenses replaced: perhaps they were blurry from being exposed to the open air for so long. Nonetheless, protests kept coming, in writing and by phone. City Hall sent out another expert to test the telescopes again. A peculiar new element emerged: the panorama from the Gianicolo appeared blurry not only through the lenses of the telescopes, but also to the naked eye. The city claimed the problem was no longer its responsibility, yet the tourists kept complaining, in writing and by phone. After gazing for a while at the expanse of rooftops, with the domes of Roman churches surfacing here and there and the white monument of Piazza Venezia, many went to have their eyes checked. Some even started wearing glasses.

A professor of panoramology was called in, from the University of Minnesota at Minneapolis. She leaned over the Gianicolo wall at varying hours; dawn, daybreak, noon, sunset, even at night. Finally she wrote a lengthy report on the distribution of hydrogen in the photosphere, on phenomena of refraction, on carbon dioxide polluting the atmosphere and even on the fragrance given off by exotic plants in the underlying Botanical Garden—without recommending any remedy.

A doorman at City Hall, who lived near the Gianicolo and who had learned of the problem, wrote a letter to the mayor explaining a theory of his. According to the doorman, the Roman panorama was being slowly worn away by the continuous gaze of tourists, and if no action were taken, it would soon be entirely used up. In a footnote at the end of his letter, the doorman added that the same thing was happening to Leonardo da Vinci's *Last Supper* and other famous paintings. In a second footnote he emphasized, as proof of his thesis, how the view visibly worsened in the spring and summer, coinciding with the greater crowds of tourists, while in the winter, when tourists were scant, one noticed no change for the worse; on the contrary, it seemed the panorama slowly regained its traditional limpidity.

Other expert panoramologists took photographs from the Gianicolo week after week, and these seemed to confirm the doorman's theory. The truth, however strange, now seemed crystal clear: the constant gaze of tourists was consuming the Roman panorama; a subtle leprosy was slowly corroding the image of the so-called Eternal City.

The City Hall Public Relations Office launched a campaign, which in order to discourage tourists, tried to ridicule the panorama in general, the very concept of a view. Their press releases had titles like "Stay clear of the panorama" or "The banality of a view." Others, more aggressive, were entitled "Spitting on the panorama," "Enough with this panorama," "One cannot live on views alone." A famous semiologist wrote a long essay entitled: "Panorama, catastrophe of a message." Some journalists abandoned themselves to malicious and gratuitous speculation on the greater corrosive power of Japanese or American or German tourists, according to their own whims or the antipathies of the newspapers where the articles were published. Fierce discussions were unleashed, which, though noisy, achieved the opposite of the desired effect: all the publicity, although negative, ended up increasing the number of tourists crowding the Gianicolo hill.

Eventually, the Roman city government, following the advice of an expert brought in from China, resorted to the stealthy planting of a row of young cypresses under the Gianicolo wall, so that, within a few years, the famous panorama would be completely hidden behind a thick, evergreen barrier.

Translated by Lesley Riva

PART I

Ruins with a View

The Keeper of Ruins

Gesualdo Bufalino

GESUALDO BUFALINO'S "The Keeper of Ruins" is the first of four late modern variations, presented in this section, on a neoclassical view: the Italian landscape with ruins. In Bufalino's story, a nocturnal invention representative of this Sicilian writer's "baroque" style, the relics of wrecked cars, like "stubborn caryatids remaining upright after the collapse of the architrave," provide the equivalent of a late twentieth-century Piranesian perspective on the ruins of civilization. Bufalino (b. 1920, Comiso, Sicily, d. 1996 in a car accident) came to critical attention only in the 1980s, when he was already in his sixties. The son of a blacksmith, he was apprenticed as a child (from 1930 to 1935) in the *bottega* of a Sicilian chariot painter. Briefly imprisoned in Friuli during the war, he fell ill with tuberculosis and after the armistice spent time in a sanatorium. Upon his recovery, he returned to Sicily and took a job teaching in secondary schools, in Vittoria, near his hometown. In 1950, he began work on his first book, *The Plague-Sower*, which remained un-published until 1981, when it was awarded the Campiello, a presti-gious literary prize. As critic Peter Hainsworth has written: "In all his books . . . [Bufalino] chooses to write in a high literary form of Italian, which he knowingly and ironically cultivates . . . [as] a bar-rier against the false certainties of the conversational, no-nonsense language which modern media and habits of mind both prefer." But his deliberate adoption of "the machinery of high literature," his "delight in literary excess," is not entirely free of parody, like "a schoolboy's, or a schoolmaster's, charade."[1]

NOTES

1. Peter Hainsworth, "Baroque to the Future," in *The New Italian Novel*, ed. Zygmunt G. Baranski and Lino Pertile (Edinburgh: Edinburgh University Press, 1993), 20 and 23. American readers have access to the three major nov-els written by Gesualdo Bufalino: *Diceria dell'untore* (1981; *The Plague-Sower*, trans. Stephen Sartarelli [Hygiene, Colo.: Eridanos, 1988]); *Argo il cieco* (1984; *Blind Argus*, trans. Patrick Creagh [London: Collins Harvill, 1989]); *Le menzogne della notte* (1988; *Lies of the Night*, trans. Patrick Creagh [New York: Atheneum, 1991]). He is also the author of a collection of stories, *L'uomo in-vaso* (1986; *The Keeper of Ruins: And Other Inventions*, trans. Patrick Creagh [London: Harvill, 1994]), and *Dizionario dei personaggi di romanzo: Da Don Chisciotte all'Innominabile* (*Dictionary of Novel Characters*, 1982).

The Keeper of Ruins
by Gesualdo Bufalino

CALL IT COINCIDENCE, call it vocation, but I've done next to nothing all my life but watch over things dead or dying. Now that I'm getting on in years, and can look back from an eminence near the summit, I never cease to be struck, among the random zigzags and paradoxes of my journey, by this persistent thread which gives them, or at least seems to give them, the lie. Maybe it is true that each man carries loyalty to a certain voice inherent in his very blood, and that he cannot but obey that voice, however many defections occasion may incite him to. Thus destiny appears to have assigned me to perpetual sentry-duty, to be keeper not of laws or of treasure hoards but of tombs and ruins; if not, indeed, of nobody and of nothing . . .

I remember that as a child, whenever we played cops and robbers, all the cops and all the robbers immediately agreed to cast me in the role of "It." All very well, had they not been equally unanimous, once I was hiding my eyes, in dropping hostilities and sauntering off, leaving me all innocent around the corner, ears astrain for non-existent enemies.

Later, one wartime Christmas night, it fell to my lot to stamp my feet for cold on picket duty outside an ammunition dump—empty and disused for years as I learnt next morning from the corporal who came to relieve me. What quaint military philosophy, to demand obedience to an heroic code even when its *raison d'être* is dead and buried . . . I (having been through high school) thought of Catherine the Great's famous sentry, destined never to leave his rickety sentry-box, and I persuaded myself that his fate was an emblem for me, maybe for all of us . . .

But to my tale. I'll mention two other periods in my life, not imposed on me by others, but sought out and chosen by me: the time I was caretaker of a graveyard; and when I was keeper of a lighthouse. The first was a task more cheerful and health-giving than you might suppose, with that smooth enamelled green on fine sunny days, and the peaceful tedium of it, the tiny lizardess cheekily peeking through a crack in a tombstone and the marble angel signposting heaven with three remaining fingers . . .

A village graveyard this, with visitors once in a blue moon tethering their mules to the gate like wild-western gunslingers hitching their horses to a post, then making for some tombstone, categorical and glum, their arms encumbered with chrysanthemums. On leaving they would hand me a tip—fruit and vegetables—and exhort me to change the water in the vases and keep the grass trim. Little did they know that every evening I had sweeter dealings with those shades, and that (better far than all these insipid wreaths) I would console them with an impromptu recital on the mandolin.

It didn't last. Migliavacca's *Mazurka* seemed a blasphemy to Rinzivillo the road-mender, as he squatted down beyond the wall on business of his own, no less perturbed than disturbed by the plucking of my strings. I was denounced, surprised *in flagrante delicto* of sound, forgiven, caught at it again . . . I got the sack, I took my leave. But not before I had rejoiced the dead, grave by grave, with one last serenade.

I had better luck with the lighthouse. If I left in the end it was of my own free will and the urge for change. Needless to say it was a derelict lighthouse, built long since at the expense of a fishermen's co-operative to pinpoint the coast with the intermittent flash of its lantern; a useless lighthouse now, since in those waters not a smack put to sea and the last fisherman was dead. Not even the steamers passing far offshore, opulent with radar and similar devilries, could now require our morsel of light, our paltry Tom Thumb's crumbs . . . So I set myself up there by general consent, and made myself master of the place, on condition that I give the machinery an occasional run to prevent it rusting, and keep the windows shipshape, and tickle the trippers on Bank Holiday nights by sullying the moonlight with the bi-chromatic hide-and-seek of my great gyrating lantern. In the summer I enjoyed this assignment as small-time pyrotechnist, nor did I crave any other contact with my fellow men than this: to look down from my eyrie on all their sheeplike meekness and count their heads from the porthole of my quarters, all high and mighty inside my lantern, unique and out of reach . . .

Winter was another story. With beaches deserted and houses

shuttered up, I devised myself histrionic pastimes. Swathed in my Man-of-Aran oilskins I'd go out of an evening on to the circular gallery, torch in hand to cleave out warnings of an imaginary cyclone or still more imaginary shipwreck. Or else (and more frequently) I would write lines to declaim before the mirror:

> As the perfidious keeper of a lighthouse
> I lure the boats that seek me on to the rocks
> And snigger to myself, and rub my hands . . .

O yes, I wrote these words and more besides, and what d'you think came of it? A customs officer confiscated my notebook when he came snooping round, convinced that from my vantage point I was tipping the wink to the smugglers' motorboats. He turned the place upside down, for those lines, the long and the short of them, looked to him like the code of some wireless telegraph; in those black and white marks he descried the esoteric *corpus delicti* of a very palpable crime. He was only half wrong.

You find me today ensconced in my ultimate stronghold: a carwrecker's yard. Here I am monarch and God Almighty on the best of all possible thrones. I even earn something. People come from all over to bring me, gratis, the wreckage of every car-crash, with the blood of the slain still wet on the mudguards. Others come searching for odd bits and pieces, spares unobtainable elsewhere, buried in the scrap-heap: a door, a baffle, a deflector . . . I am happy. Far more so than that Greek sentry of old (remember?) on the roof of Agamemnon's palace, crouched on his elbows like a dog, probing the assemblies of the stars and the secrets of their rising and setting . . . Ah no, at my side—unlike his—there stalks no fear. I still have my mandolin and if I sing it is not to banish ghosts but to summon them.

Happy: there's no other word for it. Here is the haven towards which, groping, I have moved; here I find a meaning for the race I have run, if it has been a race; for my flight, if it has been a flight.

How do I stay alive? Being moderate by nature, that's no problem. I have a small hut to sleep in. A minibus (minus the seats) does me for kitchen, pantry and dining-room. On a gas-ring I cook Spartan fare, and consume it with mock ceremonial, Grand Hotel style, playing waiter and diner in turn. A little act for which I solemnly award myself cheers or jeers before retiring to my sleeping quarters with a humdrum pack of cards to sample the delights of solitaire. I know every kind there is, but I love to think up new ones, the better to grapple with the radiant sequences of suits from Ace to King and the baffling surprises of the odd man out. And if I lose more often than I win, that merely doubles the metaphysical ecstasy of daring to wager against the vainglory of God. In any case, what is more sedative, more sleep-inveigling, than nursing the hope of getting one's own back?

As for chit-chat, I never indulge in it with a living soul, bar a yes or no to customers and a few quips to the driver of the breakdown lorry, who delivers my stock-in-trade every Monday. For all other needs I exploit every mechanical and chemical resource my quarry of old iron and sheet-metal has to offer. In the cold winter months, for instance, I burn leftover oil from some dismantled engine; in the height of summer I run a radiator fan off a battery. Lighting? From a generator. Water? From a big truck-tank hoisted above the roof. I shave with an old cut-throat razor with the aid of a rearview mirror; for my afternoon nap I seek out the reclining seat of an elderly Lancia Flaminia; the hour of noon I sound for myself on a car-horn.

You'll say it's a Robinson Crusoe kind of life, and so be it. Even though I live smack beside the motorway, and see the live cars hurtling monstrously past no more than a hundred yards away. But I'm certainly not short of space. The clearing I camp in is State property, a plot of land expropriated to give elbow room to the earth-moving operations. The debris of loose earth, brown or chalky, bulldozed at that time on to the grass, has little by little killed it. Pounded by countless feet and wheels, the soil has forgotten the seasons of sap and of seed-time, conserving a scant relict of them only in three trees in a row, like three stubborn caryatids remaining upright after the collapse of the architrave.

They it is, in my design for a city, that represent The Garden. I am, you see, pursuing a project, that of tracing the geometry of a city with the skeletons of motorcars. Not, therefore, scattering them haphazardly in the first vacant space, but arranging them in order and in line, their skulls aimed in the appointed direction, to create a semblance of buildings bordering a High Street or ringing a Circus. In my dream town I already have a gridiron of zones, according to the precepts of Hippodamus, with streets ready christened: Blue Simca Street, Three Renaults Boulevard, Lame Alfa Alley (No Thoroughfare) . . . A main square is coming into being, encompassed around with black limousines; in the centre, convoluted, for all the world like an equestrian tumour, is the carcass of a bus which impact warped and fire blackened with leprous burns. Thus, unconsciously, with these aligned and lidded sepulchres, I have been creating a replica of the country graveyard of my youth. So much so that, come All Souls' Day, I would not be surprised to see the former proprietors of each vehicle return to revisit it bearing flowers, and to hear Rinzivillo bawl me out once more from beyond the wall, before squatting down to his business . . .

No one comes, of course; but all the same, as I pace at cockcrow between scrap-metal hedges, I try to imagine in each interior the forms of life which one time hovered there. I hearken to amorous whispers, words of wrath, fevered or fatuous stirrings of the heart. A people of the dead roams my domain from end to end, an invisible flock that dotes on me and which I feed as the spirit moves me. Not without special regard for the showpieces: the Mercedes of a murder victim, its windscreen milky from bulletry; a massive hearse behind which it is hard not to conjure up a cortège, crêpe and muffled drums, black-masked horses, black-plumed cuirassiers . . .

I have particular esteem for these specimens, and never fail to bid them a fond goodnight. "Nine o'clock and all's well," I murmur, and almost feel I am putting them to bed and tucking in the blankets.

Think what you may I am not a madman, nor yet a novice in life. Who can say it is I who am wrong, not you, if I am content with my harvest of ashes, and glory only in history dead and done for, in the allurements of dereliction? In truth there is nothing in the world outside but to me is foreign or hostile: I have nothing to do with it, I don't understand it. Even of the woman who visits me occasionally from the Autogrill I ask no news of peace or war; I get the thing done with brief, technical gestures, send her packing, and become once more the voluptuary of solitude . . .

Put to the test of old age, what will become of me? When, like a noble river at the estuary, I silt up, and am myself reduced to a catastrophe to be cared for?

The future holds no fears for me. Whatever end awaits me it is sure that elsewhere, after death, I shall have to mount guard once more. I know, but will not tell you, over which absence or impotence or ruin.

Translated by Patrick Creagh

Zardino

Sebastiano Vassalli

SEBASTIANO VASSALLI'S historical novel *The Chimera* is set in a rural Piedmont village in the seventeenth century. In Vassalli's opening paragraph, the present slowly fades out and the remote past comes into focus: a cinematic technique reminiscent of Alessandro Manzoni's famous introduction to his historical masterpiece *I promessi sposi* (also set in the seventeenth century), with its long and wandering zoom into the landscape surrounding Lake Como. Yet between these two almost symmetrical openings lies the entire parabolic evolution of the modern historical novel. In the work excerpted here, the ever-present fog clouding the Padania landscape parallels the clouding of anthropological memory. The writer, as a time traveler and investigative archeologist, must first of all unearth *history*, or better his *story:* the story of Antonia, the "witch of Zardino," resurrected by its late twentieth-century chronicler. After an early start as a poet and playwright, Vassalli (b. 1941, Genoa) won recognition in the 1970s as a gifted avant-garde experimental fiction writer, influenced by Manganelli's metafictions. In the mid-1970s, he repudiated the avant-garde and went on to what critics have called a "middle period," culminating with *Abitare il vento* (*Living in the Wind*, 1980, a stream-of-consciousness record of a militant terrorist), before moving decisively in the direction of more traditional narrative codes. In *The Chimera*, he gives us an indirect explanation for his own later development into a maker of historical fictions accessible to a much wider readership: "I asked myself what on earth can help us to understand the things of the present unless they are *in* the present? Then it dawned on me. Looking out over this landscape, the nothingness of it, it came to me that in the present there is no story worth telling. The present is hubbub." Vassalli reserves the right to freely intertwine history and fiction (Antonia, the witch of Zardino, is an entirely fictional character), and he remains interested in what he calls the "archeology of the present," also the title of one of his last novels. History, Vassalli once said, is worth living and can be endured only thanks to the stories we tell ourselves.[1]

NOTES

1. In addition to *La Chimera*, Vassalli's titles include: *Mareblu* (*BlueOcean*, 1982), *La notte della cometa* (1984; *The Night of the Comet*, trans. John Gatt [Manchester: Carcanet, 1989]); *Marco and Mattio* (1992); *Il cigno* (1993; *The Swan*, trans. Emma Rose [London: Harvill, 1997]); *3012: L'anno del profeta* (*Year of the Prophet*, 1995); *Cuore di pietra* (*Stoneheart*, 1996); *La notte del lupo* (*The Night of the Wolf*, 1998); *Un infinito numero* (*An Infinite Number*, 2000); and *Archeologia del presente* (*Archeology of the Present*, 2001).

Zardino
by Sebastiano Vassalli

FROM THE WINDOWS of this house you look out on nothingness.
Especially in winter, when the mountains vanish, the sky and the
plains merge into one great blur, the motorway no longer exists,
nothing exists. On summer mornings, or on autumn evenings, this
nothingness becomes a vaporous plain with a few trees dotted about
and the motorway surfacing above the mist to straddle a couple of
by-roads, twice. Over there on those flyovers tiny cars are in motion, and trucks no bigger than models in a toyshop window. It also
happens from time to time—say twenty or thirty times a year—that
this nothingness is transfigured into a crystalline landscape, into a
glossy coloured picture postcard. Generally this happens in spring,
when the sky is as blue as the water of the paddy-fields it is mirrored
in, the motorway seems close enough to touch, and the snow-covered
Alps abide there in such a way that it gladdens the heart just to look
at them. At these times the horizon is a vast expanse: tens and even

hundreds of kilometres, with towns and villages and the works of man clambering up the mountainsides, and rivers that begin where the snows leave off, and roads, and the momentary spark of imperceptible cars on those roads; a crisscross of lives, of histories, of destinies, of dreams; a stage as huge as a whole region, upon which the deeds and the doings of the living in this part of the world have been acted out since time immemorial. An illusion . . .

At these windows, this nothingness before me, I have often chanced to think about Zardino, once a village like the others you can see over there—slightly to the left and a little beyond the second flyover—against the background of Monte Rosa, the most massive and imposing mountain in this part of Europe. On picture-postcard days the landscape hereabouts is dominated and forcibly marked by the presence of this mass of ice and granite towering above the surrounding peaks as far as they themselves turret above the plains: a "white boulder"—thus it was described at the beginning of the century by my mad adopted dad, the poet Dino Campana— around which "the peaks range/to right to left and to infinity/as in the pupils of a prisoner's eyes."

Campana arrived in Novara by train one September evening, without seeing a thing because dark had fallen; but the following morning, through prison bars, Monte Rosa is revealed to him, and "The sky is filled/with a running of white peaks": an image as elusive and remote as the love he was at that time pursuing, and which he was destined never to find, because it never existed . . . A chimera!

From those heights, from the summit of that chimera, by a tortuous route gouged more than once through the living rock, flows the river Sesia. In the local way of speech there is a gentle, feminine sound to the name: *la Sésia*, and of all the rivers that rise in the Alps it is the most eccentric and unpredictable, the most deceitful, the most perilous both for man and for matter verging on its course. Even to this day its capricious spates invade the plains with floods of muddy water metres high, and it is hard to think of the havoc it would cause if over the centuries the labour of men's hands had not hemmed it in between two endless dykes of earth and shingle and, in certain stretches, of cement, restraining and guiding it towards its confluence with the Po.

In centuries past, however, it happened that every few years the Sesia broke its banks and changed course, shifting a hundred yards in one direction or a mile in the other, leaving marshes and quagmires where once had been cultivated land, obliterating whole feudal domains and villages from the map, and even modifying the frontiers between States; which in this corner of Italy, at the turn of the sixteenth and seventeenth centuries, meant (to the west) the Duchy of Savoy (a southerly appendix of France), and the Duchy of Milan, at that time subject to the King of Spain. And maybe this was the way Zardino vanished. In the mid-seventeenth century, or a little earlier, according to historians, a village of some thirty "hearthstones" was swept away with all its inhabitants by the spate waters of the Sesia and never again rebuilt; though the facts are far from certain. Other possible causes for the disappearance of the village (the name of which, in mediaeval documents, is often to be found in the more "gentrified" form of *Giardino*, "Garden") might be the great Plague of 1630, which decimated dozens of villages in the Po valley; or it might have been some battle, or a fire . . . or the Lord knows what else besides.

In this landscape I have attempted to describe, and which today, as so often, is swathed in mist, there lies a story buried: the grand story of a girl who lived from 1590 to 1610 and was called Antonia, and of the people who were living in the same years as she was and whom she met; and of that epoch and this part of the world. For quite some while now I have had a mind to bring this story back into the light of day, to pass it on, to pull it out of nothingness as the April sun brings to light the picture postcard of the plains and of Monte Rosa; and I also had a mind to tell you about these parts, and the world Antonia lived in . . . But then I was always discouraged by the distance which separates our world from theirs, and the oblivion that enshrouds it. Who in this twentieth century of ours, I asked myself, still remembers Bishop Bascapè, Il Caccetta the bandit, Bernardo Sasso the executioner, Canon Cavagna, the *risaroli* who laboured in the paddy-fields, the *camminanti* or "strollers" who walked the roads of the seventeenth century? And then, of Antonia herself nothing was known: neither that she existed, nor that she was the "witch of Zardino," nor that she was tried and sentenced in Novara in the Year of Our Lord 1610. An episode that caused a great stir at the time had slipped out of the ken of history, and would have been irretrievably lost if the muddle of the world and of things in general had not rescued it in the most banal conceivable way, causing certain documents to end up in the wrong place, whereas if they had remained in their right place they would now be inaccessible, or for ever vanished . . . Italy, as we all know, is a land of muddle, and something is forever out of place; some story which ought by rights to have been forgotten always manages to turn up . . . But I, though I had the luck to stumble across the story of Antonia, of Zardino and the plains of Novara at the dawn of the seventeenth century, was hesitant to relate it, as I said, because it seemed to me something too remote. I asked myself what on earth can help us to understand the things of the present unless they are *in* the present? Then it dawned on me.

Looking out over this landscape, the nothingness of it, it came to me that in the present there is no story worth telling. The present is hubbub. It is millions and billions of voices all together, in every language, trying to shout each other down by yelling the word "Me!" It's all "Me, Me, Me" . . . To find the key to the present, and to understand it, we have to withdraw from the hubbub, to descend into the depths of night, to the depths of nothingness—over there, perhaps, slightly to the left and a little beyond the straddle of the second flyover, beneath the "white boulder" that today is invisible . . . to the ghost-village of Zardino, to the story of Antonia . . .

And this have I done . . .

A motorist halting today on the motorway from Milan to Turin in the vicinity of the viaduct over the river Sesia might, by looking southwards to his left, see arising from the middle of the woods the smoke from the hearthstones of Zardino—that is, if Zardino still existed, which it doesn't. In the spring of 1600, however, it was still there, and all unaware, what's more, of being fated to vanish within a few years: a small village like many another small village in the Flatlands, with its landscape of vineyards and woods towards the marshes and the river banks, its meadows and moorlands stretching towards Biandrate, its rice-paddies and fields of maize and wheat in the direction of Cameriano and of Novara. And with its two little hills, formed by deposits from the Sesia and known as the Knolls, which rose above the housetops to the north and shielded the village from the vehemence of the river when in spate.

The main street of Zardino was the road that entered from the direction of Novara and the "Mill of the Three Kings," and it ran the whole length of the village as far as the little piazza outside the church. Along this street lay the various farmyards and the houses, built part of brick and part of the very stones removed from the soil by the men who had cleared it for cultivation some centuries earlier, and were thereafter put to use either for building or for paving the streets. The balconies were made of wood, as were the roofs of the sheds for carts and implements. The cow-byres were not roofed with tiles, as the houses were, but with mud-caked straw. Everything that met the eye, as you stood among those houses, was grey, shabby, crude, and yet, in the summer months, bright with wisteria and climbing roses; ivy peeped over the walls, vine-shoots twined about the balconies and the grapes hung so low that you needed no ladder to gather them: you had only to reach up.

Inside the houses you could touch the ceiling, the doors and windows were proportionate to the rooms (that is, extremely small), and even a handful of people living together immediately produced overcrowding and promiscuity. But small chance, at the dawn of the seventeenth century, that the people living in any one of these peasant dwellings should be few in number. Out-of-doors, in the lanes, in the vineyards, in the barnyards given an air of picturesqueness by the corncobs hung up to dry, the skins of rabbits and other small animals, the strings of garlic and onions, the sheets and various garments drying on the line, human life bubbled and seethed, no more absurd than anywhere else in the world: barefoot goose-girls kept an eye on the geese wandering at will along the ditches; old men bent by the years and deformed by arthritis laboured from dawn till dusk in little kitchen gardens rendered impregnable by hedges of spiky shrubs, banks of brambles, sharpened stakes and other contrivances worthy of illustration in a present-day manual of guerrilla warfare. And all to keep out the young scamps, the donkeys, the geese, the animals of every shape and size which grazed unattended in the village, doing whatever damage they could. In the walls small niches contained miniature altars and statuettes of the Black Madonna of Oropa and of other saints who by ancient custom were thought to protect the dwellings and their inhabitants from every sort of trouble: the evil eye, diseases of men and livestock, drought, hailstorms, feuds . . .

Every morning the women were off to the pool in the Crosa (the same pool where, according to Teresina, the *Melusia* lay in ambush to grab children) balancing their washing-baskets on their heads. From that side of the village you could hear the thump and slap of the sheets as they were beaten against the stones or on the water, and the talk and laughter of the washerwomen, the *lavandere*. You heard their singing too, and their shrieks and curses if some man molested them. This business of the *lavandere* being molested by passers-by occurred fairly often at Zardino, and time was when it had even given rise to rustic wars against neighbouring villages, with punitive expeditions and reprisals on either side. These might well go on for years, but there was no solution, for the communal washing-pool, the spot where the waters of the Crosa were clearest and deepest, lay right beside the road to Novara, between the village and the "Mill of the Three Kings." At every hour of the day, but especially in the mornings, there was a constant stream of the carts and hand-carts, mules, donkeys and horses of peasants taking their grain to the mill to have it ground: *melga* and *melghetto* (maize and buck wheat), wheat and rye, and even certain pulses, such as chickpeas, had to be milled to make food for humans and fodder for animals. But always in small quantities, for grain can be stored but flour cannot. These peasants also came from other villages in the Flatlands where there was no mill, or the miller charged more, or made a poor job of it; and not all these men resisted the temptation to take a closer look at the *lavandere*, with that great gift of God which they displayed when bent over the water; or else to bandy some rustic gallantry, some passionate offer of their own persons. If the men persisted, the women replied by inviting them to make the same offer to their wives, their sisters, or their mothers, and after a few more verbal exchanges the unrequited lovers went their way. But, as I have already had occasion to say, there had in the past been some serious quarrels, when a man laid not just eyes but hands upon the plumper parts of a woman. Then husbands and betrothed came teeming out from the village, and matters passed from words to deeds. There had been black eyes and even wounded, a few over-fiery spirits had been given a chance to cool off in the perennially icy waters of the Crosa, and on occasion came the flash of a knife . . .

But all in all this was the life of the Flatlands, with all their lights and shadows, and even if after one or other of those brawls there was a corpse left on the ground the relatives would bury it and everything finished there: the constables and magistrates from the city would certainly never have come to Zardino for such a trifling matter. In the seventeenth century everyone fended for himself and his own—to care for everyone there was none but God. The lawcourts of the time had far more vital matters on their hands!

As for the mill, since we have mentioned it, we need only say that it was called the Mill of the Three Kings because of the fresco, all but erased by time and the weather, of which only a few traces remained (indeed, three bearded and crowned heads) on the façade and above the entrance; and that it was one of the most famous and ancient mills on this bank of the Sesia from Borgo Vercelli right up to Biandrate.

The market in Zardino was held in the piazza in front of the church on the first and third Monday of each month. In came the hawkers and pedlars from Novara and from the towns in the Ticino valley (Trecate, Oleggio, Galliate) to display earthenware, agricultural implements, breeding beds and other equipment for the raising of silk-worms, traps for wild animals and fishing-nets, footgear and fabrics. On those days the Lantern Tavern opposite the church burst into life as a real and proper market within the market for every sort of dealer, from the *bacialè* (marriage broker) to the tooth-puller, from the barber (who between one beard and the next busied himself with matters of health and of heart) to the vendor of marmot fat as a cure for arthritis; and the *pénat*, a hero in these villages of the Flatlands, the individual most hated and most fawned upon by the Gossips. Concerning whom there were unverifiable rumours which ascribed to him vices and wickedness such as to pale the memory of Herod, or Judas Iscariot, or the emperor Nero; but then, when the Gossips met him along the road all the frowns on their faces were smoothed out, and their eyes sparkled with joy. It was he, the *pénat*, who purchased the goose-down, paying them the lowest price they could possibly agree to, but paying in cash, and the love-hate felt for him by the Gossips can only really be understood if we remember that for the women of the Flatlands the sale of those feathers was their only means of earning money independently of their husbands; and that the little silver coins they acquired from the *pénat* the women, by ancient custom, shared with no one—it was their own money, the source of their economic independence, the very first step towards the emancipation of women in this part of the plains and of the world. Circulating among the Gossips, and passed down from mother to daughter, there were legends of certain *pénat* who had made vast fortunes by extorting high prices from the mattress-makers of Novara, of Vigevano, even of far-off Milan, for the feathers that they, poor dears!, had been forced to sell for a song. Palaces, carriages, servants; quarterings or half-quarterings of nobility, with the consequent careers in the army or the clergy; and all set up by plucking geese—or fleecing Gossips . . .

Such things were usually talked about in the winter, when they met of an evening in the cowsheds to keep warm and have a chat. And here even—though in deepest secret—they whispered the name of a recently ennobled family in Novara who had risen in the world after the coming of the Spaniards and who, without the shadow of a doubt, were descended from a long, long line of usurers and feather-mongers. These upstart noblemen—it was whispered in the cowsheds—now possessed titles and palaces, and over the great doors of the palaces were coats of arms carved in stone and representing a four-footed animal of no known species. But if they had wished to represent the true origin of their nobility, said the Gossips, those coats of arms should have depicted a goose. A fine Goose Rampant: *there* was the emblem for them!

To get a bird's-eye view of Zardino, above the roofs and chimney-pots, you had to climb either the bell-tower of the church (dedicated to St Rock) or else one of the two Knolls which the Sesia had formed over the centuries with its periodical spates, and which in the early seventeenth century were called respectively Red Stumps and the Tree Knoll. The two broad, low hills have vanished since time out of mind, as has the village. The stones they were formed of later served to construct the new river banks and the land has been flattened out, first using oxen and then bulldozers, to make room for the traditional crops of maize, wheat and forage, and the recent import from America, the Canadian poplar; so that it may truly be said that of the environment in which most of our story takes place there is nothing left, not even the memory. The plain, which in Antonia's day was undulating and in parts untilled, is now dead flat and every inch of it is cultivated; the long lines of poplars intersect at right angles along the edges of the paddy-fields, creating a landscape quite different from the primeval landscape of this region over the centuries, one of woodland and heath, marshland and meadow. Even the courses of the so-called *fontanili*, the spring-waters at one time meandering and unpredictable, here a torrent, there a streamlet, there again a pool, have now been redesigned with the set-square, and in many cases with cement. Everything is ordered and geometrical, everything is arranged to produce the maximum profit: an open-air factory for cereals, wood-pulp and fodder, practically bereft of a history.

But the two Knolls which loomed above Zardino were already very old by the beginning of the seventeenth century: centuries old, and maybe millennia. The Tree Knoll, which at one time must have had a vineyard on the village side, for the roots of the old plants still sprouted here and there, took its name from an ancient tree—a chestnut—so huge that two men alone could not encircle its trunk with their arms: it needed a third. On this trunk one could still make out an inscription carved with a knife, in capital letters with the Rs back to front; and all the inhabitants of Zardino read it, even if they couldn't read: ALBERO DEI RICORDI. Naturally, however attractive it might be to interpret this as "The Tree of Memories," it meant nothing of the sort. The real significance of the inscription was a claim to ownership of the tree and its produce by a family of share-croppers called Ricordi, immigrants from the country round Milan, or maybe even from the Veneto, who had left Zardino almost half a century earlier, having failed to put down roots there. Those who still recalled them spoke of them as arrogant, quarrelsome people, who had tried, without the least right, to establish proprietorship of a number of tracts of moorland and pasturage, the Tree Knoll included.

The other Knoll, known as the Red Stumps, was a vast bramblepatch, a mound of stones populated by large but absolutely harmless snakes to which, however, the folk imagination attributed the ability to emit sounds, to talk, to hypnotize people with their eyes and to achieve wonders if possible more extraordinary even than these. They went so far as to imagine them in the form of dragons, with wings and crests and fireworks darting forth from mouth and nostrils. The people of Zardino considered the "Red Stumps" accursed, on account of a thunderbolt that in the not-too-remote past had struck the two oak trees which graced its summit, at the same time destroying a votive image of Our Lady which, in its little wooden shrine, had been nailed to one of the trees. The stumps of the two trees, corroded by the damp and acted on by atmospheric agents, had with the passing of time become covered with a kind of lichen, a reddish mould which in the rays of the setting sun turned the colour of flame. This phenomenon, visible even from the other side of the Sesia, had caused the name of this Knoll to change rapidly in the course of only a few years, from Our Lady's Knoll, which it had always been, to the Red Stumps.

Less clear are the reasons why the inhabitants considered the Tree Knoll as ill-omened. The rumour which Teresina passed on to Antonia had already been doing the rounds for some time: that witches met there to hold their Sabbaths and worship the Devil; but how this rumour started no one had an inkling. There had been no witches in the past of Zardino, at least in the more recent past, and as for the Knoll, the village elders remembered a time before the Tree belonged to the Ricordis, and anyone who wished to climb it could do so—not right to the top but at any rate to quite some height, thirty feet or more. There used to be a number of rough-hewn ladders nailed to the trunk, and from there aloft (said the old men) when the sun was bright and the air was clear you could see the pinnacles of Milan Cathedral thirty-five miles away, as you could Moncalvo in the Monferrato, and the sanctuaries around Biella, and all the Alps from Mont Blanc to Lake Garda and the Holy Mount of Varallo. In short, you saw the world.

Then came the Ricordis with their claims to ownership. They had tried to turn the Knoll into a vineyard and quarrelled with any-one who attempted to approach the Tree. And thereafter the rumour of witches began to be whispered abroad—a thing previously un-heard of in Zardino—and people no longer ventured up the Knolls.

Life was pretty humdrum in Zardino. Especially in the winter, when work in the fields was practically at a standstill. The livestock hud-dled in their straw waiting for spring and spring sunshine to come, while every species of social activity shifted from the farmyards to the cowsheds. There the youngsters continued their games, the ancients nodded off or else, on request, told tales of times gone by to anyone wanting to hear them, and the Gossips sat in a circle sewing and spinning, as they put it, but in reality gossiping their heads off until deep into the night. It was there that the rumours started— tittle-tattle, intrigues, slanders and assorted absurdities—which still today, on the threshold of the year 2000, are an essential and indispensable element of village life in the Flatlands; only that now, thanks to progress, they can intertwine with news from the papers and the television, and may spread in ways quite different from those of yore. For example by telephone, or even—thanks to the power of literacy—by means of anonymous letters . . .

But at the dawn of the seventeenth century rumours were entirely and without exception started by the obsessions and the rancours of whoever it was set them in motion, and there was only one method of communicating them: a whisper in the ear. But the final result had no reason to envy the media of today, for the rumours circulated with extraordinary speed from stable to cowshed, entwining themselves with other voices in other sheds, other villages, other winters . . . They wove an inextricable web of lies and half-truths, a delirium of words with everyone against his neighbour, that always ended by gaining the upper hand over the truth, conditioning it, concealing it, giving it unpredictable offshoots, until it replaced the truth, became the truth itself.

When the fine weather arrived the rumours continued to do their rounds and their damage, but people began to turn their attention to other things, to "barnyard feuds" and "water feuds," two factors which for century after century stirred up the otherwise sluggish temperaments of the Flatlanders, and guaranteed the city of Novara a dense colony of pettifoggers, shysters, conveyors, scriveners, land-surveyors and others concerned with judiciary matters—a colony second only in number to that of the priests and the "religious" in general.

And may I be allowed at this point in the narrative to lay down my pen, to pause a while to draw breath and reassemble my resources? For here the matter of my discourse rises to greater heights, and the writer's task becomes an onerous one. It would require a supreme poet, a Homer, a Shakespeare, to do justice to the barnyard feuds of the Flatlands, which almost invariably sprang from a mere nothing—a sheet hung out to dry, a dead hen, a child bitten by a dog—but which could go on and on for centuries with such an accumulation of hatred between the parties concerned that, even if this did not reach the point of slit throats and corpse-laden finales, it would none the less have sufficed to confer logical form and meaning on the most atrocious massacres in history. Yes, it is here, in the barnyard feuds, that human hatred became refined and exalted, attaining the uttermost peaks of achievement, becoming an Absolute. It is hatred at its purest—abstract, bodiless, entirely impartial—that which set the universe in motion, and that survives all things. Human love, so often sung by the poets, compared to this hatred scarcely counts for a fig: a speck of gold in the broad river of life, a pearl in the sea of nothingness and no more. The water feuds also, though born of reasons of self-interest and without the least trace of idealism about them, were capable of attaining, and indeed often did attain, some species of obscure and negative grandeur. What is more, they had social implications—class warfare and so on—of the kind which have made history; the reason being that all agriculture here, especially the cultivation of rice, is strictly bound up with the presence, particularly conspicuous in this part of the plains, of either river-water or springs. It follows that the true owners of the Flatlands were not the owners of the land, then still split up into many small or even minute fragments, but the masters of the water. That is, of the vast and vastly ramified network of springs and canals, ditches and channels, sluice-gates, warping canals and so on, which was then and is to this day, and for this region, what the circulation of the blood is for the human body.

The true masters were few but mighty: the Curia of the diocese of Novara, the great landed proprietors of Novara and of Lombardy in general, the Cathedral Vestry Board, the Dominicans, the Jesuits, the Hospital (including the "House of Charity") . . . Down there in the Flatlands they fought against these overlords in two ways and in two stages. In the first place by day, when the farmers met together in their respective communities and appealed to the High Court in Novara in order to obtain the water needed for their crops, and at the proper price; after which, by night, they found their own means of unhinging the sluice-gates or piercing the dams, in the process often leaving their neighbours' paddy-fields bone dry; and achieving other feats which would be too lengthy a task to detail here.

Thus it happened that from the original trunk of a water-feud, like branches from a pollarded willow-tree there sprouted dozens and dozens of further feuds: the proprietor of the water against the individual farmer, that farmer against his whole community, community against community, or against a single farmer. And thus the canals and sluices were often guarded (as banks and public offices are guarded today) by thugs armed to the teeth, paid by the proprietors to dissuade thieves by their very presence, or to teach them a lesson if the dissuasion failed to have the desired effect. And every so often, as in the circumstances was only inevitable, the outcome was a corpse.

Translated by Patrick Creagh

The Self-Awareness of the Labyrinth

Giorgio Manganelli

WE FOLLOW Vassalli's archeology of the present with Giorgio Manganelli's labyrinthine musings. Manganelli's labyrinth might indeed be read as a biting, tongue-in-cheek metaphor for our contemporary metaphysical sense (or non-sense) of space. The piece included here is taken from the collection *All the Errors* (*Tutti gli errori*, 1986), and all the errors of the human mind form the deceptive perfection of this labyrinth: the self-deceiving quality of any attempt to find truth through fiction. It is worth noting that *Letteratura come menzogna* (*Literature as Lie*) was the title of Manganelli's first collection of essays, published in 1967. Manganelli was born in Milan in 1922 and died in 1990. A professor of English and protagonist, in the 1960s, of the experimentalist movement in criticism and fiction writing, his view of literature as a kind of endlessly multiplying maze is well illustrated in an excerpt from his kaleidoscopic *Centuria* (published in 1979, with the descriptive subtitle *Cento piccoli ro-*

manzi-fiume) and recently published in English in the journal *Grand Street*: "A writer writes a book about a writer who writes two books, both about two writers, one of whom writes because he loves the truth and the other because he is indifferent to it. These two writers write twenty-two books altogether, in which twenty-two writers are spoken of, some of whom lie but don't know they are lying, others lie knowingly, others search for the truth knowing they cannot find it, others believe they have found it, and still others believed they had found it but are beginning to have doubts."[1]

NOTES

1. Quote from *Centuria*, trans. Ann Goldstein, from *Grand Street* 59 (winter 1997): 143. Manganelli's first major work of fiction was *Hilarotragoedia* (*Hilarious Tragedy*, 1964). His previously published and unpublished work was reissued by the prestigious publishing house Adelphi in the 1980s and 1990s, right around the time of his death. Among his many recent, "posthumous" titles (the year of republication is in parentheses) are: *Dall'inferno* (*From Hell*, 1985); *Tutti gli errori* (1986; *All the Errors*, trans. Henry Martin [Kingston, N.Y.: McPherson, 1990]); *Improvvisi per macchina da scrivere* (*Improvisations for Typewriter Solo*, 1989); *Agli dei ulteriori* (*To Ulterior Gods*, 1989); *Encomio del Tiranno: Scritto all'unico scopo di fare dei soldi* (*Encomium for the Tyrant: Written Only to Make Money*, 1990); *La palude definitiva* (*The Definitive Swamp*, 1991); *Esperimento con l'India* (*Experiment with India*, 1992); and *Il presepio* (*The Nativity Scene*, 1992).

The Self-Awareness of the Labyrinth
by Giorgio Manganelli

BEING A LABYRINTH makes me uncertain of the amount of space I occupy. Indeed, I do not delimit myself with walls like a city, nor with bastions like a fortress, nor with trenches like a hilltop tower that encloses the memory of sieges. Although surely there are places where as labyrinth I have ceased to exist, I am not a surface, but rather the sum of the paths that cross me, with their turnings, gorges, underground passageways, fountains, statues and caverns. An enormous, inexhaustible gut of deceitful signs, indecipherable pathways, and a precise though unknown map, I have the girth of one of those heavy-bellied animals which, when slain and disemboweled, reveal an endless course of rosy, blood-charged intestines, here and there transparent. If I could free myself from my condition as labyrinth, these paths inside me would surely describe the confines of a world, an asteroid lost among fretful tracks of comets. But perhaps I ought to think of these lanes, avenues, and pathways as my own most intimate borders, shaping a narrow airless space saddened with odors of corruption, a habitat for omens, signs, and silent allusions.

According to the orthodox paradigm for a labyrinth, I should know myself and run my course from one place, defined conventionally as entrance, to another which would term itself an exit. And if I ascend to a vantage above myself, wanting to study myself, I espy what I might describe as a chart, enormous but none the less minute, maniacally minute, and extraordinarily sharp and clear. If I hover unmoving above this chart, my vertical bird-like gaze little by little discerns a path—or such it seems—cautiously unraveling among the numberless temptations of other, dishonest paths, avoiding enigmatic corners and proceeding with apparent rationality from one point to another, successfully bridging a frightful nexus of intervening entrails. If I rise to a greater height in the sky, this roiling mass transforms into a dusky poultice, some puddle of viscous filth defiant of description but traversable, or so I tell myself, by the unassisted violence of my members, since nothing more restrictive than a hedge seems to block my path. I will stride through the labyrinth simply by pressing my body against it. Yet my argument, naturally enough, encloses an incurable sophism: my body, after all, is itself the labyrinth. But as my winged eye descends I rediscover—or it seems so to me—the precise, fingernail wound of the path. And I find reassurance in what strikes me as the hard obstinacy of that design, which I know I can easily follow with a slow sure pace, measured and exempt from panic. I am certain of gauging every step of that path with scientific clarity, certain of knowing both start and end of the road even while wondering if they coincide with what I would speak of as entrance and exit. Thus there is a point of self-observation where the problem of the labyrinth—the problem of describing and traversing myself—appears entirely resolved. That fantastic, ingenious, and laborious design even seems imbued with the quality of something heraldic, both blazon and an endless family tree: a genealogy striking backwards to the millenarian roots of an incommensurably noble race. The precise, open path construes an image of my own secret seal; and while tracing it out with my meticulous, pedantic gaze, I delight in the hidden ruses, astute reversals, and prescient equivocations by which it overcomes obstacles, sidesteps devious paths, outflanks deceptive forkings and ignores perfidious enigmas. I tell myself that this syllogistic clarity resembles me. If surely it is true that in my entirety I am the whole of the labyrinth, it is no less true that the labyrinth harbors this lying semblance of a serpent stretched out within it. Or perhaps it is truly a serpent, cunning, agile and in its own way venomous: a snake that writhes through the whole of this grand construction, that suffers no deceptions, that advances with no trial and error, that never goes astray, that makes no plea for unearned information. This path, for me, of all of myself, is the part called "I."

If I could hover forever at these celestial heights, I would enjoy a perennial self-delight; but my task is to be the labyrinth, and my abstractions seem procrastinations. So I will descend to myself, step by step; and as I descend, the trail I have sighted grows plainer. But I realize more. The trail is continually interrupted as it blunders into obstacles I could not see from above: trenches, minuscule puddles, disrupted fords, crumbled walls, flights of stairs with missing steps. Finally I have to allow that it does not lead from any one point to any other, but is only a deception of my acute yet summary eye. This path is inept and defeated. I have reached that height at which the trail reveals its discourse to be halting and disconnected, and from that height onward—where I see its earthy, oily material, and distinguish rocks, and follow the watery troughs that run beside the trail and then cut suddenly across it—from that height, I say, the labyrinth presents itself as utterly different from all I had supposed. It is now a kind of silted, lugubrious swamp, a place of a color barely varying between mud and dead, rotted leaves. The traces that cross it with mad, maniacal insistence appear to be the hoof-tracks of un-numbered herds, the spoor of archaic beasts that marked that place from one extreme to another with ever more desperate feet: thirsty beasts, lost beasts, beasts with no herdsman: all constrained to de-sign a labyrinth that in the beginning perhaps was non-existent, beasts forced to that sad task by fury, madness, and implacable fear. So I have asked myself a question: whether once there was a time when the labyrinth did not exist, and whether, indeed, it now exists; whether it isn't instead an optical illusion, a cunning hallucination superimposing a senseless meander with neither exits nor entrances on the mire; and finally whether what I call a labyrinth is nothing more than a geogram shaped by the dementia of beasts gone mad from the fear of that death from which in fact they died: a maze of hoof-prints I do best to consider as an emblem of an animal mad-ness. Perhaps I can even amuse myself with supposing that these foot-prints, which show themselves as precisely that, are a clumsy attempt at writing, a rudimentary message, a disordered if syntacti-cally complex invocation, the remains of a massacre no one desired and that now commemorates itself with these minute, catastrophic signs. And such a case would comport even more than the labyrinth's non-existence, collapsing this description of my search for a path-

way into a tale of utter delusion: since where time had made dust of
desperate herds and hardened their tracks in the soil, such incisions
would present no obstacle to movement, and I could travel that
space in any and all directions, undisturbed by any anxiety to decipher some privileged course. All paths become equivalent; and if the
glory of exit and the delicate frenzy of entrance thus desist, all adventure likewise lapses, with any and all terror or hope of finding
oneself astray. Still, however, there is no escape from asking what
those herds might have been, where they came from, and how their
horrified hoof-prints survived their bodies, which were ponderous
enough to stamp those marks in the earth. Should I not expect to
find skeletons, skulls, tibia, horns, and hooves? On what ground, at
this point, might I possibly deny that I am the victim of an an-
guished quandary? I unavoidably perceive that the images I bit by
bit have formed of the labyrinth are mutually incompatible, and that
all of them, if not all but one, are necessarily inexact.

My only choice is to move even closer in my examination of the
labyrinth. What now resolves into focus is an intricate, geometric,
and painfully reasoned design—something no mistake might reduce
to any welter of tracks of beasts in terrified stampede. A seeing, per-
ceptive mind seems to have drawn this map with meticulous pa-
tience: every detail reveals the unstinting cunning of a craftsman
who devoted a life to it. But what life? Now I no longer distinguish
my trail; more than having crumbled into fragments, it seems to
have disappeared. It is only another of the many illusory paths that
dutifully riddle the spaces proposed for them. From here the tangle
of meanders gives no less than the impression of having been drawn
with such deliberate application as to shape a series of knots, twists,

and slings. Here and there it interrupts, truncated as though by the brusqueness of a blade, appearing more to assume the features of an ingenious prison: a place devised to prohibit all exit, and built to construe the madness not of a blinded herd, but of a uselessly thoughtful and knowingly syllogistic creature. Yet I could not call this figure malevolent; in its own certain way it is objective and necessary, deduced from a general concept of the nature of maps. In all its lethal geometry, I might dare to call the plan celestial: an accurate, rational discourse extracted from the gut of a language that tolerates propositions in no different mode of meaning. I do not intend to suggest, continuing my metaphor, that the proposition here distended before me is void of meaning, but rather that this careful sequence of signs is so fraught with meaning as to brook no translation. Perhaps I am forced to conclude that what faces me here can be no question of any single proposition as expressed within a given language, but is rather the whole of that language and the whole exhaustive chart of its syntax and morphology, now splayed out in front of my eyes. But if the labyrinth construes itself as a whole and totally impervious language, what is my own task? Am I to master a language capable of speaking only with itself and of itself—am I in fact to be that language? Am I not allowed to think of myself as a speaker of another language, and thus as a being who might pronounce some series of words that would force a response from the language now prone before me—a response and thus an arduous, though not insuperably arduous delivery from my sufferings?

Now, I cannot doubt the factuality of the labyrinth, even if I cannot assert that its construction or its present existence might possibly be unriddled into any other solution than the deaths of beasts or the madness of whoever speaks of it. Can it be that the labyrinth's objectivity coincides with its irresolvable negativity? Such a clear, if cruel conclusion strikes me neither as sensible nor as adequate to the machinery and immanent monumentality of the image I am trying to interpret. The labyrinth, I assure myself, is necessarily labyrinthine. I believe it to be inimical to all solutions; and it is indescribable. So I attempt to examine it from closer up. At this newer vantage, the labyrinth seems a place fundamentally for games: something light, laughable, and full of futile adventure seems to flow through these paths, like airy blood in the veins of a wood nymph. It might be a mythic invention, or a sylvan theater for some arcadian comedy set to music and song for a multitude of lisping infant voices, indiscernably male or female. Do I not now catch a glimpse of leafy bowers seemingly ready for fictive loves and dissembled desires? Would these, here, be anything other than rustic pedestals for tiny orchestras of strings, flutes, and mandolins; and, there, weren't those steps designed for the ease of young mothers, timid infants, girls on their first attempts at love, and clumsily infatuated boys? These paths, I tell myself, have not been built to plot my madness, but are full of gentleness and for blithesome wanderings. The path's discontinuities offer places for hiding, for games marked by innocence, or only the barest edge of cunning; and everywhere there are bowers for sweet but not unseemly conversation. Pale, elegant youths, I tell myself, have run in these places and will run here again, and they will throw harmless paper darts at one another; and surely these crumbling walls bear graffiti with arrow-pierced hearts. These dry-stack walls. So I cannot deny that I talk of paths because now I clearly see these trails, despite their mirth, to be edged by a border of ancient, fragile masonry, even if interruptedly.

Indeed, the labyrinth has ceased to seem a place of hospitable delight. Nearly at the point of immersing myself within it, I see it now as a dark, tortuous tangle of straight and curving lines, and of walls sometimes exiguous, sometimes bizarrely tall, but always spiteful, senile, decrepit, and obstinate. The trenches are villainously steep; filthy waters stink in great puddles. There are statues—I made no mistake—but now I see they are broken, gesturing with handless arms; whole arms have been detached, their shoulders shattered. That hand has no fingers; it shows no more than residues of splintered phalanges. Thick, sordid mold creeps across bellies towards the necks and faces of heroic youths and fetching nymphs, now deformed and worn; a close-grown tracery of sickly grasses sparkles with the light of petrified stupor in half-closed eyes, myopic and questioning. On the ground I see the shards of an utterly crumbled stele; perhaps the hollows are the nests of snakes, if life glimmers here at all. Everywhere on walls and statues a crawl of vegetation, invading the pathways, cancelling out all foot-tracks; no flocks or herds ever trekked across this ground, the paths among the weeds grow dubious and occult. If I rapidly skim through the airs above the labyrinth, I distinguish clearly how pathways jut into arduous turnings and stray amid the complex branchings of other routes. Arabesques unknot themselves, but become no more open, limpid, or friendly. Every voiceless byway runs toward a hypothetical goal. Yet there is no confusion. No longer geometric, the labyrinth possesses organic coherence, the appearance of an animal, flat and gigantic, whose members and organs are sinewed and firmly interconnect, effluvia in transit through soft, nervelike veins. But this complex of veins and nervatures is something less than the labyrinth, which is rather the animal itself, the enormous beast that turns this apparently crazed design into a cautious, knowing machine, something that could not be other than what it is. Yet if the labyrinth is the beast itself, how might it be traveled in any exhaustive and definitive way? If the labyrinth is a problem of not insoluble intricacy, wouldn't its solution be tantamount to destroying this wonderfully articulated marvel? Am I not then faced with the proposition—I do not know from whom—that I slaughter this creature, step by step effacing its existence as I traipse its interior roads, dismantling the coherence of its machinery of signs? And if we posit the nature of the labyrinth as an animal replete with nerves and veins, what does that make me? If I have been destined to undo this conundrum, and am thus to deal an end to this machine of itineracy, I can be nothing other than the death of the labyrinth animal; I am that demise projected in the project for the animal itself. Traveling from one end to the other of the labyrinth animal, I make myself its butcher; and by slaying the animal—my habitat and meaning—I slay myself. I am death in the absolute, the animal's as well as my own. Reaching the end of the labyrinth, nothing at all will remain. But if I am the death of the animal, I am likewise the animal itself, since the project for the animal has endowed it from the start with a labyrinth's natural death, and I can have no sense or goal if not as this animal and its animal death, and as labyrinth. If in fact the animal includes its death—a death that will issue from the labyrinth—then the animal itself is the labyrinth; and if I am this animal, then I am the labyrinth. Therefore my task is destruction; and whom or what I destroy is of little account, whether myself, the labyrinth, or the beast, since each is but one of three names for an always identical thing. I am destruction itself.

As always, I delight at finding my conclusion in a compact, coherent, and comprehensible image. Yet I know how much deception waits in my propensity for such exactitude. In this debris of defeated and treacherous pathways, I see nothing alluding to a beast's vitality, no matter how bizarre this beast might be as the single, unique example of itself throughout the world. If these are the veins and nerves of a beast, surely this beast is dead, and has been dead for a great deal of time.

I am seduced yet again by my theological lust for a harmony, no matter how sinister, in my manner of understanding the crumbling stuff I now presume to decipher. But here I have to dispense with the fiction of the continuity and coherence of supposed itineraries. My eye beholds an expanse of corruption and putrefaction: inept meanders sop through muddy fields where wisps of dying weeds begin to stink with rot; there is no unstagnant water, no tree not felled by an ancient death. The statues are mounds of dust settled from the motionless air, for I dare to suppose that the long dead beast has been interred, and I move in the space between the corrupted carcass and the sarcophagus roof, which is what I refer to when I speak of the sky. So I am in a tomb. If the labyrinth itself is not dead and decomposed, I have to suppose that it holds and conserves a path, a line, which issues beyond the limits of the tomb. I imagine the labyrinth to remain untouched by the death of the animal, conjecturing that it pre-exists and survives the beast. Perhaps it butchered the beast; perhaps the beast unknowingly swallowed it, and died from it; but surely the labyrinth is still there, since I myself pose the problem of the labyrinth. Let me invert this argument. If the beast is dead and I am not dead, then I am not the beast; if the beast is dead and I am not the labyrinth, which itself was not the animal, then the labyrinth is not dead. So there exists a dead beast, the beast is enclosed within a tomb, but the tomb is riddled by a pathway that traverses the rotted carrion from one extreme to the other. Likewise we have the circumstance that the stuff that path consists of shows no apparent difference, in color or form, from what remains of the rotting beast; it might be a nerve, but isn't; a vein, but only as similitude; a filament, but surely this filament is the only continuity. Within this cadaveric rot I have therefore imagined the existence of a path which, no matter how cautious, cunning, elusive and circumlocutional, is to lead me from one extreme of the tomb to the other. Not only am I vested to the labyrinth, but the labyrinth is consecrated to me, since its meaning lies only in my trek through this unending cemetery, then to achieve the point where the grave concludes. I have reached the conjecture that no integral labyrinth must still persist: no labyrinth as integral nexus of possibilities, of which but one is, in addition to possible, both salutary and veracious. Rather, the labyrinth has succumbed: it is rotten and corrupt, a dead and buried beast: and the path everywhere crossing it is something other than the labyrinth, something both more ancient and yet future, and which no matter how hidden, enigmatic, and mysterious can only be imagined as strong and clarion in its own intact and vital coherence—something which no matter how indirect can only be seen as rectilinear will, even if destined to the one-by-one, stop-by-stop investigation of every corner, crevice, and pit-fall in what strikes me as the demolished carcass of a creature not improbably stillborn from out of the labyrinth inside of it. Yet even as I cull this supposition, I cannot avoid admitting that this interlacing of signs reveals no unbroken path to my eye. It appears to me, rather, as a battlefield in the aftermath of slaughter, a place disarrayed by blind and ponderous violence, an expanse of corpses by now four days corrupt. Though I plane in all directions, my eye pursues no trail that does not immediately lapse. If the notion of the tomb continues to intrigue me, I have to imagine that everything—both beast and labyrinth—lies somehow within it, but I do not know whether as a living thing, or as admixture of living and dead, or as endowed with some other mode of being I have never before encountered. However, this too is something I cannot deny: that no matter what this thing may be, which I call the labyrinth—this waste of stones and spoor and tracings—it strikes me as incredibly aged: as utterly decrepit and exhausted. And no single sign presents itself as a credible wrinkle on this unknown, doltish, and obstinately ancient face. Is it therefore a city vanquished by the weight of the years; an expanse of ruins that perhaps cannot be trod; or the layered ruins of a number of cities, each containing the germ of the labyrinth destined to waste its successor, until this, the definitive labyrinth, long since self-forgetful, is all that remains of the last of them, that last city definitively dead at the end of the whole dead dynasty of cities? The labyrinth now before me is itself not dead, since it cannot die; but I see it to lie here exhausted by its unending wait for some next city it might destroy. Thus, as I prepare to descend still further, I continue to query myself. I argue: it is presupposed that the labyrinth has knowledge of itself; and no matter how greatly it may simulate disorder, putrefaction, and decrepitude, the binding conventions of the labyrinth's integrity include the certain condition that its concept of itself is complete and perfect; the certain condition that it alone is endowed with intelligence of all of its cavities, turnings, crossings and false perspectives, its misleading indications and confusing repetitions; and likewise, that in the midst all such treacherous and ambiguous substances it must have firm, clear cognition of the series of signs, no less exiguous than undeniable, abstruse as much as obstinate, which lead along that single route—amid others invoking mendacious infinity—which has meaning, continuity, beginning and end. The labyrinth, indeed, is this and nothing else: the knowledge of its numberless errors and unendingly meaningless wanderings, indeed of that near entirety of itself which it has to cancel out in order that this "near entirety"—which is the route of exhaustion and impossibility—be survived by that single path alone deserving the unspeakable name of the "way."

But let us suppose, no matter how improbably, that a labyrinth, owing to age or illness or dementia, might be ignorant of its nature and form. Is this to say that it offers no exit? Not necessarily, as I see it; and perhaps one would exit with no more trouble than otherwise. What would happen, certainly, is that no clues to the exit would propose themselves as such; all signs would show the same condition; all indications would be neither true nor false; and finally, unknown to itself in its idiocy, the unknowing labyrinth would cease to lie and betray. This, however, is not the worst of possibilities. Consider that a labyrinth endowed with self-awareness can never be other than ferociously intent upon its machinations, and will alternate series of signs with versions of themselves of opposite meaning, articulating artful mixtures of clues and traces where indications are sometimes true at face value and at other times true but meant to be taken as false, or false but to be credited as true, or false while so declarative of falsity as to excite a final fantasy of their truth. In short, a labyrinth gifted with self-awareness is a quiet and cunning enemy, an implacable sophist in its arguments, a strategist always intent on precisely insidious plots, traps, and ambush. But a doltish, ignorant labyrinth is innocent, and in its innocence can neither betray, nor, denying itself, assist. It will be merely a garbled passivity; a web of indifference. Proceeding or not, I shall find myself exempted from all interpretation or ideology of the labyrinth; and such a casual, neglectful condition might easily distract me, inviting total forget-fulness of the task of traversing the labyrinth. And I imagine, in any such case, that custody of the theory of the labyrinth would then devolve upon me alone; no matter whether aimlessly wander-ing or choosing a reasoned path, I would keep vigil, necessarily, of its dignity—my defeat restoring it to cruelty and monstrosity, or my success to its pains in service of redemption.

Yet even this reading of the labyrinth seems no more creditable than the many others I have ventured, all of them supported by the sole quality of appearing especially significant to me, and all of them almost unapprised of that artful confusion of meanings which re-mains the labyrinth's conclusive description. But by now I have de-cided to abandon my deceptive if equally seductive visions of the whole, and to seek my definitive home in the labyrinth's interior, that straitened place which proffers discernment of neither hoof-prints nor pretended paths. I see nothing but corners of totally am-biguous crossroads.

I have finally abandoned all points of view, and I do not offer my-self as a gloss on the labyrinth. In some way, no less simple than de-ceptive, I might say that finally I am inside the labyrinth. But any such phrase raises more problems, many more, than it resolves. If I declare myself "inside the labyrinth," that would first of all affirm, or presuppose, that I am not the labyrinth. I want to forward that sup-position with all the pedantry of a meticulous scholar beleaguered by self-doubt. If I am something distinct from the labyrinth, I can assert further that I am totally extraneous to the labyrinth, main-taining that I find myself in this intellectually dispersive place by chance, error, or distraction, or owing to some cosmic event I re-main unable to describe. If I am extraneous to the labyrinth, it ceases to exist as such; it is only a straying heap of refuse, illusory perspec-tives and crude theatrical backdrops, and I possess the power to cross it with an imperative, brutal, and indifferent stride. I can, simply, destroy the labyrinth, not only asserting it no longer exists, but de-claring that it never existed. Yet that would be a lie, because the point is only this: to define what relation may possibly hold between myself and the labyrinth, given precisely my inability either to de-stroy it or to confirm its existence. Even if I were able to destroy it and flee, it would always persist in my memory, and my wanderings through its deceitful and ingenious evasions would continue. So I grant that I am not extraneous to the labyrinth. There is surely, by presupposition, some difficult, obstinate relation between myself and this itinerary, similar, for example, to the liaison between dreamer and dream. Let us then propose that the labyrinth is my dream. But if I dream, I am perhaps asleep, and the dream coexists with my sleep. Dream might explain the petulance of these images—my co-existence with these images combined with my inability to govern them. But it does not explain my task, which is to make my way through the labyrinth; and it does not explain the indifference and constancy of every element of the labyrinth's structure. Moreover, there is never a moment of my not having awareness of the laby-rinth; there exists no moment prior to this labyrinthine sleep. Might

I not then conceive of an eternal dream, interminable and immortal? But if I myself am equally eternal, interminable, and immortal, the word "dream" will assume an entirely affective meaning. In reality, this notion of immortal dream implies a situation I might term simultaneously substantial and accidental: the labyrinth and myself are reciprocally accidental, yet together we constitute a substance. I realize, however, that by speaking of dream I manage to insinuate doubts about the substance of which together we consist, myself and the labyrinth; I nearly fancy that the matter of the labyrinth, as though exuded from myself, were some ectoplasmic contrivance which a single gesture of my hands might traverse. Could the labyrinth be a vision? Let us even imagine an uninterrupted and unlimited vision; but a vision: something that could not occur without me. Yet a vision does not issue from within me, I cannot search it out, I am not coextensive with a vision. The vision comes from elsewhere, some place, essence, or power. And if this is the form in which it comes, am I not perhaps to suppose—given its quality as so much more potent than my own—that I can do nothing other than entrust myself to a design that does not challenge but that includes me? So, is the labyrinth vision to be taken as a dark illumination? Am I to ponder it as a giant hieroglyph, written on the level surface of a non-existent universe? But I know the labyrinth has no ambition to communicate; it does not reveal; it has no desire to effect my illumination. Perhaps it is unaware of my existence, and its dignity is such that I cannot presume its excogitation in any palace governed by a power of perverse providence. Might not I myself have projected it, and then forgotten? Yet surely I cannot ignore that the labyrinth is infinitely wiser than I myself have ever been.

I look around and note the fragment of a wall, a statue apparently eroded by time, representing a female figure. Here a tiny moat, there perhaps the shore of a minuscule lake, and around my feet the clear trace of three paths. There is no reason to choose one rather than another. It would be sensible to begin to sketch a chart, a map of the paths, but if I had the materials needed for drawing—and perhaps I might find them in one of the grottoes—I would have to decide between carrying the map about with me, and leaving it here. In the first case, I would never know where I found myself; in the second I would find myself unable to return to the place where I had left the map. Shall I therefore proceed by chance? No. As others have done in no less insidious settings, I will leave clues behind me and take note of everything I see. For example, the statue of this female figure. Now I will look at it closely, and from here, from this female in stone, I will begin to walk.

She is draped in a brief veil, and if her hands were still intact I would discern what they grasp so tightly: perhaps a nosegay of flowers; perhaps a bow, like certain images of childish violence; or perhaps a lyre. I look with attention and attempt to remember the patterns of the shrubs and trees. But the female statue intrigues me. The face is raised towards the sky, but its posture seems to allude to inveterate blindness. The grey of the stone removes all grace from what one glimpses of her nudity; the belly might bespeak incipient maternity, or perhaps no more than a laughable windiness of the viscera. If I return to considering the face, I cannot avoid repeating that it shows no expression, and yet is blandly imperative, something I could not persuade to be different from what it is. So I start down a path chosen at random. At random? This is imprecise. I realize my instinctive choice of the seemingly most imperfect path. From such a path I can hope for nothing. I walk slowly, since I want to remember a tuft of strange flowers here, a grotto there, some-where else a stone. But soon I come to a crossing; I choose a path, up to the next crossing; and again I encounter the statue of a woman. I look at it, amazed. Is it the same one? From my memory of the other figure, it is certainly the same one; and yet I suspect a labyrinthine ruse. The trees are similar, extremely similar, to those that adorned the prospect of the statue, but perhaps nothing more than extremely similar. But if the labyrinth has sought out similar trees, couldn't it, if it wanted to trick me, have provided utterly identical trees? I begin to grasp the secret interior law of the labyrinth. It is based on suspicion. Everything is similar, nothing identical. And coming upon the statue from which I began to walk, it too would be no more than similar; perhaps a splinter will be lacking from the hand, cracked by time, by waiting, or by love. As I return to walking, I know what I will find: forkings similar to other forkings, mirroring images of lakes and streams, stones in approximate imitation of other stones; an infinite number of meetings with the female statue that looks with opaque eyes at the sky. Thus, slowly, but always less attentively, and always more amused, I walk through the labyrinth. I know this atrocious structure to be inspired by a secret irony, a minutely cal-culated sport. Perhaps there is a path that would lead me outside of the labyrinth. Perhaps I might abandon this hilarity that traps me in a limitless game of paths to no exit: I might abandon the game, and refuse to bow down to the inexact copies of the blind female figure. But now I have ceased to choose; I am no longer intrigued by the game of trying the streets of the labyrinth. I know now that the labyrinth is not a dream, not a vision, not a project of my own or of anyone else. I know that no place, no grotto, no lake or moat, I know that neither of any two forking paths of the labyrinth should be discarded in favor of the other; I know that all the errors—and I do not know whether anything which is not error exists—form the corrupt and perfect structure of the labyrinth. I abandon myself at last to standing motionless and at peace amidst the labyrinth's innumerable streets—the peace that comes from knowing, as I always knew, that I alone am the labyrinth.

Translated by Henry Martin

Lost Road

Gianni Celati

IN THE LAST piece of this section, Emilian writer Gianni Celati undertakes a perilous journey through a contemporary wasteland: "Traveling in the countryside of the Po valley, it is difficult not to feel a stranger," he writes. "Even more than the pollution of the river, the diseased trees, the industrial stench, the state of neglect blanketing anything that doesn't have to do with profit, and, finally, more than the housing meant for transient dwellers, without either homeland or destination—more than all this, what surprises one here is this new kind of countryside where one breathes an air of urban solitude." *Verso la foce* (*Down to the Delta*, the travelogue of a journey to the mouth of the Po River), published in 1989, is a work of nonfiction: the exploration of a contemporary Italian landscape, both a suburban space and a new kind of wilderness, as familiar as a childhood backyard and as unrecognizable as any foreign land. The evolution of Gianni Celati (b. 1937, Cremona) from a rebel-comedian mining an exuberant, Rabelaisian verbal vein into perhaps the most influential minimalist writer of his generation can be described as a kind of progressive sobering. *Verso la foce* consists of four pedestrian journeys (a dangerous yet rewarding proposition in a time and place dominated by the automobile) and four journals or sketchbooks (observation stories, *racconti d'osservazione*, as Celati defines them, partially inspired by the work of the late photographer Luigi Ghirri). In these fragmentary observations, the poetic objectivity of a quasi-photographic descriptive technique meets with the somewhat bewildered empathy of a nomadic anthropologist. Celati's turn to perambulatory minimalism, possessing many of the qualities and none of the mannerisms of Calvino's *esprit de finesse* and spirit of observation, is also a coherent search for a new beginning for Italian prose writing, whether openly fictional or at the boundaries of nonfiction (as in his travelogue/narrative *Avventure in Africa* [*Adventures in Africa*, 1998], recently translated into English).[1]

NOTES

1. Celati's major works include: *Le avventure di Guizzardi* (*Guizzardi's Adventures*, 1973), *La banda dei sospiri* (*The Gang of Sighs*, 1976), and *Lunario del Paradiso* (*Paradise Almanac*, 1978), collected together in *Parlamenti buffi*, 1989. In the 1980s, he published the collections of stories *Narratori delle pianure* (1985; *Voices from the Plains*, trans. Robert Lumley [London: Serpent's Tail, 1989]) and *Quattro novelle sulle apparenze* (1987; *Appearances*, trans. Stuart Hood [London: Serpent's Tail, 1991]). Among his most recent achievements are *L'Orlando innamorato raccontato in prosa* (1995), a prose retelling of Boiardo's fifteenth-century epic poem, which follows in the footsteps of Calvino's Ariosto (*Orlando furioso*, 1970); *Recita dell'attore Vecchiatto nel teatro di Rio Saliceto* (1996); and *Avventure in Africa* (1998; *Adventures in Africa*, trans. Adria Bernardi, with a foreword by Rebecca West [Chicago: University of Chicago Press, 2000]).

Lost Road

by Gianni Celati

MAY 9 1984. Saw the Ferrara countryside again from the bus. We passed close to one of those beautiful sluice gates the Este dynasty set up in the marshes to drain them by the differential drainage method. Built maybe in the sixteenth century, a little narrow-arched bridge surmounted by a square turret. The four right-angled triangular segments of the roof are still the model, I believe, for the contractors who build the houses in this area.

Before I dropped off to sleep I could hear the slats of the roll-down window blinds rattling in time to some distant vibration, and the thought came to me that here at night the land falls off all the way down to the Po Delta. At dawn I thought I heard a radio commercial for a furniture store being broadcast out in the streets, here in Finale di Rero, this village at the back of beyond, in the district of the great land reclamation. It sounded like a car with a loudspeaker was driving through the deserted streets.

The landlady of the café-hotel asked me if I'd slept well, with a smile which I read as a pucker of loneliness. Later, when she served me my coffee, she smiled the same smile, which made me feel like shaking her hand as I was leaving. She wiped her hand on her apron and held it out awkwardly, saying: "Excuse me!"

Her son offered to give me a ride in his minivan as far as Tresi-gallo, and he wanted to know what I was doing in these parts. He must have found it comical that I was here to write, because he said, joshing me a bit: "What are you writing then, a book for the farm-ing cooperative?" Evidently a lot of people here write books for farming cooperatives, I don't know why.

The Tresigallo town-square is a shapeless opening at the junction of four streets, flanked on the one side by fascist-vintage buildings with epic bas-reliefs, and by a parking lot crammed with compact cars, in front of the low-rise city hall, on the other. The latter is a modernistic structure made up of cubes of diminishing sizes. An avenue leading out of town, with young trees recently pruned and low-built old houses, runs by the cemetery, where I see a number of women coming out wearing head scarves.

At the far end of the opening, a narrow street lined with low-rise apartment buildings painted in acrylic colors, and this is the road I take.

The sensation of being among peoples who live on a reservation on some continent, in some outlying province or other, where things have lost some of their urgency by the time they get here. Maybe this is what I was looking for, yesterday on the bus.

The road from Tresigallo to Jolanda di Savoia, a straight narrow road lined with plane-trees. The yellow wheat fields, the corn fields still green, the furrows of the other crops, all form straight lines that appear to converge in perspective towards the same point on the horizon, and that point moves along with me as I walk. Houses and trees and church steeples stand out, very low on the horizon, off in the distance and spread out over space.

The cars go by at high speed, and I am forced to walk on the shoulder. Up above a crow sails slowly by, I see it come down onto the asphalt to pick up something that looked to me like a piece of plastic. White cumulus clouds along the line of the horizon, hanging over scattered clusters of houses, with stands of poplar trees in the background.

I pass a group of old abandoned farm buildings, the walls all grey with mildew, windows broken, crows pacing up and down in front of the cowshed waiting for something. On the other side of the road, a pink villa, with weeping willows in the front yard. No one in sight for several moments, then a truck went by, its flatbed loaded with tractors.

The bus was coming, and I ran towards the bus stop to get on. Jolanda di Savoia is this wide main road with two service roads, with building estates of contractor-built houses scattered everywhere you look. An agricultural settlement, developed in the fascist period, under the auspices, I imagine, of Italo Balbo. When my mother was a child, it didn't exist, and here there were marshes.

Along the main road a row of stores, with all the modern trimmings, and women on their way to do the shopping, pedalling as if time had no weight for them. A Gothic-style chapel built in the fascist period, a fine crop of TV antennas on the roofs, and here too that same sense of life on a reservation. A bit like being below par as compared with the overall financial project for universal life.

Just outside town, out in the fields and by the side of the road, lots and lots of little houses painted in bright colors, well kept, and modest. They all have acute-angled roofs, aluminum window-frames, a yard fenced off with a plain wire fence, a glass-covered porch over the front door. They don't look like prefabs, but old houses remodeled by their owners in keeping with a common trend.

From the bus they seemed to be standing there waiting, like everything else. Everywhere the same feeling of waiting—for time to pass, for the day to go by, for another season to come—a feeling you don't get in town.

I thought the bus was going to Codigoro, instead, at the boundary of a farm, it turned around. Stares when I asked the driver to let me off with over-hurried gestures. At times I can feel the difference between the town and the country from the way people have of staring at me as if my behavior were incomprehensible. The woman in the bus was staring quite hard, but she was staring at me without staring, as if she were looking at something in the air around me.

The bus went back the way it had come, leaving behind a huge cloud of dust. Here the dirt road takes off across the fields, after a little bridge over a canal. In front of me empty countryside with lots of sky overhead, a wide wide sky above an expanse of rectangular parcels, divided up by ditches and cart-tracks.

I have been walking through the fields for an hour, following a canal called Canale Leone on my military map. Nobody ever comes along, I don't know for sure where I am going, I head more or less east by my compass.

There's a kind of happiness out there, in those lines of earth that go off in all directions without a rise or a dip. They're so flat I seem to be standing on an elevation simply because the path is six inches higher than the fields. As far as I can see into the distance, little bright-colored houses, emerald green, pink, egg-yolk yellow, meadow green, are like indistinct visions.

I hadn't realized that these fluorescent-green sheets, like big meadows, that my track cuts across are rice paddies. Rice stalks at water-level all around, like a submerged prairie. The sky overcast again, low clouds that flatten out at the bottom, getting darker towards the top. Surprised to be among rice paddies, with rice paddies on all sides, as far as the eye can see.

Three p.m. I come out on an asphalt road, across from a heap of rubble on which a fine specimen of ailanthus has sprouted. On the far side of the road, another group of abandoned farm buildings. Cowshed, barn, farmhouse and yard, all locked up with heavy padlocks, with the tang of manure still in the air. Here the level of the road is two or three meters above the surrounding countryside, and I can finally see the rice paddies properly.

A sea of green rectangles that look like fields of grass, if it weren't for the sparkling of the lines of water that separate them. Very attracted, happy to be here.

A man with a three-wheeler Vespa minivan gives me a lift to a village called Le Contane. Driving between the rice paddies, we saw a number of herons. The man was talking about the weather forecast, but I think he took me for a foreigner, because at a certain point he said: "Do you follow what I'm saying?"

When you're on foot, the line of the horizon constantly reminds you that you are displaced somewhere or other on the surface of the earth, like the things you can see in the distance. You have to look for another point you can use as an axis, and imagine you'll get there sooner or later. You always have to be able to imagine what's out there, otherwise you couldn't take a single step.

After Le Contane, it's another eight kilometers to Ariano Ferrarese, I pass between fields planted with tomatoes, with one or two more rice paddies. On a strip of grass between the rice paddies, hundreds of milling seagulls shrieking all at the same time, like people at their wits' end.

A young man driving a Volvo took me all the way to Mezzogoro and told me he was going to university and studying for a business degree.

I got out on a ring road in front of a white villa, built in what some people might refer to as a postmodern style. A bulldozer was finishing clearing away the remains of an old farmhouse, to make room, I imagine, for another white villa in the same style. In the rubble I spotted a colored print of Venice and a picture of the Virgin Mary.

I'm writing on the bus, as we drive alongside a canal that flows between two concrete embankments, with the water up to the level of the road. This is the land of canals.

On the outskirts of Codigoro, residential villas everywhere you look. A big ultramodern-looking supermarket, with diagonal green stripes. De luxe clothing stores with English names practically at a country crossroads.

June 10 1984 (Sunday in Codigoro). Waking up in this rented room, with somber-colored curtains and a bedspread with a big allover floral pattern. Outdoors right away, strolling in the direction of the little remodelled railroad station, a neighborhood of new houses.

At one time this was all marshes. Dammed up and filled in manually for centuries by peasants in the grip of malaria, taken over again by the water and filled in by peasants in the grip of malaria and of agribusiness consortiums, and finally reclaimed by the pumps of the great land reclamation authority, becoming fertile ground for the social projects of fascism. Now modern houses stand here, orthogonal and faceless.

In the main square of Codigoro, in a café, lunchtime.

Behind the square is a street that runs alongside the Po di Volano, with art nouveau villas down past the bridge. A low bridge, almost on a level with the water, maybe it was once a drawbridge. Further along, the two banks fan out in perspective, and the flow of the water opens everything up and makes it easier to breathe.

Delighted with the houses along the canal, the ones with the Venetian-style pediments with three windows, three little windows lined up along the eaves with pretty green blinds. The power of the frontal view in Venetian architecture: it accustoms you to looking at surfaces as something joyful, the rejoicing of things in appearing.

The houses along the canal, on either side, all built in former days and embellished by the simple rhythms of the windows, open up the space in a sort of very broad curve and together create a real sense of place. Nothing abstract or planned, you can see how time has become a form of space, one feature has grown bit by bit on top of another, like the wrinkles in our skin.

Afternoon in my room. On my map the district of the great land reclamation is a crisscross of canals which cover the area that used to be marsh, while to the south a former branch of the Po River passes through here as the Po di Volano. The Volano debouches today in appalling places completely paved over with asphalt, the so-called Lidi Ferraresi, the Ferrara seashore, designed for vacationing and the summer trade, jam-packed with faceless buildings, and as deserted in winter as a graveyard.

I came here to see the great land reclamation district, the land rendered uniform and productive, and what there is left of the country. All of life, the whole earth nowadays, is a part of some project. But I must swallow my diffidence and observe what takes place day after day for no reason, that most unshowy of spectacles.

Still the urge to write, after dinner outside town looking for a telephone booth. Across from the great pumping station are canals in which one or two people are fishing.

A red glow at sunset, and an immediate sensation of remorse for something I didn't do or am not doing, along with the thought of people I'm far away from, and the certainty we will grow further and further apart. On the towpath by the canal I can now see a lot of men fishing with fishing poles, sitting on folding stools.

You can sense a slowing down of the pace, even in the bird cries, in the cars that pass on the main road, in a dog barking in the distance. In this light the fields in perspective, intersected by canals, look like the surface of a game board. One or two fishermen have already lit their kerosene lamps, in a willow thicket there is only indistinct shadow and the abstract calm of this hour of the day.

June 11 1984. Leaving Codigoro on the Migliarino road, past the bridge over the Po di Volano. Cottages with kitchen gardens by the side of the road, a fine morning, the activity of a back-to-work day. There's something you can't put your finger on that distinguishes Monday-morning behavior.

Eight a.m. Before reaching the railroad crossing, a long two-story structure with a row of statuettes on top, neoclassical peasant lasses and lads in rustic poses. A former agribusiness cooperative maybe, it has a great arched gateway with a wooden door studded with nails. A minivan is unloading something outside the gate, a woman is leaning out for a laugh with the delivery man, and he comes up with a clever wisecrack for the woman whom he certainly desires.

The main road widens and I meet up with the Volano canal again as I walk, then the pumping station. There is a bronze plaque: FER-RARA LAND RECLAMATION AUTHORITY, CODIGORO PUMPING STATION. There is a pumping plant shown in relief on the plaque, but it looks like a huge dam, with sheets of water pouring down like Niagara Falls. The artist must have exaggerated a bit.

The pumping station is a rigid tower-like structure in exposed brick with big pipes coming out at the bottom. In the little entrance lodge the watchman looks up, afraid I may want to go in, then goes back to reading his newspaper.

The straight road runs along the canal, and beyond the canal the horizon opens up, with stands of poplar trees in the distance. On the right here, the enormous grey structure of the Codigoro sugar re-finery, now in ruins. All the windows on all three floors are broken, walls with patches of mildew, and a skylight on top also has its win-dows broken. Weeds grow in the yard in between what's left of the paving stones, and you can still make out the inscription on the gate: "ERIDANIA," NATIONAL SUGAR REFINERIES.

At one time it was the only industry in these parts, everybody wanted to join in the sugar harvest; and "Eridanos," the Greek name for the Po River (connected with the myth of Phaethon), came back to me, thanks to that word in quotes. A bit like the thought of an old girlfriend. Those were times when the family brought everyone to-gether, and they still gave industrial concerns mythological names,

because the industries were mythical giants. Now a sign reads: ERI-
DANIA INDUSTRIAL PARK. And below a telephone number for
information and sales.

Across from the ruined sugar refinery, on the banks of the canal,
there are heaps of trash. Somebody dumped an old refrigerator, a box
spring mattress, a broken chair. Near the trash, two elderly gentle-
men on bicycles had stopped to talk, and we eyed one another.

Walking along the canal still, now this landscape reminds me of
Texas. High tension pylons cross it from one end to the other, with
wires drooping down over long distances. The road is on a higher
level than the fields, and all you can see is the color of the clay, way
off into the distance. On my right, nothing but flatland, with the
desert colors the ochre soils have in these parts.

At a gas station I chat for a while with the pump attendant, it's
windy and the air is very clear. On the horizon I see another abandoned industrial complex: smokestacks and buildings with empty
windows.

Wooden telegraph poles by the side of the road, and now over
there beyond the canal the local train from Ferrara to Codigoro is
going by. Green, with only three cars, it sails through the countryside through the clear air like a migrating thought.

The grass on the shoulder of the road is tossed by violent gusts of
wind. Seeing me standing there taking notes, somebody shouted
from a passing car: "Hey, egghead, you walking?"

Now the Volano winds this way and that, and the road alongside
it is full of bends. In the fields on the far bank I caught sight of an old
truncated watchtower. On the right many canals intersect against
the chequerboard background, and one of them reaches all the way
here, flowing under the road.

If I could, I'd go look at all those canals one by one, they strike me as being so fabulous. That's where the ages of myth are: in the landscape, in the roads and canals that crisscross the terrain, and all this use of the world that is going on everywhere.

One thirty p.m. The bridge that takes you into Massa Fiscaglia. As you enter the village, a block of mustard-colored modern row houses. Each house has its own spiral staircase, two massive balconies one on top of the other, and rough-hewn corner walls jutting out to keep it separate from the rest. Mustard-colored houses for poor unfortunate rich people whose homes just have to have style.

The street winds back and forth, and you finally come out in a big empty asphalt-paved space that is supposed to represent a townsquare. Here there is a four-story working-class apartment building, with all those identical balconies with the flimsy metal railings, and here am I in the café across the street.

A man with a pencil moustache gave me a lift along the Migliarino road, grudgingly. Sitting behind the wheel, he said: "If people can't afford it, they shouldn't travel. Anyway, what's there to see? Good God! What's gotten into people? I can't take you very far, you know. Hitchhikers! Good God! If it were up to me I'd get rid of the lot! Where the hell do you think you're going, on foot?" He was one of those Southern Italians who come north to work and pick up the local dialect so they can pass as locals.

A relatively deserted road, very winding; it's not too hot because there's still a wind coming off the sea. It's only now that I notice that, to the right, through a stand of reeds, you can see the outlines of the mountains in the distance. The gas station attendant had said so this morning, today it's so clear you can see the Alps.

What I see is an intenser blue shadow to the northwest, up above there are white clouds that make its contours uncertain. It must be the foothills, the Pre-Alps.

A minibus goes by, and the driver gives me a good long stare, but without stopping for my signal.

On the bank of a canal choked with reeds and rushes, I come across a notice board that says: FISHING WITH RODS ONLY. A row of plane trees bordering the road begins here.

The horizon is an unbroken green line, apart from the tip of some distant church steeple or the darker outlines of the clumps of willows among the plantations of fruit trees. White clouds rise from the direction of the sea, and on the other side you can see the blue line of the mountains, now barely visible.

Under an umbrella up ahead a woman selling potatoes and peaches and watermelons comes into view, with her crates laid out by the side of the road. Sitting on a little folding stool, she is reading an illustrated magazine.

The fruit lady under the umbrella sold me some peaches and handed me a bottle of water to rinse my hands. Around fifty, she didn't seem surprised to see me on foot, and she informed me there was a bus stop up ahead. I told her that today the air is so clear you can see the Alps, and she answered that nobody has ever seen the Alps from here because they're too far away. Whereupon I looked for that blue line, but I couldn't see anything for the reeds growing next to the canal.

I was sorry to leave the fruit lady, but she'd gone back to reading her magazine. And as I went on my way I looked for that blue line of the mountains again, but I couldn't see anything, and I began to think I'd imagined it all along. Then there were white clouds covering the horizon; probably nobody has ever seen the Alps from here, but a lot of people must have imagined them, like I did.

Imagination is part of the landscape as well: it gets us into this state of love for something out there, though it's more likely to put us on the defensive with too many anxieties; without it we couldn't take a single step, but then she invariably leads us we know not where. Ineliminable goddess who guides our every glance, figure of the horizon, so be it, Amen.

I arrived at the station of Portomaggiore by bus.

Six p.m., I'm about to go home. Remember that hedgehog run over on the road with his jaws open. Remember that roadsign which said: "STRADA SMARRITA," LOST ROAD. Remember that woman in the dairy store who greeted me with: "Good morning, young fellow," and, when I pointed out I wasn't young, replied: "Well, it's what people always say, isn't it?"

I think I was the only passenger to board the train at Portomaggiore.

I dozed off for a while. After Consandolo, Traghetto, Ospedale, now we are at the Molinella halt.

I'm amazed these places are so big, that there are so many houses and so many streets and factories and inhabitants. How many places like this there are all over, places few people have ever even heard of. Think of the ones you saw, travelling in America, how godforsaken they seemed. Odd-sounding names, that give the idea of a little tiny settlement, and instead always complicated places it would take months to begin to get to know.

It's a surprise every time, you discover you know nothing for certain about the outside world. Then you feel like apologizing to everyone: forgive us our presumption, forgive us our speechifying, for-give us for taking you for a fistful of flies to mouth off to.

Forgive us, forgive us, we are heedless and incompetent, not even smart enough to stay put, not to move, not to talk, to be like the trees.

Translated by Anthony Oldcorn

PART II

Memory Lanes

The Penumbra We Have Crossed

Lalla Romano

IN HER introduction to *The Penumbra We Have Crossed*, from which this piece is excerpted, Turinese writer Lalla Romano (1902–2001) notes that her book describes a journey or, better, *is* a journey. Yet it "is not a journey in time to retrieve the past; it is a short journey in space to the home village," where "the past is eternally present." In this intimate and somewhat ghostly domestic territory, immortalized by old daguerreotypes, a new literary space awaits us, a space where poetry and truth belong to each other and to the collective memory of literature. *The Penumbra We Have Crossed* is a Proustian title, taken from *Le temps retrouvée*. As Romano paraphrases Proust in the introduction to her book: "Only that which we bring to light truly belongs to us, drawing it out of the obscurity we contain." The "redemption of time" is the true motivation and leitmotif in Romano's writing. Indeed, Italo Calvino, while recognizing the Proustian inspiration of her work, wrote that her discreet and rigorous poetry consists in collecting and revealing precisely those moments of life that we call scattered or lost. *The Penumbra* originally appeared in 1964, somewhat outside the parameters of this anthology. It is included here because although her work found renewed fortune and recognition in the 1980s and 1990s in Italy, Romano remains substantially unknown to the American reader.[1] In her books, fiction and autobiography interweave in the narration of often painful family relations: between mother and son in *Le parole tra noi leggère* (*Light Words Between Us*, 1969) and grandmother and grandchild in *L'ospite* (*The Guest*, 1973), justifying the comparison to the work of another great (and better known to the American reader) Turinese writer, Natalia Ginzburg. Both contributed to "the retrospective construction of a tradition of women's writing . . . [a] canon [that] emphasized the themes of family, history and memory, but did not, generally speaking, mount a strong critique of the patriarchy" (perhaps because this generation of Italian women did not perceive themselves as overshadowed by their fathers and husbands).[2]

NOTES

1. *The Penumbra We Have Crossed* only recently became available in a translation by Sîan Williams (London: Quartet Books, 1998). Her *Lettura di un'immagine* (*Reading of an Image*, a photographic family album, published in 1975 and republished in revised and enlarged versions in 1986, *Romanzo di figure*, and in 1997, *Nuovo romanzo di figure*) was reissued along with all her other major works. As Romano, also an accomplished painter, wrote in the preface: "the images are the text and writing an illustration." Another "visual" type of narrative is *La treccia di Tatiana* (*Tatiana's Braid*, with photographs by Antonio Ria, 1986). Her more recent books, such as the novel *Nei mari estremi: Ro-*

manzo (*On Extreme Seas: A Novel,* 1987) and the journal/travelogue *Lune di Hvar* (*Moons of Hvar,* 1991), confirm the interlacing of image and word as her constant stylistic and subjective preoccupation. Other recent titles are: *Le metamorfosi* (*The Metamorphoses,* 1983); *Un sogno del Nord* (*A Northern Dream,* 1989); *Un caso di coscienza* (*A Case of Consciousness,* 1992); *Ho sognato l'ospedale* (*I Dreamt the Hospital,* 1995); and *In vacanza col buon samaritano* (*On Holiday with the Good Samaritan,* 1997).

2. Michael Ceasar, "Contemporary Italy (since 1956)," in *The Cambridge History of Italian Literature,* ed. Peter Brand and Lino Pertile (Cambridge: Cambridge University Press, 1996), 590.

The Penumbra We Have Crossed
by Lalla Romano

FOR ME the Farm and the Cemetery didn't qualify as "places"; the Cemetery was an extension of the town, the Farm was home. But other localities too were just as much witnesses to our lives, practically participants. What's more, they had a history that had taken place "beforehand," which meant that they had distinguishing marks and characteristics: like people. But they put on the ornament of the seasons, and as a result their history was so to speak veiled, hidden, removed to an indefinite distance.

I believe that the intimacy I felt for the Castle was due in the first place to the fact that I constantly had it in view from the windows of our house. My parents were attached to it too; for Papa it was the favorite backdrop for his photographs.

For me, when I was a little girl, the Castle was the site of everything beautiful.

It had almost gone back to the wild state, but it was not wholly natural. You could still sense the echo of bygone histories. There was evidence of gentility, avenues, clearings; but also traces of military installations, huge walls, the remains of the demolished fort. Everywhere in the Castle there was a rapt silence, the silence of places that have been battlefields, the theaters of forgotten defeats. The entrance was located after the last houses of the Lower Town: a high gate between two pillars. Now the gate is open because the Castle, these days, is public property (and maybe nobody goes there). The cripple told me that in the summer it hosts a children's summer camp.

The avenue of horsechestnut trees is as dense, high and dark as ever. But the great ring at the top of the first ramp has been thinned out, it lets in too much light: the circle of tree trunks is no longer complete. From there the avenue makes a bend and proceeds uphill along another ramp we never took. We used to stay in the ring. All around there were strange stone seats set in the ground; fragments of an architecture: segments of arches, capitals trimmed with mouldings. They were concave, like chairs. It was they that gave the ring its solemn and ornate appearance, reminiscent of a stage-setting.

In those days the grass was fresh, thick and level, scattered in places with clumps of little daisies. Now it is uneven, dried-up, trampled here and there. In the avenue you can make out tire tracks. All the signs of a new life are signs of violence, they accelerate decadence, ruin. Whereas, in those days, the Castle was the very place where time seemed to have stood still.

I used to play with pebbles and horse chestnuts, leaning on the buried capitals. Mama embroidered in silence. Like me, she preferred the Castle to the esplanade, because there we were alone. Occasionally she would have with her a lady who was staying for the summer at the Hotel Europa.

A vague feeling of apprehension hung over us from above, from the house of the caretaker, which we avoided approaching. Up there was where the Dumb-girl lived.

I saw her once up close, when I was already grown-up and we used to go to the top of the Castle to play—going up the back way, from the road to the Podio—among the ruined walls. We had come upon the entrance to a tunnel and we planned to explore it. We found the Dumb-girl right next to us, making signs with her hands and her eyes. Perhaps she was trying to dissuade us; we ran off pretending it was a joke, but in reality terrified by her presence.

At a certain point along the road to the Podio the wide path that the Marchesa's carriage used to go by on forks off.

I failed to locate, along the initial stretch of road, Photograph Rock. Perhaps it is that big rock lying slantwise below the edge of the road: it must have been uprooted and rolled to one side to make way for the army tanks during the war.

In those days the rock that jutted out over the edge of the road was shaped more or less like a log; it seemed to have been put there on purpose to sit on. I thought it was "Papa's rock."

Papa would pose the group. Mama sitting down, a flat beret perched on her curly hair; me with my little white topcoat, leaning up against her; Papa stood behind us, with his hunting jacket buttoned up to the neck and his fur cap. In front of everybody, our dog Murò. In the background, the road lined with oaks and emaciated wild elms. Papa looked serious, with a trace of pride, and with the ghost of a smile in his half-closed eyes. Murò was serious too; but in some photos, distracted by a butterfly, he had turned his head to one side. Mama looked out with her deep, slightly mocking eyes. (She found this photography business rather boring.) Still a little girl, I stared with almost painful astonishment.

Papa was able to get into the pictures because he operated the shutter with a rubber bulb held in his hand behind his back. The bulb was connected to the camera, which stood on a tripod, by a long thin rubber tube.

Photography, which only Papa went in for in Ponte Stura, was a complex affair with a magical side to it. It involved secret operations that were conducted under "red" light. I was allowed to watch. The plates were wrapped in red paper. There were wooden frames with steel clips, into which the plates were inserted, white enamel basins with blue rims, in which the liquid was gently agitated until the picture appeared. I don't think I paid much attention to the pictures; when they came the exciting part was over.

When he was "developing," Papa did not speak, he only whistled, with modulations that imitated a flute, and this too added to the pleasure.

Mama was interested in the pictures; but she often fell asleep waiting. She got teased for this; she would laugh and say that her brothers used to make fun of her at home: even as a little girl, she used to fall asleep early in the evening. (I saw this as evidence of her naïveté, one side of her inferiority compared with Papa.)

Papa took the art of photography seriously; he had had his name embossed in gold on the red binding of the album with the words: Amateur Photographer. (Mama found this droll.) Papa used the same term—I thought it was his exclusive property—for his activities as a painter and as a flutist, if he happened to talk about them to somebody; but he certainly considered photography a simpler art.

The style of his photographs was similar to that of his paintings. The images were calm and delicate, with no pronounced shadows or stiffness, captured, so to speak, with a light hand.

As time went by the poses changed a little. Mama held my little sister on her knee, and it was obvious that my sister was not aware she was in a photograph; I would lean on my hoop—almost as tall as I was—and look impatient. Papa looked less romantic and more cheerful, Mama more fulfilled perhaps, more serene. Is that where her happiness lay? ("Don't I have two lovely little girls?" she said when she was dying and time for her had ceased to exist.)

Papa had also taken a lot of photos at the top of the Castle, always in the same location, with a pine tree with a forked trunk in the background.

In one, Papa rested his head against Mama's (it belongs to the "romantic" period); Mama is lost in thought, as if she were all alone, toying with my hair with one hand; I am in front of her, still small, about two or three years old, with thin legs, and in my eyes that ill-at-ease astonished look that I always had.

But the picture I was looking for now was of Mama by herself. Mama, dressed in white, with the pine trees behind her, leaning slightly, with one hand, on her parasol. Her slim waist was enclosed in a wide belt with a silver buckle. If I didn't have the photo, I would only have remembered the belt. It was a strip of heavy silk with pale yellow and pink stripes and a very high buckle. Mama gave it to us later to play with. Her blouse was made of lace, her skirt smooth, flared at the bottom. A little above the wrist the puckered lace fell down soft and wide. The wrist was slender, the hand thin and tired-looking.

I held her hand in my hands when it was once more like the hand in the photo: I picked it up as it lay on the coverlet. The small hand with the little finger slightly crooked had a shy, so to speak secret grace. It was abandoned, but at the same time it gripped faintly, and the delicate warmth it gave off was like a final silent devotion.

There were women around us: unspeaking, attentive, almost holding their breath. But not all the time. Often they had things to do: clean, dust, change the flowers. Things that "had to be done." She would praise their work: "Good, very good." But with me she would exchange a glance of regret: they had interrupted the silence, the contemplation. I suffered for these interruptions, but I was also ashamed of not being able to make myself useful like the others. I was happy just to be able to sit at her side and look at her face, at her hands, white and slender again as they had been when she was young.

I compared, inadvertently at first, her hands with those of the visitors and relatives. Next to hers, their thick solid wrists stood out more. They suggested a hardness almost, something heavy and wooden about the persons. And her gracefulness seemed without defences and in a way fatal. As if it was as a consequence of that gracefulness that she was dying now.

At the top of the Castle, among the scattered trees, I felt the wind coming up from the valley as it used to. The overgrown clearing still bore the imprint of the ancient construction: remote, unwonted in its size.

The caretaker's house had been spruced up; the arcades bricked in. It was impossible to get up close: there was a fence and a locked gate.

I climbed once more the pathways half-hidden among the acacias, and they all ended up against a wire fence. Lumps of scrap metal, relics of the war, showed that soldiers had passed through, maybe stayed there. It was not possible to reach the tunnels or the rocky ledges: they continued to be off limits, even if only as the result of an oversight.

Still, I found what I was looking for, that precise point of reference: the pine with the forked trunk. Mama had posed there, among the prickly junipers that brushed against her dress.

The forked trunk had gotten stockier, like a person who has put on weight with age. In those days, the two slender branching stems had been spread apart like the two arms of a lyre. The terrain was steep, slippery because of the dry grass.

The Podio with its gentler contour is a prolongation of the Castle heights, which are solid rock. The road is on the side looking over the Cemetery and, across the fields, towards the Stura river. The road to the Podio is paved with dry moss like an old carpet; it runs between hummocks cropped close by the wind, between barren little fields white with stones and stubble.

I had always associated that feeling of life suspended, of "a road that leads nowhere" with my own roads "of vice and virtue." But the going was too easy to symbolize the harsh road of goodness, too arid to represent the allurements of evil: I called it "the road to nothingness." Perhaps I meant "death"?

I took the road again and it still seemed familiar to me; and I to it. At the edge of a field, long and swift, the bound of a hare went by, and immediately afterwards, on its scent, a black and white dog (a pointer like our Lisa). He was seeking, quivering all over, on edge. The hunter's whistle called him back: the hunting season wasn't open yet.

Translated by Anthony Oldcorn

On the Neverending Terrace

Anna Maria Ortese

Taken from Anna Maria Ortese's remarkable 1986 collection *In sonno e in veglia* (*Asleep and Awake*), "On the Neverending Terrace" introduces us to a strange subliminal dimension reminiscent of her 1965 masterpiece *The Iguana*. All classic perspectives are disrupted in this story: the house with its peculiar feeling of isolation and its strange layout "stretched out like a long tram, or a goods wagon left on a disused track," swiftly expands into a whole nightmarish landscape where bizarre mechanical creatures, migrating from the realm of folktales, are connected to a sinister and haunting presence. The story's final twist, however, is laden with Ortese's own molten material, leaving a personal mark on this parody of a gothic fairy tale. Born in Rome in 1914, one of seven children, Ortese grew up in southern Italy and in Tripoli. Her formal education ended at age thirteen. She died in 1998. Her highly original work spans at least four decades.[1] As critic Sharon Wood has written: "Ortese's protest against 'realism' is more than stylistic and expressive dissent. . . . Her stories and novels consistently challenge elements of conventional narrative structure such as plot and character, dealing instead with the ebb and flow of experience, emotion, thought and dream which escape the constraint of logical reasoning. . . . Ortese's is a quest for light in darkness, for reality in a world of sham and illusion, and her fantastic fictions lightly mask a seriousness of purpose rarely to be matched in modern Italian fiction."[2] As Ortese herself writes in her "literary testament," a short autobiography: "I have sometimes managed, in the course of at least some fifty years of adult life, to reach the luminous shore—I think of myself as eternally shipwrecked—of a form of self-expression and creativity that find their unswerving goal in the hope of capturing and fixing—if only for an instant, meaning the span of time encompassed by a work of art—the marvelous phenomenon of living and feeling."[3]

NOTES

1. Her works include: *Il mare non bagna Napoli* (*The Sea Doesn't Touch Naples*, 1953), *Il porto di Toledo: Ricordi della vita irreale* (*The Port of Toledo: Memories from the Unreal Life*, 1975), *Il cardillo addolorato* (1993; *The Lament of the Linnet*, trans. Patrick Creagh [London: Harvill, 1997]), and *The Iguana*, trans. Henry Martin (Kingston, N.Y.: McPherson, 1987). Some of her short stories are now available to the American reader in *A Music Behind the Wall: Selected Stories*, trans. Henry Martin (Kingston, N.Y.: McPherson, 1994). Among her most recent titles are: *Il mormorio di Parigi* (*Paris's Whispers*, 1986), *In sonno e in veglia* (*Asleep and Awake*, 1987), the travelogues *La lente scura: Scritti di viaggio* (*The Dark Lens*, 1991), *Il mio paese è la notte* (*My Country Is the Night*, 1996), *Alonso e i visionari* (*Alonso and the Seers*, 1996), and *Corpo celeste* (*Celestial Body*, 1997).

2. Sharon Wood, "Anna Maria Ortese and the Art of the Real," in *Italian Women's Writing, 1860–1994* (London: Athlone, 1995), 173 and 183.

3. Ortese's entire text, *When Time Is Another,* can be read online in Henry Martin's translation at http://www.archipelago.org/vol2-4/ortese.htm.

On the Neverending Terrace
by Anna Maria Ortese

IN A HOUSE where I lived before, here in Liguria, strange happenings occurred. But I must briefly describe it. Tiny, for one thing, yet, through a peculiarity of its layout or the structure of the premises, such as to appear quite large. Five or six doors lining a very long, not quite straight corridor paved with violet-coloured tiles, and two other doors, one at each end of the corridor, but situated in such a way that they were not directly facing, were perhaps the secret of the house's illusory size. In the middle of the corridor was the door opening on to the stairs, and immediately opposite, as a feature of the corridor itself, was the little door of the lift, which thereby gave direct access into the house. Just the two large rooms stood precisely at each end of the corridor: one, north facing, had a yellow floor; in the other, which was southwest facing (the house being somewhat crooked), a fine violet-coloured floor met the eye. The north-facing room had a narrowish balcony, and because of its situation, it got the sun for *only* one hour in the morning. For the rest of the day it was sunk in a sad half light. The southwest-facing room, because of its situation, was brightened by the sun *only* in the evening, and never in winter. And the whole house was stretched out like an old tram, or a goods wagon left on a disused track, in the middle of a terrace so limitless—I'd have no way of knowing where it ended— that I've never seen anything like it, and it seemed more akin to a valley. Now, around it, there were mountains and more mountains, hills so-called, but strictly mountains, and rising so high above the room as to cast a shadow on the inner walls and the furniture itself. This, northwards. In other directions—south most of all—were more and more new houses, some of them quite pretty, but all shut up tight because they were completely uninhabited, redolent of an ancient, vast necropolis long since forgotten in that valley. Which gave the house on the terrace a peculiar feeling of isolation. Bearable in summer, but in wintry weather rather sinister. The wind whistled, the rain drummed on the roof or streamed incessantly down every wall of the house, and a fluffy towel with a big brightly-coloured sailor on it that I'd attached to the walls of the lift flapped backwards and forwards somewhat foolishly, because the wind blowing through the doors of the lift kept puffing it out and in. And all the time, through the window panes of the balconies, those great mountain slopes thick with vegetation, and clouds, and the smokiness of fog and the smoke of shepherds' fires. And, to the south, that huge great valley of empty houses, where the sun, whenever it came out, seemed almost paler than the fog.

Now, this is what happened. But, another thing before that, I ought to say that the perpetual sensation of an invisible *third presence* was a torment both to me and to the person who lived with me in that house. This person, who for now I'll call Trude, didn't realize it, but it cast a gloom over her, while the thing always just put me on a knife edge of dread and *dumbfoundment.*

Apart from the *presence* (just as if some uninvited guest were living in a room or even inside a seemingly innocent wall of the apartment, a room or wall whose *charged* atmosphere had long since even escaped the notice of the occasional tenants, and maybe at the time, even of the builder); apart from this *presence*, there were phenomena: the first of which, more garish than any of the others, was, one morning, a kind of immense dawn, coloured a pink very close to cyclamen, which terrified me more than I can say, and lasted for two hours. The mountains were rose-pink, the valley and November storm clouds roseate. There wasn't a gleam of sunshine, nor a single sign of life. Trude, to whom I didn't venture a word, was equally dismayed, thunderstruck. But since there was no janitor, nor any tenants in the little block, nor any shops whatsoever in the neighbourhood, and not even any smallholders digging their plots, we had no idea who to ask, who to turn to for an explanation. This dawn-phenomenon had a second occurrence, but its effects—in comparison with the extent and intensity of the first—were considerably less.

And then, the clocks. In the house at that time, there were a lot of little clocks in coloured wood, German made, the gift of a worker who had been for many years in Stuttgart, or rather a small town nearby, famous, it seems, for these delicate little timepieces. These toy-like clocks, decorated with birds and branches and tendrils of gold-brown wood, and little blue doors that opened intriguingly to allow a glimpse of two little figures, hadn't worked for years, but in that house they all started up again, striking the hours unsynchronized and almost without interruption, and the little blue doors would open and shut, and the two little figures would go up and down with ecstatic faces. And all of them together—fortunately not all day long—would make an artless, grating noise, as if a rapt, invisible hand had wound them up, though only so as to hear again the sound of music heard before, and to be listened to again with an urgency that came from genuine desperation; and then, abruptly, just as it had begun, the horrid little music died away. And I ought to add here the business with the house keys, which were to be found one minute on the floor of one room, the next on the floor of another; you would go to pick them up, they would fly off, and you would hear the unmistakable sound of them falling ten yards away. I won't talk about the spiders. The valley was full of them, a variety of fast, reddish-coloured spider, with a kind of curly fuzz, rather like a beard, round the head and the little legs covered in what looked like boots, reddish coloured too. Despite the house being awash with insecticide, they never went away, they were everywhere, in fact I suppose they were the worst thing. Sometimes, motionless on the walls, they seemed to be listening. The minute an eye fastened upon them, then, as people say about flying saucers, they were off. And this brings me to the pack of cigarettes.

One morning, on the table in my room, there was a pack with red wrapping and big white lettering, bought in the nearby resort town a week before. I didn't like them in the least, I far preferred the cheap, grey national brand cigarettes. That morning, though, I didn't have any national brand. I leave the room—just long enough to answer the telephone ringing in the corridor (nobody!)—I go back, and there, on the table, *just one cigarette*—all the others had vanished— half of it a normal white cigarette, the other half entirely black.

Broken open, it was shown to be made of totally *black* tobacco, and I looked at it for two solid days, doing not a stroke of work. Then, after gathering those nasty little shreds into a piece of paper, I threw them from the top of the terrace, abetted by the gushing stream of rainwater, which whooshed them right away.

Another phenomenon, one a bit less disturbing—if you could bring any more or less into these things, their being all equally inscrutable— was the sudden cutting off of the television screen in the west-facing room in the evenings, even though everywhere else the power was still on. Then, after a few minutes, the picture came back, but with little figures moving about in the background (with their backs turned), little figures that weren't part of the programme. These had made me start to dislike the TV. However, I imagine this phenomenon was some kind of technical fault, nothing out of the ordinary, it was just that, combined with so many other things, it too had a bad effect.

Whereas there were other phenomena, like the sudden and inexplicable moving together of two *similar* objects, right before my eyes, let's say *two* nails, *two* used matches, *two* screws—even outside the room, on the terrace, and in the raging wind and rain—I didn't take much notice, they hardly seemed anything to do with me. Before my very eyes, from being essentially *motionless*, these small objects would begin to move, and after rushing together, they would stop, settle at rest. Sometimes, a day later, even so much as a month later, they would still be there, impervious to the wind and rain. Or else, *suddenly*, they'd have gone. And who's to know where these paltry objects go, and what could have been the reason either for their convergence, or for their final departure.

One autumn night—or spring perhaps? the air was so serene!—I was taking a walk on that terrace, having been sleepless for some hours. Trude was sleeping soundly, and I was going backwards and forwards along the neverending terrace, peering about among the mountains, looking out for a light, even a glimmer of one, any sign of life. Nothing, nothing! And, thinking of this, such a deep despair, such a wordless despair took hold of my spirits. I wondered whether—not just in cities, but throughout the limitless universe—the human soul is everywhere so alone and lost in such a profound silence and accursed solitude. I had been told as a child that on earth there lived, invisible, the guardian spirits of men, and I recalled that for many, very many years, I had ceased to bother with mine, I hadn't even remembered its existence. Perhaps it had grown, like me, or become, instead, very tiny? To cut a long story short: without thinking, in a sudden fit of foolishness, I called him: "If you're there, answer, and hurry up please," I said. "If you're there, *creature*, or dear *angel* of mine, answer," that's what I said.

No sooner said than done—well, let's say a moment later—a tiny little light began whirling round in front of me.

"Huh, you're a firefly!" I said laughing.

And, just as I said it, I immediately realized that there were no fireflies left in the whole world, and at that time of year, cool as it was, at night, they would never have stirred themselves.

"Well . . . do you mind telling me who you are?" I said, trembling.

And right after this:

"Oh Firefly, Firefly, pray for me."

She gave a little whirl, as if to say: " . . . yes . . . yes . . . well . . . we'll see . . . but you'd forgotten all about me, hmm?" And with that—and a whirl or two as she went—she was gone.

First thing the next morning—it was still dark outside—there was a knock at the door.

It was the postman, with a letter bringing me wonderful news.

I can leave this house and this town of mysteries and harrowing presentiments, for the lovely life-filled, happy place where I lived before. My joy made it seem like a dream. I call Trude. She's happy too, she laughs, she can't believe it:

"So, everything'll change! So, no more wracked nerves, no more mystery! Oh, how marvellous! Oh, how could it have happened?"

She comes up to the door beside me, to give the postman a tip if he's still there. She's so delighted she wants everybody to be happy. But we can't find the key. The door hasn't been opened since the night before. The key—we see now—is in its usual place, on top of a chest.

"Oh!" cries Trude. "So who brought the letter? So, there was nobody here! So it isn't true, the letter's a dream!"

And she bursts into tears.

But it was true! We made a telephone call, as soon as it turned nine o'clock, and had it confirmed.

Only, no news of the postman.

But a woman who was going to mass around that time says she saw a lovely little girl about six years old coming out of our house, wearing a dark cloak and carrying a lantern.

She skipped, like any schoolgirl, loose-limbed, and, the woman says, almost *flew* above the shrubbery.

Translated by Liz Heron

The Piazza

Fabrizia Ramondino

WHAT BETTER site of collective memory in the Italian literary subconscious than a piazza? All memory lanes seem to converge on it. "A most civilized piazza, sunlit . . ." begins this excerpt from Neapolitan writer Fabrizia Ramondino's 1981 novel *Althenopis*, the mythical name of the fictional Neapolitan village of Santa Maria del Mare. As Ramondino (b. 1936) explains in a footnote: "The name of my native city. Originally its name meant 'maiden's eye.' But it seems that the Germans, during the Occupation, finding it so decrepit compared with Mozart's descriptions . . . changed its name to Althenopis, as if to mean 'hag's eye.'" Like a stage, her piazza soon fills up with swarming crowds of people and objects that, were they not rescued by the powerful magnet of memory, would remain forever buried within our subconscious. Ramondino, like Romano, is "concerned with the recuperation of memory, from childhood and from the most recent past, and the difficulties of remembering," interweaving in her work autobiography, meditations, and storytelling.[1] Her work has often been compared, rightly or not, to that of Elsa Morante. In fact, Morante's "southern" legacy, that collision of collective memory, history, and personal mythology, does seem to form the backdrop of Ramondino's work, more evident than any direct stylistic influence. In the words of critic Jonathan Usher, *Althenopis* "is a partially first-person re-evocation of a series of lost worlds which are presented to us via a fascinating potpourri of unbridled poetic suggestion and conscientious, almost academic regard for authenticity."[2] Ramondino is like an exile in her homeland, and her work the gentle salvaging of an anthropological archive which, precisely because it is so familiar, risks being irretrievably lost.

NOTES

1. Michael Caesar, "Contemporary Italy (since 1956)," in *The Cambridge History of Italian Literature*, ed. Peter Brand and Lino Pertile (Cambridge: Cambridge University Press, 1996), 601. Among Ramondino's other works are: *Storie di patio* (*Patio Stories*, 1983); the travelogue *Taccuino tedesco* (*German Notebook*, 1987); *Un giorno e mezzo* (*A Day and a Half*, 1988); *Star di casa* (*To Be at Home*, 1991), *Terremoto con madre e figlia* (*Earthquake with Mother and Daughter*, 1994); *In viaggio* (*On the Journey*, 1995); and *L'isola riflessa* (*The Reflected Island*, 1998). Also noteworthy is her "anthropolinguistic" work *Dadapolis: Caleidoscopio napoletano* (*Dadapolis: A Neapolitan Kaleidoscope*, with Andreas Friedrich Muller, 1989), a playful collection of Neapolitan quotations, maxims, and proverbs.

2. Jonathan Usher, "Fabrizia Ramondino: The Muse of Memory," in *The New Italian Novel*, ed. Zygmunt G. Baranski and Lino Pertile (Edinburgh: Edinburgh University Press, 1993), 166–67. The variable, semiautobiographical voice, interlacing first and third person, "encourages the reader to assume an autobiographical identity between the author and the narrator, much as close friends often feel no need to call each other by name."

The Piazza

by Fabrizia Ramondino

A MOST civilized piazza, sunlit, Mediterranean, poor but never mean, smiling with flowers on window-sills, the area outside each house swept every morning; conceived and built, it seemed, in a single moment, from a single plan, such was its harmony, usefulness and grace. A notary, a pharmacist and a landowner had built, it seems, the three large houses that bounded it, and which stretched or spread loosely beyond the piazza into other buildings rich in stairways, arches, gardens of orange trees and courtyards. Pink, yellowish, washed-out blue were the colours of the houses. The other side of the piazza was bounded by the church and the priest's house. From the villages higher up, Monticchio, Schiazzano, Termini, L'Annunziata, Aiello, Anteselva, Nocelle, and from the villages lower down, Metamunno, La Marina, Sistri, Alisistri, Marciano, you could see the round and familiar asphalt-covered dome of the church brooding lovingly over the village. And thick around the village the straw mats that roofed the lemon and orange groves.

We lived in what had been the notary's house. Stone lions orna-
mented the balustrade of the stairway. Facing ours was the house
that must have belonged to the pharmacist, with a pink façade, where
some old women lived upstairs, while below there was the bakery.
The house continued on from the bakery in more genteel form, and
this wing was occupied by spinsters who lived by sewing. Their balconies, with sharp-pointed railings, always had geraniums in flower.
Next to the bakery was the tobacconist's where our mother used to
send us to buy Nazionali cigarettes, and once in a while for a few
pence we would buy large white knobbly comfits or pink ones like
shells or mint caramels thin and round as lentils. The tobacconist's
was a place of perdition, for it also sold wine and the whole day long
three or four men would sit drinking inside, in woollen vests, their
lean white arms covered in flies. It also sold postcards with pictures
of loving couples: they sat beside a trellis of roses or an ivy garland;
the girls wore flowered dresses and their lovers had jackets and ties
with a gold stripe; their cheeks were painted pink. The tobacconist
also sold black exercise books with red borders, pens and pencils,
little bottles of ink, and those "Giotto" coloured pencils whose
points were forever breaking, or would slip out whole from the
wood, and served better for cleaning our teeth than for drawing.

In the house that had belonged to the landowner—the largest in
the piazza, almost a palace, divided into two wings by a central arch
leading to the rest of the village which terminated, as rosaries do
with the crucifix, in the ruins of the castle—there lived dozens of
families, most of them heirs of the one-time owners. One of these
families was very influential and the father, among his many other
dealings, looked after the interests of the Gargiulos who lived in the
capital. The wife, who was ever so fat, was a seamstress and they had

an only daughter, rotund and blonde. Mariarosa was treated better than we other children, always had impeccable flowered dresses, gleaming hair, carefully combed, washed with shampoo and not soap like ours. They gave her dolls taller than herself which she kept on top of the wardrobe, laid out in cellophane boxes like fairytale tombs, or propped up on her mother's bed like oddly dressed visitors. One wasn't supposed to touch them. She seemed like a doll herself and was careful when she played, so hardly ever scraped her elbows or knees. She was an only child, in line with her mother's decision when a second child was born dead and deformed. Now and again Mariarosa would tell us that her mother had taken an infusion of parsley and was in bed with a colic and shitting a lot, all soft; at times she would shit blood or angels, little angels, she would tell us, like the cherubs in the big painting at the foot of her bed who played the harp and, glorious and triumphant, blew on trumpets and flutes.

When birthdays came round in Mariarosa's house, lavish parties were held and guests streamed in from the nearby villages. The feasting took place in the lemon grove where the clustered trees thinned out towards the vineyard; the father sat on a plank with his legs crossed and his white shirt open down to his hairy belly; the women went in and out with *guantiere** heaped with pastries ordered from the pastry-cook in Corento, and handed round glasses of vermouth or lemonade. Mariarosa's father would laugh indulgently and lend an ear to the confidences of his guests. He made his money managing property, in setting up deals and acting as middleman. Occasionally he would go off to Althenopis in a trap, his pockets bulging

*Althenopis dialect: salver for gloves. Because it was on this that gloves were handed to the master. The Spanish grandeur in the offering of food and drink wouldn't be conveyed by the Italian term.

with bundles of thousand-lire notes tied with string. On his return he brought presents for his wife and daughter, filling the house with bric-à-brac: a music-box ballerina, a huge painted shell, fans, glass balls in which snow fell when you shook them. After the war he brought a photograph in a silver frame of an actress called Shirley Temple. Once he turned up with some canaries; another time he promised a monkey but his wife was afraid and didn't want it.

Next door to Mariarosa was the cobbler. The cobbler was skinny and sad—all the family was skinny and sad—and wore glasses; in the village only he and my mother wore glasses. He had six children; the older ones were tainted with consumption and were being looked after in a hospital in Althenopis, though even when they got better they never worked in our village but only in the neighbouring ones. Every now and again the house was whitewashed; through the open door one could see the interior: large green plants near the sewing-machine in the living-room lapped the sisters in shadow as they worked. The village girls did not go there for their Easter dresses, but every fortnight a woman would appear, puffing and perspiring, with a lad who took away trousers in a bundle humped on his head. Once out of the piazza, just before turning the corner, he would look back and stick his tongue out. We weren't allowed in that house because they all spat blood. The mother wore a hair shirt under her dress to punish herself and expiate the malady; but we played in the piazza with the two youngest girls, Anna and Immacolatella, and sometimes, to spite my mother, I would go into their house to drink a glass of water and then spit to check the colour of the saliva.

Next to the cobbler's, in a house that looked out on a shady lemon grove, lived a young woman who had been evacuated from Althenopis because of the air-raids. She was about thirty years old, very beautiful, with a large bosom and wavy hair, who was said to have worked in the land registry and to have lost her job when the offices were moved underground because of the bombing. Signorina Angelina lived with her invalid mother and was very fond of geraniums. Hers was a true passion. She didn't like simple geraniums—or at least she despised them as commonplace—and looked instead for complicated hybrids, violets and reds, whites and purples, pinks and lilacs, with black stripes, with colours that blended into one another, with pointed or jagged petals. When we returned with a rare species from our sorties in the countryside or the villages or deserted villas roundabout she was delighted, and rewarded us with sweets or thirty lire; and if the species flowered we were called to inspect it, while she looked on, her eyes shining with a moisture that seemed anointed and perfumed. She would bend over the plant with her large bosom, not like that of the other women, compressed by a bodice, but wearing an indecent brassière, my mother said, which supported each of her breasts singly instead of squeezing them together. Coral pendants tapped lightly against her cheeks, and the strange shape of the geranium seemed to expand into the shape of her ears. She took care of the geraniums at dawn after cleaning out the hen-coop, and she used a special fertilizer which required that Signorina Angelina crap not in the toilet but in a little pisspot which she covered with a chipped flowered plate to keep off the flies.

In the house adjacent to Angelina's lived three young men, probably with their families, but we knew nothing about them. They rushed through the piazza smoking cigarettes, and occasionally gave an idle kick to our ball. We began a relationship with the young males only when one of them died. There was one whose house lay in the stretch between Santa Maria del Mare and Metamunno. We all went into the bedroom: he was lying on an iron bedstead against the wall, a white damask cloth strewn with comfits covered him chest-high, all around there were lilies, sprigs of jasmine, freesias, and a profusion of roses with worm-eaten petals. He was as beautiful as could be, dark-skinned, his hair cropped because he was a soldier, the face plump and tranquil. He seemed to be lying there waiting to become part of one of those loving couples in the postcards; all he needed was his cheeks to be painted red; or, with that elegant suit and tie, he might have been ready to set off on a rapid trip to the Americas.

In front of the landowner's house were the three church buildings: the façade of the church itself, the bell-tower, the house of the parish priest. A single gateway led to the priest's house and to that of Antima and her children. Don Candido, always up and about, went through the village umbrella in hand even on fine days, as if to give himself standing; in fact almost nobody had an umbrella and when it rained they shielded their heads with bits of waxed cloth. Donna Antima was in service with the priest; and the word was that her daughter, Antonia, was having it off with him. Antonia was blonde with curly permed hair and washed-out blue eyes in a pale and bony face. Donna Antima and her daughter would address us in honeyed tones and almost always in Italian. And when they drove us away, they never used bad language like the other women, but said "Shoo, shoo" as if we were chicks. Criato, Antima's other child, was the village idiot; he would leave the piazza in the early morning with five sheep and come back in the evening. Sometimes as we played we came across him in the countryside and made fun of him; his blurred and guttural voice would follow after us.

When Criato was very unhappy he would take his clothes off in

the fields and shake them threateningly in the direction of the village. We liked to watch him piss. "Go on, have a piss!" we would say.
He would pull out his part*—which was what we children called
it—and point it upwards to make as high a jet as possible, then he
would hold it in his hand smiling proudly, catching the last drop on
his fingertip and putting it in his mouth.

The interior of the church was in that rustic baroque one finds in
the fondant-covered biscuits the nuns make in those regions, or in
certain Easter cakes covered in meringue and tiny coloured comfits.
On the right of the high altar, balancing the pulpit, towered a large
white marble statue of the Madonna, donated in 1915 by the mother
of a minor aristocrat from the village, sister to our grandmother, as
an offering for the safe return of her son from the war. Above the
high altar there was a fresco showing an extraordinary young man
with an azure tunic and blond hair, hugging a lamb in his arms, who
seemed intent on informing me that I wasn't fit to live.

All the flowers in the village and the surrounding area, apart from

---

*It has cost me much fatigue to go through all the facts recounted in this
tale. Then to revise the text, so that it satisfies memory and the reader, has required a certain labour. Here, for example, in the first draft I had written
"prick." That was a lazy accommodation to fashion, a sign also of a certain se-
nility of thought, but above all a serious mis-use of language because in those
days this part of the body, like many another thing, had for us no name. It was
in fact called "the fact," "the whatsit," or "the this," or "the that." Correct, in
fact, was "the part" or "the piece," at least for us girls, while the remainder was
the body. Part, therefore, not of a boy's body, but of a cosmic and mysterious
body. With this "part" was associated a numinous quality which therefore cannot
be rendered by terms like "penis" or "prick." The first because of the obvious
limit of the exact sciences, the second because, as with all obscene language, it
reduces the numinous to a merely base and infernal force, whereas an essential
feature of the numinous is its ambiguity.

the geraniums, seemed to be grown for the cemetery or the church which were always decked out with them: white, blue, purple irises, stupid and puffed-up calla lilies towering over the other flowers, hawthorn, jonquils and carnations, dog-roses and garden roses, yellow, white, sometimes of an emphatic red, swollen, soon blown and drooping, wasp-eaten and infested by ants, no sooner open than the petals would fall. In the half-shadow there would be a busy coming and going of old women changing the water, trimming stems, stripping off rotten leaves and replacing the flowers in the vases of blue opal or frosted glass; a heavy odour always hung about inside, putrid and sweet.

At Easter, corn-stalk wound round with strands of red wool germinated in dozens of vases; on the side-altars bizarre compositions appeared: pine-cones in which, weeks earlier, lentil seeds had been set and which germinated with a Germanic gentleness; or twisted and dwarfish succulents in small vases, the childish sports of the old women. The church would be hung with black and silver and banners of varied and conflicting colours. When newly-weds left the church the fathers threw sugared almonds to the watching children— coins even, if they were rich—and we would dive into the scrimmage to grab them. The smaller children cried since they never got anything.

On Sundays everybody went to church in their best. In spring after the war the young women and the girls were a gala of clothes. A young man came from Metamunno to play the organ.

For its flowers, for its scents, for its splendours, for its moulderings, for its stucco, for its frescos, for its hangings and its embroidered cloths, for its gilded missals, for the solemn fervour of its sermons and its music, for its festive flowered dresses, the church was a magical sphere enclosing all the luxuries and secret unbridledness of the world. And in this fulgid great sin which was the church, each Sunday I had to confess my sins. On the first occasion I said to Don Candido: "I haven't committed any sins." I was kneeling in the confessional, my eyes in the half-dark screwed up in an effort to make out his face behind the grille, where it sometimes seemed like a beast's in the shadow of the stables or of certain dreams. "It's a sin of pride not to have any sins," said Don Candido, and from then on, scared by the long silences between us, and by that horrible verdict, I went round my friends asking for sins. And then I would say: "I stole some beans, I stole some money or some sweets." Or: "I've been envious, I've been gluttonous." But all these things didn't seem like sins to me. The only great sin that I knew I daily committed was that of being different from the marvellous youth in majestic movement over the high altar. My swarthiness, my dark eyes, my skinniness, my nocturnal frights—those, for example, were sins.

And sins, too, were my pelting races in the rain to meet my father from the motor-coach on the New Road, running till I dropped breathless and lay abandoned with my cheek on the road surface; or when I ran in one breath from the rock of the Annunciata to the piazza, with my arms over my head, never stopping; or when at nine in the evenings I wouldn't come in from play in the piazza and heard my mother's futile calling, mingling or alternating with the other women's. Each window had its voice, whether tired and tame, or imploring and nagging, or furious, or sharp and peremptory, or uncaring and distracted, or loving and fetching. These were sins. They were not sins of disobedience as I confessed to Don Candido, but of incontinence, even if I didn't know how to say so because it was not among the words I knew then.

Also a sin was my terror of lightning, when I hid trembling under the table in the kitchen, which looked out on the open country where the storms crossed the valley.

Certainly Don Candido had no understanding of sins: in the great sin of his church he moved about like a book-keeper, ministering the sacraments and quick slaps to the children.

With the profound contempt that I felt for him, contenting himself with silly little sins and fooling himself every Sunday when he thought he was absolving my torments and my unconfessable rapture, there was mixed a kind of social contempt inculcated by our mother, who was sceptical about church matters; and, with opposite motives, by our grandmother, who compared Don Candido to altogether different priests and especially to the saints. So going to church on Sundays became part of one's social duties, from which, by a privilege reserved for grown-ups, our mother was exempt.

Flanked by the bakery and the wall of the church was the opening of the little street that led to the New Road. On the right was the carter who sold vegetables and slept in front of his store in the early afternoons. He was fat with a large belly half uncovered—he could never find vests his size—and had a son as fat as himself called To-tore, who was one of our playmates. The carter was a jovial man and a great gossip. It was he who brought the news from Althenopis where he went one night a week to sell his vegetables in the market. Beside him on the cart he would set a basket with his bite for two days, a flask of wine, and two copper pans that he used in the city as helmets against the bombing. We gave bits of carrot and mouldy fennel to the donkey and he patted it and promised it a fabulous harness if it would take him quickly into town. The least ornamental was to be red with brass buckles, but he also promised twenty-four-carat gold with silver bells and velvet cloth. "When the war is over I'll buy them for you," he would say in a singsong.

One time he brought back a large blonde doll with its belly torn open and a missing leg, almost as big as my sister; he had come across it in a bombed-out house. Once a week he took a soup made from seven particular vegetables to a woman in Althenopis. Should he add *borrana** and a bit of pig's skin she would give him a tip with tears in her eyes. "It's as if the war were over," she would say; and she tipped him almost every time with a *bonbonnière* for she was the midwife of the Decumani district and everyone took her sugared almonds. After the Liberation the tips were more substantial because an American soldier, the son of her brother who had emigrated, kept heaping her with tins of stuff, cigarettes and candies.

The carter also took baskets of lemons to a place in Via del Serraglio where the lemons were just a front for anti-Fascist propaganda. He would laugh till his belly shook as he told us this but we couldn't understand the reason for his chuckles. Often in the city women ordered large bundles of parsley and on those occasions also

---

*Althenopis dialect: borage, medicinal herbaceous plant, with oval leaves covered in rough hairs. It has a blue flower and the tips and leaves can be cooked. The Decumani midwife used to prepare her "married" soup even in wartime, to comfort the offence to her bowels of so many deaths—she, who aided entry into the land of the living. Some skin from a pig, and where possible even a bit of meat, is set to simmer in salted water. When the skin is almost cooked the vegetables are added: chicory, various kinds of broccoli, cabbage, etc., and the essential ingredient, borage, which is rare in city markets because it grows wild and since it is prickly, children, whose allotted task it is to collect such things, avoid it as they do thistles.

When skin or meat are not included the soup is simple and no longer "married."

he would laugh and chant: "It's not bad, it's not bad, parsley and *purchiachella** salad!" When he loaded the lettuces on the cart, in neat rows with the hearts all opening one way, he would sing a song about a lettuce on the bottom of the sea, pat the donkey on the back, do the same for his son, and then make a waltzing twirl with another bundle of lettuce before setting it alongside the others. He always had a flask of wine beside the door of the shop, wrapped in cabbage-leaves when the sun was on it, which he offered to the men going by and to the old women, who waved it away. He would drink, wipe his mouth with the back of his hand and tell us how his great belly had saved him from the war, since they hadn't been able to come up with a uniform his size. He had got himself diagnosed as dropsical. And he laughingly claimed that it wasn't water swelling his belly but wine. He hid bottles of olive-oil under the vegetables on the cart to sell on the black market, and when he went about at night he was more afraid of the customs and excise than he was of bandits.

One evening the carter came dancing up to the tobacconist's entirely drunk, shaking a bundle of newspapers like a tambourine. "The war's over!"—he clamoured—"The war's over!" It was true. The war was over. His loud summons at the edge of the village boomed through the piazza and everybody came to windows and out on to the street in wonder. We stopped our playing and crowded round the tobacconist's in mute expectation. He had heard it that morning in Althenopis. And he waved the newspapers he had got from the opponents of Fascism, the people who pretended to sell lemons, until the tobacconist snatched them from him and set about

---

*Althenopis dialect: purslane, lit. maiden's vulva. Infusions of parsley are a well-known abortive agent.

reading them. And while people were running up he went down towards the piazza with the cart; and we, our first surprise over, skipped round him while the tobacconist brought up the procession spelling out the headlines. All the village gathered in the piazza, and from window to window and door to door the word ran: "The war's over!" Everybody began hugging everyone else; the women were crying; Don Candido was called to open the church. Criato, Donn'Antima's son, went to ring the bells. Don Candido wept on the steps of the church and said: "Thanks be to God, the war is over!" Our mother had heard it on the radio two hours earlier but hadn't said a word, either because she didn't think the news of any great importance, or because, distrustful and hard to convince, she had thought it a lie. She didn't believe in the radio or the newspapers, but only in books. And then, whom should she have told? She wasn't like the others. She didn't even tell Granny. Only when she saw the crowd in the piazza and heard the word going round from door to door, from window to window, did she pull herself together, get out of bed, and lean on the window-sill with her hair damp from vinegar. Grandmother ran down the stairs, her hair in a mess and covered in the dust of the attic she was tidying.

With tears in her eyes, careless of the conventions of her rank, she knelt on the steps of the church to thank God and beseech him to bring back soon from the Indies her prisoner grandson.

When Criato finished ringing the bells and came down into the piazza red and panting, radiant with joy and self-importance, the carter took his hand, and with a gesture half burlesque and half serious, bent and kissed it. Criato burst into tears and in his blurry voice stuttered out a sound which seemed to want to mean "The war's over!" "ar's . . . ar's . . . ," he went on saying. We gazed in silence and nobody mimicked him.

The women carried chairs out into the piazza, the men began to arrive with the *cacciate*,* some bringing out fennel, some cheese, or wine, walnuts, hazelnuts. Somebody brought out good bread, not the everyday bread that tasted of diesel. And all evening long people stayed up drinking, dancing, chatting, and with an extension from the church the radio was set up to address the piazza. From the window Mother called us in, but to no point; then, as if ashamed, she withdrew into the shadow.

Some days later we were playing on the New Road. Two jeeps arrived with the Americans. They seemed like royal swans. The moment they saw us lined up on the road, as if in church or school, they came to a stop. Out of a truck they dug wrapped white loaves cut in slices, and we devoured those heavenly slices with our eyes half-closed. They also took out packets of sweets, round with a hole, yellow, green and red and strawberry flavoured, blocks of chocolate, little tubes with strange pastes, light and dark brown, which we couldn't even guess at. They also gave us pamphlets and we all wanted one, and we went down to the village waving them, with our pockets and aprons crammed; the boys had taken off their shirts to hold their goodies. The soldiers followed us, they hadn't known that the fork off the New Road led to a village. Santa Maria del Mare wasn't marked on the map. Everybody came to the window to look at them and they waved back. They began to take photographs, picking out

---

*Althenopis dialect: offerings of coffee, cakes, liqueurs and ice-cream on holiday occasions or when visitors come. Though the offering can also be of olives, cheese, salami, wine.

children, myself and my sister and brother among them, and posing us against the wall. They handed out money to everyone, hundred-lire pieces the like of which we had never seen, and in a waving of arms and smiles they disappeared in an azure cloud, like gods.

Translated by Michael Sullivan

Great Bear, Little Bear

Ginevra Bompiani

GINEVRA BOMPIANI takes us, in this piece, far from home (wherever home is, in space or time). Her journey back to adolescence involves the patient retracing of footsteps in an effort to unearth her past self. We wander with her, first on a Parisian street and then, suddenly evoked by the name *rue Marmousets,* up the narrow lanes of a mountain village where the protagonist went to a boarding school, also named *Les Marmousets,* years before. Bompiani's fragmentary road to remembering (somewhat reminiscent of another writer, already familiar to the American reader, Fleur Jaeggy) follows a different path from that of Romano or Ramondino. The sites she evokes are not patiently retrieved from the penumbra, like Romano's photographs, or illuminated in a single blinding moment, like Ramondino's piazza: they are shattered, glimpsed only bit by bit. Born in Milan in 1939, the daughter of Italian publisher Valentino Bompiani, she studied at the Sorbonne in Paris and until recently taught English and comparative literature at the University of Siena. Her writing aims at "introspective precision," as Italo Calvino once wrote, whether she writes about fantastic creatures or more concrete things, dreaming hermaphrodites or the insomnia of centaurs (*The Species of Dream*). "The landscape created by her prose recalls those paintings in which peaceful figures are asleep in a quiet wood, or a solitary house, or any place where the senses can dim and reason's guard is dropped. . . . It is precisely into that borderland—where reason dozes off, making room for myths, fables, and dreams—that Ginevra Bompiani's prose ventures."[1]

NOTES

1. Sergio Parussa, introduction to *The Great Bear* (New York: Italica Press, 2000). Bompiani is the author of several essays and books of fiction: *Le specie del sonno* (*The Species of Dream*, 1975); *L'incantato* (*The Enchanted One*, 1987); *Vecchio cielo, nuova terra* (*Old Sky, New Land*, 1988); *L'orso maggiore* (1994; *Great Bear*, trans. Brian Kern and Sergio Parussa [New York: Italica Press, 2000]). Among her recent and highly original works of nonfiction are: *L'attesa* (*Waiting*, 1988) and *Tempora* (1993). Available in English is "The Chimera Himself," in *Fragments for a History of the Human Body*, 3 vols., ed. Michel Feher, Ramona Naddaff, and Nadio Tazi (New York: Zone, 1989), 1:364–409.

Great Bear, Little Bear

by Ginevra Bompiani

November 11, 1993

Marmousets

It's a sunny day and I went out to stretch my legs. Strolling not far from home along a street I'd never taken before, I suddenly came upon a street name: Rue Marmousets. I'll explain later just why that name took me by surprise. It is a very short street, and since only the backsides of houses face onto it, there are no doors, either of houses or of shops. No one can say they live on that street, even though their windows face onto it. But this is not the only strange thing about it. On one side, around a metal garage door, the wall has been painted, and the painting depicts—on closer inspection—a mountain landscape, golden, barren, and crowned by snowfields. Within the landscape is a small blue square in which the same mountain landscape is depicted, lush and verdant, as if another season, *en abîme*, had been opened, green and warm.

Fortunately, in this city one can stand staring dumbfounded at something without anyone turning their head. On the roof of one of the two tall houses, a cat is walking warily along the eaves, in search of a place from which to jump. Maybe, I thought, as small and uninhabited as it is, this street can't even be found on the city map. Yet there it is, the name longer than the street. I went back home.

Les Marmousets was the name of the boarding school where I spent two years of my childhood. It was a boarding school in the mountains, and when I say "childhood," I immediately see a mountain landscape like the one painted in the street and the chalet of ancient black wood with that peculiar name inscribed on the balustrade of the balcony on the second floor.

I think *marmousets* are small elves, spiteful as children, and that's what we were. Spiteful, cruel, and enchanted, all of us, without any other dimension than that of an eternal childhood, absolute and ruthless. Above us were the governesses and the headmistress, but they didn't count. We were the only ones who did—we, our own masters and slaves, actors and audience, savage and abandoned.

We knew all the passions, envy and jealousy, fear and desire, contempt and veneration, all fierce and burning passions. We alone tried them, tasted them, spat them out. Today when I feel a passion of such raw and desperate force, I don't recognize it. But I know that it had to have been born then, because it has the same savage anxiety, the same rapacity that we learned then.

Cabins

Behind the chalet, the ground rises along a narrow, damp embankment. That is the space for the cabins. The hedge is thick with rather tall and slender shrubs, so that we can pull them up and construct four walls. When I say "we," I mean "they," my subjects. The band is formed and I am its leader. Tiana is my second-in-command. Through her I command all the others, but she too can incur punishment. That's when the bushes provide quick and nimble whips that strike the bare backs of the disobedient with precision. The times have changed. The persecuted become oppressors, eyebrows narrow into a grimace, hands behind the back agitate the thin switch, the victims remove their clothes patiently.

The males, previously full of jokes and sticks, now obey muttering. No more the small, brief punches on the floor, the chance alliances, the tearful surrenders. Those blows did nothing worse than cause tears. The whip is prickly but no one cries. Every offense is punished; there is no remission. The discipline is forceful; it is delicious. Everyone tastes it; they have its flavour in their mouths. Victims and tyrant, everyone smacks their lips.

In the rooms they try kisses; in the garden, whips. Once in a while someone rebels, and it begins all over again. A new leader is elected: it's always me. Sometimes the rebellion gets to the point of wanting to subject me to the same punishment, of sharpening the whip for my back. I produce a revolution, the cards fly, the voices rise, and once again, I'm the leader.

The cabins serve to hide the cruel games, the new laws. If a governess wants to surprise us, all the worse for her. The headmistress comes out of the kitchen door that faces out back, I intercept her at once, tripping her up, and she is on the ground.

No one touches me anymore. No one dares beat me. Not even the governesses scold me. I enjoy unlimited indulgence. The mountains have strengthened my body, the battle has transformed my meekness into metal. I have understood. Or better, without understanding I have learned.

Little Bear

Along the path that leads from the small gate to the chalet, my mother, young, slender, unusual, advances against the wind and the snow. Something has happened.

Our dog has died, the Maremma sheepdog, the first one I learned not to be afraid of. I was six years old, there was the house at the sea and, with the house, the big white dog, its tail sticking up. I am afraid of dogs: during the war we had a cocker spaniel, left by friends, frightened and growling. It huddled under the furniture, trembling at the air raids. It didn't like anybody. The fear remained with me, cured by Totò, and then it returned, indelible, at the age of twenty. My father says, "Don't be afraid. Pet it." I timidly hold out a hand, Totò accepts the caress. After that, he doesn't accept any others. Whoever comes close to me has to watch out for him. We talk for a long time, back and forth in the garden, with that familiarity that children and loners have with dogs.

Now I am in tears. My mother, who has foreseen it, has made this long trip and will depart again in the evening. She's taking me to the village, dragging me mourning past the shops to awaken a desire in me for something. In front of one shop window I see a small stuffed bear. I am big for a teddy bear, but the fact is that I have never had one before. I was never allowed to sleep with an animal, real or fake, between my arms. I tug at my mother who enters the shop. It's a scrawny bear, standing upright, light brown. Then we go to the usual pastry shop of consolation. To console me, my mother spends everything she has and leaves without dinner.

The teddy bear will sleep in my bed. No one at the boarding school will forbid it. It is such a relief that something can be a consolation for something else.

Forest

In the morning we study in the dining room around the oval table from nine to noon. I don't know anymore who is teaching us. They are easy classes, a year behind the class that in the month of June I will take to prepare for the Italian school. When I am in the third class there, here I am in the second, and so on. I mix the two languages, I muddle the spellings. But in the afternoon we all go out in double file, climbing toward the forest. We climb singing in chorus. Sometimes on the way we come across a procession from another boarding school, the Beau Soleil, for example. It's a bigger boarding school, richer: we look on it with envy. Why? It lies along the street that separates the two villages and we pass by it when we go to the village on Sundays for the Service or on Saturdays to spend our weekly fifty cents on red candy dolls. It is big, famous, expensive. I don't know what it has that's better than ours, small, homey, affectionate. But I envy its guests: they say at night the boys climb up into the girls' rooms (at our place, there's no need); that they have thousands of ways of entertaining themselves; that they don't suffer from homesickness. We see them coming down from the forest with a longer, more resolute stride, without singing. We huddle together, clumsy, ashamed, whispering. A friend of mine who was in that boarding school (though I didn't know it) will tell me that, while passing by one day, she saw me with my arms on the fence, "so sad." I'm surprised. I thought I had buried all my sadness so well in those two years that I myself had forgotten it. Maybe I was careless, maybe I was looking at the meadow without thinking, and the sadness found a forgotten door and emerged to look out at the forest.

The imagination populates the meadow with wolves, lambs, and hunters. The forest with satyrs and nymphs. The house is a human place, the outdoors is animal. I dream of a future house with a garden around it, inhabited by children and animals. It is the very boarding school of which I would become the owner. Because the boarding school is the absolute place of imagination, I cannot think about anything that is not among its folds, in its myriad interstices. Snow, meadow, forest, stairs, balcony, window, boots, scent, piano, hedge, song, sleep, fir tree—everything has its mold there and awaits only a new draft, a new imprint, immutable in every line, in its definition of space, proportion, and contour. A new thing appears and the model moves, adapts, grows or diminishes, one or another detail enters the frame, like a lens, which moves slowly over an illustration, bringing into view the wing of an angel or the donkey climbing the path.

Great Bear

Above the big meadow there is an abandoned house. It is summer, time has passed, the rhythms have changed. Now I live in the city in winter, and I come to the boarding school in the summer. I have my band, grown, all the girls, adolescents like me, ten, twelve years old. The house is newer than the chalet, the wood is lighter, the stone more abundant. It doesn't have an air of abandonment, but no one ever comes here; it's abandoned to us. We walk about it each and every afternoon (in the morning the choral walks through the forest continue) looking for an opening where we can slip in. Finally we find one under the garage. The garage door is a few centimeters away from the ground. Our thin bodies slither into the empty room. From here, through a door easy to open, we enter the house.

There is a stairway in the middle that goes up to the second floor. The most reckless of us ventures up there alone, arrives at the top, lets out a scream, and tumbles down.

"There's a man," she stammers, "a beast!"

We remain in silence at the foot of the stairs. Then I go up, one stair at a time, while the others hesitate behind me, copying step by step. The stairway rises quickly, sharply, decisively. At the second floor, it looks into a large hall. On the outside the windows are blocked by shutters, and on the inside, by curtains. The furniture lies in the shadows. In the middle of the room between two windows, an immense bear raises its paw menacingly. We all scream. We remain on the last step, trembling. Even the bear holds his menace motionless. And little by little, while the sweat runs cold between our shoulder blades and our hearts pound in our ears, the penumbra fades and the bear reveals its eyes of glass, its stuffed flesh.

Translated by Brian Kern and Sergio Parussa

PART III

Vanishing Points

Windswept Lane

Antonio Tabucchi

IT IS to a haunted space of memory, both familiar and disorienting, that we are led in this excerpt from Antonio Tabucchi's short novel of 1986, *The Edge of the Horizon*. An air of mystery pervades this sleepy Mediterranean harbor city (Genoa?), captured at an indeterminate moment in time. The protagonist, a coroner named Spino, attempts to trace the footsteps and discover the identity of a mysterious Carlo Nobodi, nicknamed "The Kid," a suspected terrorist murdered under murky circumstances. Tabucchi suggests in a postscript that "Spino" could be an abbreviation for Spinoza: "Spinoza was a Sephardic Jew, and like many of his people carried the horizon within him in his eyes. The horizon is in fact a geometrical locus, which moves as we move. I wish that by magic my character had reached it, since he too had it in his eyes." Spino's fragmentary memories slowly take over the investigation, which becomes a slow approximation of his own death (or disappearance). As A. L. Lepschy has noted, in Tabucchi's fiction "the intellectual quest, which may be expressed as travel to foreign lands, or as a journey of the mind, allows [the creation of] realities which prove ephemeral, enigmatic and uncertain."[1] The reader is slowly lured into a strange temporal dimension, a past-perfect that is more like a faded present tense—not an *is* but an eternal *has been*. A scholar of Portuguese literature, Tabucchi (b. Pisa, 1943) began his prolific career as a novelist with *Piazza d'Italia*, published in 1975 and inspired, despite its de Chirichian title, by García Márquez's *One Hundred Years of Solitude*.[2] Tabucchi's sensibility is perfectly summed up by one of his characters (inspired by the Portuguese poet Fernando Pessoa): "My emotions only come through true fiction. . . . The supreme truth is fiction." The pure emotion (and supreme truth) of fiction is conveyed by Tabucchi with superb technique, borrowing from a theatrical and, especially in this piece, an exquisitely cinematic vision.

NOTES

1. Anna L. Lepschy, "Antonio Tabucchi: Splinters of Existence," in *The New Italian Novel*, ed. Zygmunt G. Baranski and Lino Pertile (Edinburgh: Edinburgh University Press, 1993), 200. As Michael Caesar has written, Tabucchi's protagonists are plagued by "a pervasive sense of anxiety and guilt . . . they carry their imprisoning horizon with them . . . a horizon that is neither waiting to be crossed nor crowding in on the protagonist, but always there, at the same distance, always unreachable" ("Contemporary Italy [since 1956]," in *The Cambridge History of Italian Literature*, ed. Peter Brand and Lino Pertile [Cambridge: Cambridge University Press, 1996], 602).
2. To the American reader, he is among the better-known contemporary Italian writers since many of his books were translated into English in the 1980s. To mention a few of his titles: *Il gioco del rovescio* (1981; *Letter from Casablanca*,

trans. Janice M. Thresher [New York: New Directions, 1986]); *Piccoli equivoci senza importanza* (1985; *Little Misunderstandings of No Importance*, trans. Frances Frenaye [New York: New Directions, 1987]); *Notturno indiano* (1984; *Indian Nocturne*, trans. Tim Parks [New York: New Directions, 1989]); *Donna di Porto Pim* (1983: *Vanishing Point: The Woman of Porto Pim*, trans. Tim Parks [London: Chatto and Windus, 1991]); *Requiem: Un allucinazione* (1992, originally published in Portuguese; *Requiem: A Hallucination*, trans. Margaret Jull Costa [London: Harvill, 1994]); *Sostiene Pereira* (1994; *Pereira Declares: A Testimony*, trans. Patrick Creagh [New York: New Directions, 1995]); *I volatili del Beato Angelico* (*The Winged Creatures of Beato Angelico*, 1987), *Sogni di sogni* (*Dreams of Dreams*, 1992), and *Gli ultimi tre giorni di Fernando Pessoa: Un delirio* (*The Last Three Days of Fernando Pessoa: A Delirium*, 1994), which were translated together from the Italian by Nancy J. Peters (San Francisco: City Lights Books, 1999); and *La testa perduta di Damasceno Monteiro* (1997; *The Missing Head of Damasceno Monteiro*, trans. J. C. Patrick [New York: New Directions, 1999]).

Windswept Lane
by Antonio Tabucchi

THERE ARE days when the jealous beauty of this city seems to un-
veil itself. On clear days, for example, windy days, when the breeze
that announces the arrival of the south-westerly sweeps along the
streets slapping like a taut sail. Then the houses and bell towers take
on a brightness that is too real, the outlines too sharp; like a photograph with fierce contrasts, light and shade collide aggressively without blending together, forming a black-and-white check of splashes
of shadow and dazzling light, of alleyways and small squares.

Once, if he had nothing else to do, he used to choose days like
this to wander round the old dock area, and now, following the
dead-end sidings the wagons use along the quay, heading back to
town, he finds himself thinking of those days. He could catch the
bus that goes to town through the tunnels of the beltway, but instead he chooses to walk across the docks, following the twists and
turns of the wharves. He feels he wants to dawdle slowly through

this grim landscape of railway lines that reminds him of his childhood, of diving from the landing stage with the tires along its sides, of those poor summers, the memory of which has remained etched inside him like a scar.

In the disused shipyard, where once they repaired steamships, he sees the hulk of a Swedish vessel lying on its side. It's called the *Ulla*. Strangely, the yellow letters of the name somehow escaped the fire that devastated the boat leaving enormous brown stains on the paint. And he has the impression that this old monster on the brink of extinction has always been there in that corner of the dock. A little further on he found a battered phone booth. He thought of phoning Corrado to put him in the picture. Anyway it was only right to let him know, since to a certain extent he owed the meeting to his friend.

"Corrado," he said, "it's me. I managed to speak to him."

"But where are you? Why did you disappear like that?"

"I didn't disappear at all. I'm at the docks. Don't worry."

"Sara was after you. She left you a message here at the paper. She says they're extending their vacation for three days, they're going to Switzerland."

A seagull, which had been wheeling about for some time, landed on the arm of a water pump right next to the phone booth and stood there quietly watching him while at the same time hunting through its feathers with its beak.

"There's a seagull next to me, it's right here next to the phone booth, it's as if it knew me."

"What are you talking about? . . . Listen, where did you find him, what did he tell you?"

"I can't explain now. There's a seagull here with its ears pricked, it must be a spy."

"Don't play the fool. Where are you, where did you find him?"

"I told you, I'm at the docks. We met at the Boat Club. There are boats for rent and we went out for a trip."

Corrado's voice dropped, perhaps someone had come into the office. "Don't trust him," he said. "Don't trust him an inch."

"It's not a question of trusting or not. He gave me a tip and I'm going to try it out. He didn't know anything about the business. But there's someone who maybe does know something and he told me who."

"Who?"

"I told you I can't tell you, I don't want to speak on the phone."

"There's no one here who can hear you. You can speak on my phone. Tell me who."

"Come on, you don't imagine he went and gave me name and surname, do you? He's very smart. He just gave me an idea."

"So then give me an idea."

"You wouldn't understand."

"So how come you understood?"

"Because it's someone I happened to know years back. A musician."

"Where does he play?"

"Corrado, please, I can't tell you anything."

"In any event I don't like it, and you're too naive, understand? It's quicksand. Anywhere you put your feet you risk sinking in."

"Sorry Corrado, have to say goodbye, it's getting late. And then this seagull is getting annoyed, he wants to make a call, he's waving his beak at me furiously."

"Come straight here, I'll wait for you at the paper. I won't go home, just so I can see you."

"What about tomorrow, okay? I'm tired now, and I've got something to do this evening."

"Promise me you won't trust anyone."

"Okay, talk to you tomorrow."

"Hang on a second, I heard something that might interest you. The coroner has arranged for the burial, the case has been dropped."

Twenty years ago the Tropical was a small nightclub with a shady atmosphere catering to American sailors. Now it's called the Louisiana and it's a piano bar with couches and table lamps. On the drinks list, on a green velvet noticeboard near the main door, it says: *Piano player—Peppe Harpo.*

Peppe Harpo is Giuseppe Antonio Arpetti, born in Sestri Levante in 1929, struck off the register of doctors in 1962 for his overlavish prescription of addictive drugs. In his university days he played the piano at little parties. He was quite talented and could do perfect imitations of Erroll Garner. After the drug scandal he took to playing at the Tropical. He played mambos and pop songs through evenings thick with smoke, five hundred lire a drink. The emergency exit, behind the curtains, opened onto a stairwell where, above another door, a neon sign said: *Pensione—Zimmer—Rooms.* Then at a certain point he disappeared for six or seven years, to America, people said. When he reappeared it was with small round eyeglasses and a greying mustache. He had become Peppe Harpo, the jazz pianist. And with his return the Tropical became the Louisiana. Some said he had bought the place, that he'd made money playing in bands in America. That he had made money no one found strange.

He seemed capable of it. That he had made money banging on the piano left many unconvinced.

Spino sat down at a table to one side and ordered a gin and tonic. Harpo was playing "In a Little Spanish Town," and Spino supposed his entry had passed unobserved, but then when his drink came there was no bill with it. He sat on his own for a long time, slowly sipping his gin and listening to old tunes. Then towards eleven Harpo took a break and a tape of dance music replaced the piano. Spino had the impression, as Harpo came towards him through the tables, that his face wore an expression at once remorseful and resolute, as if he were thinking: ask me anything, but not that, I can't tell you that. *He knows*, a voice inside him whispered, *Harpo knows*. For a second Spino thought of putting the photo of The Kid as a child down on the table and then saying nothing, just smiling with the sly expression of one who knows what he knows. Instead he said straightforwardly that perhaps the time had come for Harpo to return him that favor. He was sorry if that was putting it bluntly. The favor, that is, of helping him find somebody, as he had once helped Harpo. A look of what seemed like genuine amazement crossed Harpo's face. He waited without saying anything. So Spino pulled out the group photograph. "Him," he said, pointing at the boy.

"Is he a relative of yours?"

Spino shook his head.

"Who is he?"

"I don't know. That's what I want to find out. Perhaps his name is Carlito."

Harpo looked at Spino suspiciously, as if expecting a trick, or afraid he was being made fun of. Was he mad? The people were wearing fifties-style clothes, it was an old photograph. The boy must be a man now, for God's sake.

"You know perfectly well what I'm talking about," Spino said. "He's got a dark beard now. His hair is darker too, not as light as in the photo, but his face still has something boyish about it. He's been in my freezer for a few days. The people who knew him are keeping quiet, nothing, not even an anonymous phone call, as if he'd never existed. They're wiping out his past."

Harpo was looking around rather uneasily. A couple at a nearby table was watching them with interest. "Don't speak so loud," he said. "No need to disturb the customers."

"Listen Harpo," Spino said, "if a person doesn't have the courage to go beyond appearances, he'll never understand, will he? All his life he'll just be forced to keep playing the game without understanding why."

Harpo called a waiter and ordered a drink. "But who's he to you?" he asked softly. "You don't know him, he doesn't mean anything to you." He was speaking in a whisper, uneasy, his hands moving nervously.

"And you?" Spino said. "Who are you to yourself? Do you realize that if you wanted to find that out one day you'd have to look for yourself all over the place, reconstruct yourself, rummage in old drawers, get hold of evidence from other people, clues scattered here and there and lost? You'd be completely in the dark, you'd have to feel your way."

Harpo lowered his voice even further and told him to try an address, though he wasn't certain. His face told Spino that in giving him that address the favor had been repaid in full.

It's called "Egle's." It's an old pie-house, or that's what he's heard people call it. The walls are covered in white tiles and behind a zinc-topped counter Signora Egle bustles about a small wood-fired oven serving cakes and pies. Spino sits at one of the little marble tables and a grey-aproned waitress with the haggard look of a cloistered nun comes with a cloth to wipe up the crumbs the last customer left. He orders a chickpea pie and then, as instructed, lays a copy of the *Gazzetta Ufficiale* on the table in full view. He begins to check out the other customers and speculate as to who they are. At the table next to his are two middle-aged blonde women chattering in low voices, occasionally exploding in shrill laughter. They look well-heeled and are wearing gauche, expensive clothes. They could be two retired whores who've invested their earnings well and now run a shop, or some business related to their previous profession, but dignified now by this façade of respectability. Sitting in a corner is a young lout bundled up in a thick jacket and engrossed in a magazine from the cover of which a fat orange-clad guru wags a warning finger at the plate of pie in front of him. Then there's a spry-looking old man, hair dyed a black that takes on a reddish tint about the temples, as cheap dyes often do. He has a gaudy tie and brown-and-white shoes with patterns of tiny holes. Wheeler-dealer, pimp, widower in the grip of a mad desire for adventure? Could be anything. Finally there's a lanky man leaning against the counter. He's chatting to Signora Egle and smiling, showing off an enormous gap in his upper teeth. He has a horsey profile and greased-back hair, a jacket that doesn't manage to cover his bony wrists, jeans. Signora Egle seems determined not to concede something the lanky character is insisting on. Then, with an expression of surrender, she moves

to one end of the counter and puts a record on a decrepit phono-
graph that looked as if it were purely decorative. The record is a 78
and rumbles; there are a couple of bursts from a band and then a
falsetto voice starts up, distorted by the scratches the disc carries in
its grooves. Incredibly, it's *Il tango delle capinere*, sung by Rabagliati.
The lanky character sends a nod of complicity in the direction of
the waitress and she, unresisting but sullen, lets herself be led in a
long-stepping tango that immediately captures the attention of the
clientele. The girl leans a cheek on the chest of her beau, which is as
far as her height allows her to reach, but she's having all kinds of
trouble keeping up with his powerful strides as he leads her aggressively about the room. They finish with a supple *casqué* and everybody claps. Even Spino joins in, then opens his paper, pushing his
plate away, and pretends to be absorbed in the *Gazzetta Ufficiale*.

Meanwhile the boy with the guru on his magazine gets up
dreamily and pays his bill. Going out he doesn't deign to give anyone in the room a single glance, as if he had too much on his mind.
The two big blonde women are repairing their make-up and two
cigarettes with traces of lipstick on the filters burn in their ashtray.
They leave chuckling, but no one shows any special interest in
Spino, nor in the paper he's reading. He raises his eyes from the
paper and his gaze meets that of the spry old man. There follows a
long and intense exchange of glances and Spino feels a light coating
of sweat on the palms of his hands. He folds his paper and puts his
pack of cigarettes on top, waiting for the first move. Perhaps he
should do something, he thinks, but he's not sure what. Meanwhile
the girl has finished clearing the tables and has started spreading
damp sawdust on the floor, sweeping it along the tiles with a broom

taller than herself. Signora Egle is going through the day's takings behind the counter. The room is quiet now, the air thick with breath, with cigarettes, with burnt wood. Then the spry little old man smiles: it's a trite, mechanical smile, accompanied by the slightest jerk of the head and then another gesture that tells all. Spino sees the misunderstanding he's been encouraging, immediately turns red with embarrassment, then senses, rising within him, a blind anger and intolerance towards this place, towards his own stupidity. He makes a sign to the girl and asks for his bill. She approaches wearily, drying her hands on her apron. She adds up his bill on a paper napkin; her hands are red and swollen with a coating of sawdust sticking to their backs, they might be two chops sprinkled with breadcrumbs. Then, giving him an insolent look, she mutters in a toneless voice: "You're losing your hair. Reading after eating makes you lose your hair." Spino looks at her astonished, as though not believing his ears. It can't be her, he thinks, it can't be. And he almost has to hold himself back from attacking this little monster who goes on giving him her arrogant stare. But she, still in that detached, professional tone, is telling him about a herbalist who sells things for hair, on Vico Spazzavento.

Vico Spazzavento—Windswept Lane—is the perfect name for this blind alley squeezed between walls covered with scars. The wind forms a whirling eddy right where a blade of sunshine, slipping into the narrow street between flapping washing seen high above against a corridor of sky, lights up a little heap of swirling detritus. A wreath of dry flowers, newspapers, a nylon stocking.

The shop is in a basement with a swing door. It looks like a coal cellar, and in fact on the floor there are some sacks of coal, although the sign on the doorpost says: "spices, paints." On the counter is a pile of newspapers used to wrap up goods sold. A little old man dozing on a small wicker-covered chair near the coal got to his feet. Spino was first to say hello. The old man mumbled a good evening. He propped himself up against the counter with a lazy and seemingly absent expression.

"Someone told me you sold hair lotions here," Spino said.

The old man answered knowledgeably. He leant over the counter a little to look at Spino's hair, listed various products with curious names: *Zolfex, Catramina.* Then some plants and roots: sage, nettle, rhubarb, red cedar. He thinks red cedar is what he needs, that's his guess at first glance, though one ought to do some tests on the hair.

Spino answered that maybe red cedar would be okay, he doesn't know, he doesn't know what properties red cedar has.

The old man looked at him doubtfully. He had metal-framed glasses and a two-day growth of beard. He didn't say anything. Spino tried not to let his nerves get the better of him. Calmly, he explained that he hadn't checked out his hair type, it was just brittle. In any case, he doesn't want a commercial product, he wants a special lotion. He stressed the word special, something that *only* the shopkeeper knows the formula for. He has come on the advice of people he trusts. It's strange they haven't mentioned it to him.

The old man pushed aside a curtain, said to wait and disappeared. For a second Spino caught a glimpse of a poky little room with a gas-ring and a light bulb switched on, but he didn't see anybody. The old man started to speak, a few yards from Spino, in a whisper. A woman's voice answered, perhaps an old woman. Then they fell silent. Then they began to speak again, their voices very low. It was impossible to catch what they were saying. Then came a squeak as of a drawer being opened, and finally silence again.

The minutes passed slowly. Not a sound came from beyond the curtain now, as if the two had gone out by another door to leave him waiting there like an idiot. Spino coughed loudly, he made a noise with a chair, at which the old man reappeared at the curtain with a look of reproach. "Be patient," he said, "another few minutes."

He came out round the counter and went to close and bolt the swing door that opened onto the street. He moved somewhat cautiously, looked at his customer, lit a small cigar, and returned to the back room. The voices began to whisper again, more urgently than before. The shop was almost dark. The daylight coming in through the small barred window had grown dimmer. The sacks of coal along the walls looked like human bodies abandoned in sleep. Spino couldn't help thinking that the dead man might also have come to this shop once and like him have waited in the half-dark; perhaps the old man knew him well, knew who he was, his reasons, his motives.

Finally the little man came back all smiles. In his hand he had a small brown bottle of the kind they use in pharmacies to sell iodine. He wrapped it up carefully in a sheet of newspaper and pushed it across the counter without a word. Spino looked at it now, paused, smiled perhaps. "Hope you're not making a mistake," he said. "It's important."

The old man released the bolt on the door, went back to sit on his seat and started on the accounts he had previously broken off. He made a show of pretending not to have heard. "Off you go now," he said. "The instructions are on the label."

Spino slipped the little bottle into his pocket and left. When he said goodbye, the old man answered that he had put some sage in the lotion too, to give it some fragrance. And Spino had the impression he was still smiling. There was no one on Vico Spazzavento. He felt as though time hadn't passed, as though everything had happened too quickly, like some event that took place long ago and is revisited in the memory in a flash.

Translated by Tim Parks

Reaching Dew Point

Daniele Del Giudice

THIS EXCERPT from Daniele Del Giudice's second book translated into English, *Staccando l'ombra da terra* (*Takeoff: The Pilot's Lore*), springs directly from the writer's passion for flying: the "dew point" of the title is a technical expression used by pilots, hinting metaphorically at a shifting point of no return, a paradoxical vantage point on the invisible horizon suspended over the hazy plains crossed by the Po River. Evidently the view of these deceptive and foggy flatlands is not much clearer from the air than from the ground (witness Celati or Vassalli). If Tabucchi's prose contains multiple echoes of popular 1930s cinema, Del Giudice (b. Rome, 1943) offers a cooler, almost abstract modernism reminiscent of the cinema of Michelangelo Antonioni. He made his literary debut with *Lo stadio di Wimbledon* (*Center Court*, 1983), which showed a metanarrative obsession with the productive moment, the coming to being of (narrative) language.[1] His next novel, *Atlante Occidentale* (*Lines of Light*, 1985), set in the cosmopolitan milieu of Geneva, also dealt with the unfathomable threshold between the visible and the invisible. Here, too, Calvino's lesson is undeniably at work (coincidentally, Del Giudice worked for the publishing house Einaudi of Turin, in a position similar to the one once held by Calvino): in Del Giudice's musings one can recognize Calvino's profound preoccupation with the technical, material and immaterial, referential and self-referential nature of writing (after all, if the writer is a pilot, in "Reaching the Dew Point," the pilot *is* the writer).

NOTES

1. In addition to *Atlante Occidentale* (1985; *Lines of Light,* trans. Norman MacAfee and Luigi Fontanella [San Diego: Harcourt Brace, 1988]) and *Staccando l'ombra da terra* (1994; *Takeoff: The Pilot's Lore,* trans. Joseph Farrell [San Diego: Harcourt Brace, 1996]), he published (also with Einaudi) *Mania* in 1997. He is also the creator of an interesting experiment with visual narrative, in collaboration with painter Marco Nereo Rotelli, *Nel museo di Reims* (*In the Museum of Reims,* 1985).

Reaching Dew Point
by Daniele Del Giudice

ONE MORNING, while airborne, you lost your way, as people do in life, without ever being quite aware that they are lost but drifting bit by bit into a zone where their bearings are gone: first the country-side was not what you expected, then the river which ought to have come into view did not, and finally the heat haze which hung over the Po valley crystallized into a more unyielding, impenetrable opaqueness. Any minute now I'll be out of this, you thought, and the minute passed, then another, one by one the windows of the plane turned frosty white and you came to realize that there was no way out of that hot, daytime mist. It is not the case that people lose their way in an instant, the process will be under way over time, you had, in reality, already got lost earlier, at the last checkpoint, when you called Air Traffic Control confirming your position as the spot where you ought to have been as per flight plan; pure nominalism, the victory of the plan over reality, since you were nowhere near

there. At that point, you made a descent to a lower altitude, following closely a railway track, but when the line came to a halt in a little
village, you were reduced to flying low over the village station in an
effort to make out its name, but the name, glimpsed as you flashed
by at speed, was of no great help; wherever you were, you were lost
and climbing once more into the haze; you lost your bearings more
comprehensively until you found yourself where you are now, which
is to say, you have no idea where. The last sure position was Abeam
Boa, a nautical point on the map a dozen or so miles to the east of
Bologna, above various tiny huddles of houses—Budrio, Medicina
or San Lazzaro di Savena, who could say?—the one indistinguish-
able from the other; the village name not being written on the house
roofs; no one ever heeded Rodchenko when he proposed that the
roof become a heaven-facing façade which would offer aviators something more than the monotony of rows of tiles. This occurred in the
thirties, but the roof-façade never caught on after that; roofs have
remained uniform, as uniform as the villages which do not carry
names on their roofs, and as a result you were lost, and lied about
your fix to Air Traffic Control.

Fear is composed of liquids in the act of drying up: you stared at
the altimeter, you grabbed at the map, searching wildly for those
dark-colored areas in shades ranging from warm yellow to dark
brown, where the mountain peaks are clustered; if you were off
course to the northeast, Monte Venda should be there, if to the
north, the Lessini mountains and the Pre-Alps should make an appearance; but you would hardly have time to see a cliff face emerge
from the whiteness in front of the windscreen. It was the first time
you had got lost in a plane and, not having yet acquired expertise in
instrument flight, you celebrated the event with a phrase produced

spontaneously by the mind; the phrase ran, "I do not want to die," a phrase which came so naturally that of its own accord your voice spoke it aloud, as though it were the voice of another person reproaching you for exposing him to such a situation. In order to cheat death I must climb, you immediately thought, it is senseless to plough blindly forward. And climb I do, in spirals around the vertical axis of my present position; if I manage to hold perfectly the center of the rotation, if I do not waver on the first or second loop, I am safe. You read on the map the heights of the most likely peaks, adding another thousand feet for safety, and started to climb towards the five thousand mark. In the opaque darkness of the sky, in the infinity of space, slowly drifting upwards in fibrous mist, you closed yourself inside the safety cylinder of your circling flight. All around, everything prickled with invisible menace; with each circle you reduced the radius to reduce the threat, or that was your hope, but each circle was never-ending. Fog is infertile cloud, so Aristotle held, place no trust in that all-permeating, all-enveloping substance, water of that sort is only humidity, not impregnating rain, which sows life in the fields and swells the course of the rivers. Fog is a backdrop, fog lurks; on fields, in the space between earth and sky, fog is sterile, the trusty crony of crime. Unconscious crimes, indifferent to the fog, but crimes nonetheless.

Such were the thoughts in your mind as you kept an eye on the instruments, variometer five-hundred-feet climb-rating, sixty knots for the steep ascent, turn-and-slip indicator with ball centered and needle tilted for two-minute turn. And yet when you are not flying, you are fond of fog, when a fog descends on the city, you respond first to its scents and changing noise patterns, you feel yourself irresistibly drawn by the night and the mists, like a dog called to heel by its master's whistle. That apart, what did you know about fog, pilot?—that it is born of a coincidence, a coincidence of dew temperature and air temperature, temperatures which you studiously avoided asking the meteorological office to check before takeoff. You could, of course, do so now, you could ask the Air Traffic Control Board if they had any information on the mist, on how widespread it was, on what height it reached, but then you would have to clarify other matters with the Board, so you put it off. Board: philosophically, a concept not amenable to definition, but merely to clarification; Board, one and indivisible but distinct from all others; Board, intelligible and lovable in and of itself alone. Even the Air Traffic Control Board could be understood in these terms; in the last analysis it is the disembodied voice grasped in the mist, the unseen voice speaking from earth, the reversal of the higher and lower orders, with us poor mortals wandering lost in the skies and the Immortal at peace on earth, a pursuing eye in the dark inside the luminous dial of the radar tracers. Eye for eye, Board for Board, there is nothing to be seen here, you caught yourself muttering nervously to yourself; the mind was protecting itself from terror by generating a brand of nonsense which resembled the "white vision," that gentle flooding of light which those who pass through death but make their return claim to have witnessed at the last moments, the ultimate analgesic with which the mind gives you its final embrace even as it extinguishes itself and prepares to depart.

Outside the windows, the fog seemed to come to life in thick, darting, smoky forms. It took you some time to realize that these were not crags, trees or bodies looming out of the darkness, about to collide with you, but swirls and empty volumes of the humid mass; you leaned over towards the instrument panel, you looked upwards

in the futile hope that the light of the sun might dilute that gluti-
nous brightness, but instead, as you climbed, the opaqueness, growing ever darker, turned a gloomier grey. The pitching and rolling of
the plane increased, there were sudden updrafts and downdrafts and
a yawing from side to side, swinging the aircraft around without al-
lowing it to bank, sending it into a flat roll around an imaginary
vertical pivot bored through from the top, as though it were a fish
on a skewer. You rammed down your foot the moment you heard the
propeller roaring as it bit into the air at a different tempo, you
rammed down your foot to regain balance. Had you any idea where
you were? Clear of the fog, certainly, but not in the open sky; you
had gone directly from fog to cloud without as much as glimpsing a
patch of blue, and there you were in the heart of a cloud, a cumulus
to judge by the turbulence shaking the plane and by the dark sur-
roundings, as livid grey as a bruise. And just how much did you
know then about a *cumulonimbus*, pilot?—that it held everything inside it, strong rising and falling air currents, rain and hail, the
prospect of instant ice; that a cloud of this sort is produced when
the air freezes to dew point, and the idea of dew as a thermic reference point, the idea that dew was related to events of might and
menace so much greater than itself, dew which has always been consolation, relief, comfort? . . . well, it was not easy to credit. In summer, you had been able to fly around a storm because you had seen it
in good time; some miles off you had made out this congested,
cylindrical squall stretching from earth to sky, as humid and opaque
as a jellyfish, sometimes so precise and fixed in mass that it is possible to circumnavigate it, flank it with one wing, keeping it to the
east, since virtually everything in our skies moves from west to east.

But this time you had blundered into cloud without knowing where it came from, and not imagining where that sky might end.

The aircraft was buffeted by gusts of wind from below, which raised it onto its side only to let it fall with a dull thud against fresh layers of rising air, as though it were dropping into the furrow of a wave so hollow that the sea itself seemed to have run dry. You had instinctively reduced velocity when you felt the plane twist and turn, you had already lost all sense of direction long before, and after all those climbing turns and that turbulence you had less idea of bearing than ever; you could no longer delay making contact with Air Traffic Control. Hand on microphone, gaze fixed on the blackness of the sky, you worked out what to say. In reality, the words had already shaped themselves in your mind into one natural, grand sentence: "Treviso radar, I do not want to die. I repeat, I do not want to die." Aeronautical jargon, however, leaves no space for wishes, not even for heartfelt wishes, only for positions and directions, although this might well turn out to be an advantage, considering that the terror of being lost in the midst of those clouds was now more or less equal to the fear of having to admit as much to Air Traffic Control. To discover where you are, or to be located again from the ground, all you have to do is own up to your present, miserable condition without wasting a second searching for the aeronautically most accurate, and least humiliating, formula. Call Air Traffic Control, call at once; while you dither, things at this end are getting out of hand, any time now you will fall prey to those illusory sensations which until now you have only read about in the handbooks you flick through last thing at night, before dropping off. You refuse to give in, you simply refuse to face the fact that you are lost, you are still putting the final touches to the words, you fail to notice that the plane is falling on one side, until finally you switch on and declaim in the most impersonal, flat tone you can manage: "Treviso radar, India Echo November is no longer in Victor Mike Charlie. Request a Quebec Delta Mike."

If your aim was to take cover behind a wall of words, you have carried it off. Treviso radar is the authority you are calling, a military authority as it happens; India Echo November is the abbreviated name of this poor machine lost in the skies; Victor Mike Charlie, VMC, are the initials for *Visual Meteorological Conditions*, so you are no longer flying in meteorological conditions of visibility. They might believe that you were not to blame for ending up in fog and cloud, that the state of the sky, the cosmos around you, just happened to alter, that visibility was snuffed out, that previously excellent conditions faded as inexplicably and suddenly as lights fail in a house. (Away from flight and the present situation, in the domain of *everything else*, you would have detested such a use of words as a way of hiding behind "objectivity" and "putting on a brave front"; for years you had heard people speak in this style, using words as though they were precious stones. Through objectivity, that is through omissions, they managed to attribute to things a plausibility they could never possess, making them appear the opposite of what they really were.) The *Quebec Delta Mike*, QDM, you requested is a dated term of the old Q code, the code used by Faggione and Buscaglia. Nothing in the world is more conservative than aeronautical and maritime jargon, QDM, qudimike, an old term much loved by pilots, a term redolent of home comforts, but it is untranslatable because these are not initials but three letters which codify and seal the following, lifesaving question: Be kind enough to inform me of the direction I must follow if I am to reach my destination, *destino* in Spanish, the only language in which the geographical goal coincides with the completion of the individual, personal adventure.

"India Echo November. Position?" replied the voice at the other end. Air Traffic Control's voice was Neapolitan, military and impassive, seemingly emerging from nowhere.

He's got you there. Now what can you say? Where are you? Once more you attempted to play for time, the aircraft tossed about, the sky grew darker by the minute, the voice repeated with a touch of alarm: "India Echo November. Are you receiving? Over."

"Affirmative . . . Four-fifths . . . India Echo November has left Abeam . . . " This much was true, you had left Abeam Boa, but when, how much time previously, and for where? In addition, you were supposed to declare your new altitude. "Levelled at five thousand."

"What do you mean at five thousand?" Neapolitan Air Traffic Control came back immediately, shaken rudely awake. "You're at five thousand? You should have told us if you were going up to five thousand. It's your responsibility to inform us of any change of altitude . . . Do you have a transponder?"

"Yes, we have a transponder." Of course you had the automatic reply mechanism to radar signals, but the royal plural had a merely grotesque, hypocritical and pretentious ring in your present solitude; all those "Do you all have? We have"'s were designed to give the impression of a full crew, the copilot busying himself with inserting the four-figured code the moment it was transmitted, the engineer keeping his eye on the levels, the navigator in charge of the route, the radio operator overseeing communications with the world at large.

"Squawk ident six four six seven," Air Traffic Control insisted.

"Ident six four six seven." You insert the four figures into the instrument, you observe the panel light flickering, a sign that the radar equipment is interrogating the metallic mass in the sky perceptible to it alone, but holding you inside it: the transponder replies, and on the ground, in the luminous dial which records the traces, the indeterminate point which corresponded to your plane lights up with the number 6467: no longer indefinite, you are now distinct, individualized, singular and knowable.

"Sorry about the altitude," you proceed in the plural, "we've left Victor Mike Charlie. We'd be glad of a Quebec Delta Mike for the Chioggia VOR," indicating that you always think it's better to climb to a safe height before making radio contact.

"The qudimike's one zero three," concedes the Neapolitan voice, in a businesslike tone.

One hundred and three. You began a one-hundred-and-three-degree turn, heading southeast, a turn in the clouds in the midst of nonstop bumpiness and updrafts; Air Traffic Control could see where you were and where the VOR was, relativity of positions, inevitability of positions, as in the classical conundrum on free will—two people, each unaware of the other, are heading for the same street corner, a third party at a window sees them approach and foresees the collision but can do nothing to prevent it; destiny is foresight minus the power of intervention. At that moment of your life, destiny was a one-hundred-and-three-degree rotation, and on that figure on the face of the gyroscopic compass, pulling out of the turn, you halted, or rather, in the general shambles, attempted to halt, the body of the plane.

It was then, looking at the artificial horizon, that you realized the plane was rolling to one side and had almost overturned. You drummed one finger on the instrument, it must be out of order, you felt the plane to be perfectly horizontal and level after the completion of the turn; you peered through the windscreen for confirmation, but everything outside was grey and opaque, giving no fixed point for checking; turning back to the instrument panel, you became aware that the ascent ratings given by the variometer were extremely high while velocity was falling. You could not make out what was happening to the plane, you still seemed to be maintaining perfectly level flight, but was it possible for the entire instrument panel to have broken down all at once? You wondered if, as you travelled through the clouds, ice had formed on the instruments' external air ducts, but you could not remember the means by which each instrument, once it stops receiving the air it requires, indicates position. A pilot in an emergency situation can only make effective use of five percent of what he knows, says Bruno, and if he knows very little at the best of times, what will he be like when the odds are against him? That's why, every night, before going to sleep, you used to read the handbooks leading to further qualifications, and from one of the pages on instrument flight, flicked through when you were half asleep and the book about to drop from your hand, you managed to regurgitate the notion of illusory sensation. Such sensations had to do with the perception of space, they were a function of the fluids in the canals of the auricular labyrinth, whose flow is determined by a movement which causes them to stimulate the cilia in the ear walls and alert us to our own position. So, pilot, you carry flight instruments inside your ears, except that your instruments are a little slower; those dense bodily fluids move more slowly than does the turning aircraft, the cilia in the labyrinth take note and transmit, all in order but all delayed, and so produce a false present in the mind while the aircraft, and your body, are already living in the future, in a different position. You are not at all straight and level, as you believed, and as a true horizon would confirm to you; sight being preeminent, a visible line between heaven and earth would override any other representation of things, and then you would realize, if the clouds were ever again to open, the position you really are in—sitting over to one side inside a plane tilted over on one wing, nose pointing upwards. Be a believer in instruments, Bruno used to say with that ironic imperative he loved to use, if you can't see out, never raise your eyes from the panel, place your trust in instruments alone, and you indeed began to believe and trust blindly, peering at dial hands and figures, constantly tugging at levers, working at pedals and columns until the control column, after a bout of odd vibrations, all of a sudden went limp and weak in your hands, and you knew exactly what was wrong, oh yes, this time you had no doubts: this was a stall, you were going into stall. I do not want to die, your voice rang out loud and clear, I cannot die here, it would clash with my survivor's nature, and while you were speaking or thinking or yelling these words, the aircraft plummeted, tumbling over on its side.

Translated by Joseph Farrell

Montedidio

Erri De Luca

WITH THIS selection we turn again to the south. Erri De Luca's
Montedidio (*God's Mountain*), from which the following piece is
taken, is an unconventional novel, the journal of an adolescent living and working as a carpenter's apprentice in one of Naples's poor-
est neighborhoods—an area called Montedidio, giving the book its
"biblical" title. De Luca, who taught himself Hebrew in order to
translate the book of Ruth, Ecclesiastes, and several other Old Testament books into Italian, borrows the voice of a young scribe who
writes his own coming-of-age story in the foreign idiom (Italian) he
has learned in school: a quiet, *silent* language, a language "without
spit," whereas his native *Napoletano*, the deafening and expressive
tongue of everyday life in the *vicoli* (alleys) of Montedidio, "fills your
mouth with spit to stick the words together." The difference is more
physical than cultural. To express himself in this acquired language
means, for the narrator and protagonist of this apocryphal contem-

porary tale, to "emigrate" from his mother tongue ("like going to America but without leaving") and embark on a symbolic journey that requires both a transformation of his body and a transfiguration of his soul. Neapolitan, with a militant past in the Italian New Left, Erri De Luca (b. 1950) worked as a truck driver in Africa and a mason in France and Italy until the publication of his first book, *Non Ora Non Qui* (*Not Now, Not Here*), in 1989. His short fictions are told in an array of strikingly versatile first-person voices, always compellingly embodied and suffused with a palpable need to tell their particular story.[1] They also show an almost theological concern for the resilient fragility of life and a bent for short, aphoristic sentences. "De Luca," critic Katia Migliori has written, "is aware of living in a 'dark time,' when language—our whole body is language—is a constant challenge, an opposition to something or somebody. . . . His writing refuses to be homologated by the code of the cultural industry."[2]

NOTES

1. In addition to *Montedidio*, De Luca's books include: *Aceto Arcobaleno* (*Vinegar Rainbow*, 1992); *Tu, mio* (1998; *Sea of Memory*, trans. Beth Archer Brombert [Hopewell: Ecco Press, 1999]); *Tre cavalli* (*Three Horses*, 1999), all published in Italy by Feltrinelli of Milan.
2. Katia Migliori, "Erri De Luca: Aceto Arcobaleno," in *I tempi del rinnovamento*, ed. Serge Vanvolsem, Franco Musarra, and Bart Van den Bossche, Proceedings of an international conference, "Rinnovamento del codice narrativo in Italia dal 1945 al 1992," held in Belgium May 3-8, 1993 (Rome: Bulzoni, 1995), vol. 1, 643.

Montedidio

by Erri De Luca

'A JURNATA È 'NU MUORZO—the day is a morsel, reads the sign over the doorway to Master Errico's workshop. I'd already been standing out front for a quarter of an hour to start my first day of work off right. He gets there at seven, rolls up the gates, and speaks his words of encouragement: the day is a morsel. One bite and it's gone, so let's get busy. Yes, sir, I answer, and so it went. I'm writing my first entry today to keep track of these new days. I don't go to school anymore. I turned thirteen and my dad sent me to work. It's the right thing to do. It's time. You only have to stay in school till third grade. He let me stay until fifth because I was sickly and also because that way I'd have a better diploma. Around here all the kids go to work even if they never went to school, and Papa didn't want that. He works at the docks. He never went to school and is just learning to read and write at the night school run by the longshoremen's cooperative. He only speaks dialect and is intimidated by proper Italian and people with an education. He says that you do better in life if you know Italian. I know Italian because I read library books, but I don't speak it. I write in Italian because it's quiet. I can put down what happens every day, sheltered from the noise of Neapolitan.

I'm finally working, even if I don't make much, and Saturdays I bring home my pay. It's the beginning of summer. At six in the morning it's cool. The two of us have breakfast together and then I put on my smock. We leave the house together. I walk up the street with him a ways and then head back. Master Errico's shop is in the alley down from our building. For my birthday Papa gave me a piece of curved wood. It's called a boomerang. I took it in my hands without asking what it was. A tingle, a little electric shock went through me. Papa explained that you throw it far and it always comes back. Mama was against it. "*Ma addò l'adda ausa*"; where's he gonna use it? She's right. In this neighborhood of alleyways called Montedidio there's not enough room to spit between your feet, no room to hang out the wash. All right, I said, maybe I can't throw it, but I can still practice the moves. It's heavy, like iron. Mama gave me a pair of long trousers. She got them at the market in Resina. They're good quality. American. Rugged, dark. I put them on and rolled them up to my knees. "Now you're a man," an *ommo*, "you bring money home." Yes, I bring home my pay on Saturdays, but it'll take a lot more than that to make me a man. Meantime I've lost my voice and have a frog in my throat.

Papa got the boomerang from a sailor friend. It's not a *pazziella*, a toy. It's a tool that ancient people used. As he explains, I get to know its surface. I rub my hand over it, in the direction of the grain. From Master Errico I learn about the grains of wood. There's a right way and a wrong way. I follow the boomerang's grain when I polish it and it shakes a little in my hands. It's not a toy, but it's not a tool either. It's something in between, a weapon. I want to learn how to use it. I want to practice throwing it tonight, after Mama and Papa have gone to sleep. Italian has one word for sleep and another for dream. Neapolitan has just one—*suonno*. For us they're the same thing.

I swept the floor of the woodshed today and got attacked by fleas. They went for my legs. At work I wear shorts, and my legs turned black. Master Errico stripped me and washed me down at the pump in front of the shop. We were laughing like crazy. Thank goodness it's summer. There were mice in the woodshed, too. We put down some poison. "*'O súrece! 'O súrece!*" he screamed. They give him the creeps, not me. Then I got paid. He counted out the money and gave it to me. At night I started to practice with the boomerang. I learned that it didn't come from America. It came from Australia. The Americans are full of new things. The Neapolitans gather around when their ships weigh anchor and they come ashore. The latest thing is a plastic circle. It's called the Hula Hoop. I saw Maria spinning it around on her hips without letting it fall to the ground. She told me, "Try it." I said no, that I didn't think it was for boys. Maria turned thirteen before me. She lives on the top floor. That was the first time she talked to me.

I squeeze the boomerang. It gives me a shock. I start going through the moves to throw it. I wind it around behind my shoulder, then thrust it forward like I'm going to release it, but I don't. My shoulders are quick, like Maria's hips. I can't let the boomerang fly free. We're too cramped on top of Montedidio. My hand grips the last half inch of the wood and pulls it behind me. I keep doing this, back and forth. My back loosens up. I work up a sweat. I keep a tight grip. All it takes is a flick of the wrist for it to slip from your fingers. After a while I can see that my right hand's getting bigger than my left, so I change hands. This way one side of my body keeps up with the other, equal in speed, strength, and exhaustion. My last few unreleased throws really want to fly. It hurts my wrist to hold them back, so I stop.

I didn't want to stay at school. I was bigger than the other fifth graders. At snack time some kids used to take cakes out of their bags. To us poor kids, the janitor would hand out bread with quince jam. When it got hot the poor kids would come to school with their heads shaved like melons, on account of lice. The other kids still had hair to comb. There were too many differences between us. They went on in school. We didn't. I had to repeat grades a lot because I used to get sick with fevers. Then they promoted me but I didn't want to go to school anymore. I wanted to help out, to work. The studying I've done is enough. I know Italian, a quiet language that sits still inside books.

Ever since I started working and training with the boomerang I get hungrier. Papa is happy to have breakfast with me. At six the first rays of sunlight slither into the street and make their way into the houses, even the lower floors. We don't turn the light on. In summer the sunlight treads lightly over the ground before climbing up and becoming an oven that sits on top of the city. I put bread inside my cup of milk, which is darkened with coffee substitute. Papa used to get up alone every morning and now he's happy that I'm there, to talk to, to leave the house with. Mama gets up late. A lot of the time she's weak. At lunchtime I go up to the washbasins on the roof to hang out the laundry, then I pick it up in the evening. I never used to go up to the terrace before. It's high above Montedidio and gets a little breeze in the evening. No one can see me so I practice there. The boomerang quivers in the fresh air. My sleeve gets twisted when I squeeze the boomerang to keep from letting go. It's wood that was grown to fly. Master Errico is a good carpenter. He says that wood is good for fire, for water, for wine. I know that it's good for flying, too, but I won't say so if he won't. I was thinking I'd like to throw the boomerang from where the washbasins are, from the highest rooftop in Montedidio.

My arms are tired, sweaty, so I stretch out for a bit on the pavement by the clotheslines. By now there isn't even a sliver of the city above me. I close my good eye, and look up with the other one, the blind one, half open. Instantly the sky grows darker, denser, closer, right on top of me. My right eye is weak, but it can see the sky better than my good eye, which I need for the street, to look people in the face, to do my job in the shop. My left eye is sly, fast, understands things in a heartbeat. It's Neapolitan. My right is slow. It can't focus on anything. Instead of clouds it sees the scattered tufts of the mattress maker in the street, when he combs and twists the wool and breaks it up into tufts on a sheet spread out on the ground.

I go back to the washbasins, carrying the clothes basket. In the darkness of the stairs someone spies me going by. I can feel other people's eyes, even in the dark, because when they touch, when they look, it's like a slight current of air passing under a door. I think it's Maria. The building is old. Spirits pass you on the stairs. Once their bodies are gone, spirits start to miss their hands. The desire to touch makes them throw themselves at people. Despite all the effort they put into it, all you feel is a caress. Now that it's summer they rub against my face. They dry away the sweat. Spirits are happy in old buildings. But if someone says they saw them they're lying. You can only feel spirits, and only when they want.

Master Errico gives space in his shop to a cobbler named Don Rafaniello. I clean up his space, too, around the workbench and the pile of shoes that he fixes. He came to Naples from somewhere in Europe after the war. He went straight to Montedidio to Master Errico's and started fixing the shoes of the poor. He makes them new again. They call him Rafaniello because his hair is red, his eyes are green, he's short, and he has a hump on the top of his back. In Naples, it took one look for them to nickname him *ravanello*, radish. That's how he became Don Rafaniello. Not even he knows how many years he's been in the world.

Kids don't understand age. For them forty and eighty are all the same mess. Once on the stairs I heard Maria ask her grandma if she was old. Her grandma said no. Maria asked if her grandpa was old. Her grandma answered no. Then Maria asked, "So there's no such thing as old people," and got smacked across the face. I can tell how old people are, except for Rafaniello. His face is a hundred, his hands are forty, his hair, all red and bushy, twenty. From his words, I can't tell. He doesn't talk much, and when he does, it's in a teeny tiny voice. He sings in a foreign language. When I sweep up his corner he smiles at me, making his wrinkles and freckles ripple like the sea in the rain.

He's a good man, Rafaniello. He fixes the shoes of the poor and won't take money from them. One guy came by who wanted a new pair. Rafaniello took his measurements with a piece of string, made a few knots, and got to work. The guy came back to try them on for size and there they were. They fit like a glove. Rafaniello cares about people's feet. He wouldn't hurt a fly, so the flies never bother him. They buzz around him but never land on his skin, no matter how many there are. Master Errico shakes his neck like a carriage horse to get them out of his face when his hands are busy. He even snorts like a horse. I swat a rag around him and they leave him alone for a second.

I wear sandals even in winter. My feet are growing and this way they can stick out a little without having to buy a new pair. They're small on me. I sweep the floor in my bare feet, so as not to wear them out. Rafaniello took them one morning, and when I put them on at noon they fit me so well I was afraid they were the wrong sandals. I looked at him and he nodded yes, yes, with his head. I tell him, thank you Don Rafaniè. He answers, "You don't have to call me don." But you're a good Christian. You do acts of charity for the feet of the poor. You deserve to be called don. "No, call other people don if you want to. I'm not even a Christian. Where I'm from I had a name that was almost the same as Rafaniello." I didn't say a word. Till then we'd almost never spoken. The sandal leather smelled nice. It had come back to life in his hands. At home Mama complimented me, saying that I was good at getting people to like me. But with Don Rafaniello it doesn't count. He likes everybody.

I hear screeches and Neapolitan voices. I speak Neapolitan but I write Italian. "We're in Italy," Papa says, "but we're not Italian. To speak the language we have to study it, like being abroad, in America, but without leaving home. Many of us will never speak Italian and will die in Neapolitan." It's a hard language, he says, but you will learn it and be Italian. Me and your mother won't. "*Noi nun pu, nun po, nuie nun putimmo.*" He's trying to say "we can't," *non possiamo,* but the words won't come out. I tell him how to say it the Italian way. "Good boy," he says, "good boy. You know the national language." Sure I know it and I even write it in secret and when I do, I feel a little like I'm cheating on Neapolitan, so in my head I conjugate the verb "can," *potere. I' pozzo, tu puozzi, isso po', nuie putimmo, vuie putite, lloro ponno.* Mama doesn't agree with Papa and says, "We're Neapolitans and that's all there is to it." "*Ll'Italia mia,*" she says, doubling the *l* of the article. "*Ll'Italia mia sta in America*"—my Italy is in America. That's where half my family lives. "Your homeland is what puts food on your plate," she says, and stops. To tease her, Papa says, "Then you must be my homeland." He doesn't want to disagree with Mama. In our house we never raise our voices, we don't get into arguments. If something bothers him, he puts his hand over his mouth and covers half his face.

Master Errico has me spreading pore-filler on wood and sanding it down. Then I polish the doors of a wardrobe for clothes. How many clothes does this family have? We're making eight doors, two levels. They call it a "four seasons." Today I tested the latch on the first door and it fit so well that it made a vacuum sound. The air escaped from inside. Master Errico made me put my face near the door. I could feel the air stroking my cheek. That's how the spirits rub up against my face. Then Master Errico took it apart and covered it. It's a big job. He's been tinkering with it for a year. The drawers are made out of beech, the joints are dovetailed. It feels great to run your hands over them. He checks the squaring again and again, greasing the runners until the drawers don't make a sound when he pulls them out and slides them back in. He says it's like dropping a fishing line in the sea. They rise and fall silently in his hands. Master Errico, I say, you're a genius, a fishing cabinet maker.

Translated by Michael Moore

Leo's World

Pier Vittorio Tondelli

HOMECOMING is the theme of "Leo's World," by Pier Vittorio Tondelli (b. Correggio, Reggio Emilia, 1955), an excerpt from his fourth book, *Camere separate (Separate Rooms)*. Considered Tondelli's most mature work, *Separate Rooms* was published only two years before his premature death of AIDS in 1991. Tondelli is perhaps the most convincing example of a "postnational" type of author. His protagonists (including Leo, the autobiographical main character of *Separate Rooms*) are gripped by wanderlust and move with ease across Europe (and the world), following the migratory currents of the new "urban race."[1] As critic Diego Zancani has written, "Pier Vittorio Tondelli fits the image of a young 1980s writer almost perfectly. . . . He [was] interested in youth culture, contemporary music, jazz and American novels of the 1960s. He [had] a penchant and a very good ear for the language of teenagers."[2] He was also instrumental in providing media and publishing exposure to a number of young writers under twenty-five. The link between living and writing, typical of the Beat generation but also shared, in a peculiarly Emilian fashion, by Tondelli's favorite Emilian masters (the writers Antonio Delfini and Silvio D'Arzo), is a leitmotif of his fiction, described by critics as adhering to a postmodern mode and mood.[3] But *Camere separate* ("the story of a journey divided into three concentric and contiguous movements/chapters, like an operetta of environmental music," as Tondelli described it) is written from the vantage point of an author who knows it is "no longer suitable to define himself as young."[4] "In this book the individual self who had been occasionally suppressed or pushed to the margins of the narrative re-emerges in a glorious, even a religious context," writes Zancani.[5] Leo's visit to his provincial hometown and his crumbling paternal house is the second movement/chapter of his journey: his room, where "he wrote his first words, his diaries," is now "a sort of box room," half shelter and half reliquary, where literary ghosts of beloved, eccentric and melancholy Emilian writers hover among the remains of a vanishing adolescence.

NOTES

1. Bart Van den Bossche, "La geografia letteraria nei romanzi e nei racconti di Tondelli" (Louvain, 1997), readable online at:
http://www.comune.bologna.it/iperbole/assrere/autori/tondelli.htm.
2. Diego Zancani, "Pier Vittorio Tondelli: The Calm after the Storm," in *The New Italian Novel*, ed. Zygmunt G. Baranski and Lino Pertile (Edinburgh: Edinburgh University Press, 1993), 239.
3. Tondelli's books include the stories of *Altri libertini* (*Other Libertines*, published in 1980), the novels *Pao-Pao* (1982), *Rimini* (1985), and *Camere separate*

(1991; *Separate Rooms*, trans. Simon Pleasance [London: Serpent's Tail, 1992]). *Un weekend postmoderno* (*A Postmodern Weekend*) is the title of Tondelli's last book, published in 1990 and in his words: "a travelogue made of fragments, reportages, interior enlightenment, reflections, shared and direct descriptions, in the more creative and experimental years of the 1980s."

4. One can read this quote (quoting Ingeborg Bachmann) and other excerpts from various Tondelli interviews on the Web site documenting his work created by his hometown of Correggio (Reggio Emilia) at: http://www.rcs .re.it/correggio/pvt/e_camere.htm. The home page opens (somewhat eerily) with Tondelli's voice pronouncing a sort of personal mantra: "A writer is somebody who tries to live by his writing, and tries to let his writing help him live."

5. Zancani, "Pier Vittorio Tondelli," 236.

Leo's World

by Pier Vittorio Tondelli

A SMALL town in the lower Po valley. It has colonnades, cobble-
stones on the main thoroughfare, a church consecrated to the town's
patron saint, a Renaissance palace, towers and belfries, a castle, an
old quarter with 19th century houses, and one or two 18th century
mansions. The fabric of the town is still intact, gathered about the
old city walls now in ruins. Leo was born here in a large, old house
looking out on to the main square. It is still there, but not for much
longer. It has been abandoned. The tenants have gone, and with the
exception of the barber all the storekeepers on the ground-floor
have abandoned their shops. Demolition work will start before
long, and the town will be given another building with neither history nor style.

A building filled with one- or two-room apartments, low ceilings,
faceless windows, and post-modern in salmon-pink or bluish-green
plasterwork. But he is not shocked. His parents would see things in

exactly the same way. Only prisoners need space. And city-dweller Leo would keep everything as it is, with his reverence for the past. He is dumbfounded, for example, that a small devotional chapel, built in the 19th century, and still standing on the main road just a few yards from his birthplace, should have been left in a state of total neglect.

When he was a boy, Leo's grandmother would walk him in front of this little church, take him by the arm and show him the altar inside, with the painting of the Virgin Mary and the vases of flowers. For many of the townsfolk there is a tree that records the changes and developments, and the passage of time. Many of them remember that that sixty-five foot fir tree was planted by their father when they were children. Leo also recalls planting the poplars, tall now, in front of the high school buildings one October day that had been dedicated to trees. But he feels nothing when he sees that line of poplars. Not so when he walks past the chapel in the street. It reminds him of when he was a boy, and had to clamber up the iron grille to see inside. Now he can see inside with no trouble. He is taller. And the chapel has grown smaller, more huddled, and its outline is sharper. It is possible that the chapel is more alone too. But for him it is still a way of measuring time.

He parks his car on the tree-lined boulevard, not far from the chapel. He notices that they have put two metal rubbish bins close by it, and one side of the chapel is covered with flyers and posters. It makes him realize that his sense of preserving reality, or rather preserving what he has known, or been fond of, is very different to other people's sensibilities. He is quite sure that if he were to ask his fellow citizens—all several thousand of them—where he might find a certain chapel, built in a certain style, with a particular religious painting inside, and vases of flowers and a rusty grille with the initials of the Virgin Mary, nobody would be able to tell him. Maybe not even his own mother. He realizes that the way he is able to see and perceive the town where he was born is radically different. He remembers it with affection, tempered now by distance and detachment.

When the house he was born in has vanished, when the chapel he clambered to see inside has been demolished, when all the old stones have gone, it is not only the memory of the people he loved in his childhood that will die, it is he himself who will die as well. The next generation will not know anything about these small people who have punctuated the history of the place—people who will leave no trace, people whom nobody will remember. Humble, anonymous folk, but people he felt at one with, people who in a certain sense embraced him, just as they embrace the whole future. When the little chapel stands in ruins, which is undoubtedly what will happen to it, he will feel even more alone. And without noticing a thing, the town will lose another small, infinitesimal fraction of its sensibility.

The cemetery stands on the far side of the house his parents now live in, which, in turn, stands right opposite the house where he was born—the house his family left more than twenty-five years ago. At the end of the boulevard, a mile or so away, the road makes a sweeping bend where it joins the new ring road. This is where the cemetery is, close by the municipal water-tower. No matter how much Leo has travelled the world, no matter how many places he has lived in, or will live in across the length and breadth of Europe, his whole life will be contained in this walk that leads from his birthplace to the graveyard. A mile or so that he will walk down like the stations of the cross, along a path of incarnation and suffering. "Here and yonder" is a mental attitude that he now repeats as he looks along the boulevard and then back to the windows that gave him the first view of his life. "Here and yonder" sums up his whole life.

His mother is waving to him from the balcony. She has spied him standing still in the middle of the roadway and called out to him in her shrill voice, the voice of a young country girl, that has not changed from one decade to the next. She is still that lass who used to run through fields shouting, calling out to her sisters through the rooms of the large farmhouse where she was born. When these other women get together, they also use the same gestures and make the same din that they made in their far distant communal youth. Four sisters parted by marriages and the different towns and cities where life had led them, into small apartments where they yelled from one room to the next as if they were still in the country.

When the four of them get together, in a bedroom before Sunday mass, and parade in front of the mirror, and perfume themselves and adjust each other's clothes and the bows on their blouses and their head-scarves, chattering excitedly all the while, about who has had a house built, and who has died, and who has been unfaithful to whose wife, and who has been elected to the town council, and gossiping about trains and buses, grape-harvests and grandchildren, Leo watches them in awe, standing in a corner, feeling a sense of complicity. He would like to be invisible so that he could watch them more closely. He would like to record the interwoven strands of their chatter—as, indeed, he had secretly done now and then— the way they speak, their little shrieks, their cursing, their huffing and puffing, and those signs of the cross that they each make so swiftly, like spells. He sees how hierarchy and seniority are mirrored in their group. He notices the coalitions that are struck up between the two youngest and the two oldest. Or the sudden alliances whereby one sister is suddenly ostracized by the other three. And all of it happening in a whirligig of high heels, furs, mothballs, face-powder, earrings, and foundation creams that none of them, past sixty, has ever learned to apply without exaggeration. And all of them yelling and shouting in their rapid, shrill dialect, with each one trying to outdo the others. The end result: a babble made up of gestures, and sisters darting to and fro across the room, and laughter in front of the mirrors, and sudden lulls—a stampede, in a word, such as probably went on in their own house on Sunday mornings, before they all stepped up into the carriage to go off to mass in the village church. And when he sees them filing out one after the other, each one of them closing and reclosing the doors, with much slamming and flapping of doors and windows and shutters, because none of them trusts any of the others to close up properly, so they each open and close everything all over again with a fine sneer of self-satisfaction and spite, then Leo joins the end of the line, quiet and a little hunched, quite sure that the people who hold the reins of power on this earth are not men, but women. He sees these ladies, who are well past sixty, still showing all the vigour of young girls. He has seen them bury their husbands and withstand the slings and arrows of time, never, never ill in hospital, but always ready to assist their recuperating menfolk suffering from the frailty of their sickly bodies.

When he imagines his mother walking through the colonnades in the town, wrapped in her fine fur coat, with grandma's gold earrings and always just a bit too much make-up and face-powder, or when he hears her "amens" rise up through the church as if she were back in the days of her childhood, he experiences a split second of terror. He prays that a chicken will not start strutting down the middle of the nave, or that a pheasant will not run across the main aisle, because if such a thing happened he would see her throwing down her fur coat, hoisting up her skirts, pulling off her orthopaedic shoes, and chasing the hen through the churchgoers, yelling and clapping her hands until she had caught it. And once she had grabbed it, she would wring its neck with a broad smile across her face, or snap its spine with a swift twist of the head. Then she would return to the congregation in church, or the crowd in the square, proudly displaying her trophy. When he finds his mother in a crowd of people he always has this same feeling of dread, and he looks anxiously and nervously about him, checking to see if there is not some poor unsuspecting chicken near at hand. Because despite all the years that have passed, he still sees his mother as a young and frisky peasant girl. And when he imagines her, thousands of miles away, trying to clutch at the image of her, he always describes her to himself with the same words, just to remind himself: "Like a poor, everlasting, most beautiful Jewess."

Now she comes towards him by the lift. She hurries to take his bags before she even says hello. He steps back abruptly: "Let me take them, mama."

They go up to the apartment. It is dark, with just the bluish light from the television to lighten the gloom in the living-room. His father is stretched out in an armchair fiddling with the remote control in an endless search for thrillers and mini-series. They say an awkward hello to each other, with that alien feeling that comes from their mutual awareness that their lives are so very different. His father gets to his feet and turns on the light. Leo makes to stop him, not wanting to disturb him.

In the kitchen one half of the table is laid with a small clean tablecloth. There is a bottle of red wine to open and a bowl of salad. His mother heats up the stew. They both eye each other without a word passing between them. Next door the room resounds with gunshots and screeching police cars. Leo runs a hand through his hair, wondering if his mother is thinking he is much balder than the last time she saw him. Then he notices her adjusting her skirt, straightening it at the sides with a quick unconvincingly absent-minded gesture. Maybe she is wondering if Leo has noticed that she has put on a little weight. At the same moment they both look up, and their eyes meet, and they ask each other: "How are things?"

Leo adds quickly: "I'm not that hungry, mama." Then he regrets his words, because now he will trigger off his mother's reaction about all that muck that people cook the world over and how he will always eat his fill in restaurants, not to mention that insult, that sacrilege—Chinese cooking. I've seen those Chinese people, where your father works. A boiled fish and a couple of pounds of rice, all mixed up and cooked together, guts, blood, onion, rosemary, the whole lot in the same pot, just like during the war, and then they all eat from the same pot with their hands. Go to your restaurant, go on with you.

Leo smiles because what he really cannot digest any more is his mother's cooking—the food from his own land. But he does not let on. He pours a glass of wine and drinks it down in one gulp. He will always have fond memories of this fresh, aromatic wine.

His father is a man who has not been successful in his life. He has not made much money. He does not talk much. He still gets up at dawn to go hunting in the Apennines. Or beating in the countryside nearby with his dog. The most recent thing he has done, as far as anyone knows, is to build a small bird pen around a natural spring, out in the country. Every day he prepares the feed for the fish and the birds—ducks, peacocks, pheasants and chickens. An Egyptian friend has given him a pair of pink flamingoes, and they are managing to survive in what he stubbornly calls his oasis. He wants them to mate and reproduce and start a colony. Every now and then, with his friends and their wives, they organize fishing competitions, or they wring the necks of a dozen chickens and cook them in a prefabricated shed. They will spend a whole Sunday there, from dawn until dusk.

The women knead dough and fry dumplings. The men besport themselves angling for handsome pike, catfish and perch. Among their friends, with every passing month, there are always more widows or women who have lost their lifelong companion. But there is nothing sad about their gatherings out at the oasis.

It is just some overgrown pond gone wild with a few fish and a few animals, but Leo feels that his father really loves the spot. It is his private paradise, a place where he can do what the hell he likes. It probably reminds him of his own childhood and his life in the country. It reminds him of his solitude. Leo appreciates this solitary, unsociable side of his father's character. He feels the same. They are two men who have not communicated with one another, or had any physical contact with one another for at least twenty years. They avoid each other. They certainly do not seek each other out. And they ask absolutely nothing of each other. One mirrors the other, and Leo is well aware of this. He wonders if his father is aware of it, too.

After supper he chats with his mother in the kitchen. To stop her asking questions, he asks her what has been happening in the town, who has got married, who has been burgled, who has got divorced and who has given birth. All it takes is one small question to set his mother off telling him about the whole world and his wife, darting pell-mell from one story to the next. He laughs and chuckles and surreptitiously pours himself more wine until his mother whisks the bottle off the table, still chattering, and still fixing him with her slightly severe gaze. The news she gives him is comforting. Even when they talk of friends ailing with cancer and close to death, and his mother sniffs and wipes an eye with the hem of her apron, with a shake of the head, Leo finds nothing "tragic" about it. It is as if it were all part and parcel of town life. Birth, death, people parting, they are all just stages in the collective life of the place. This life always leaves room for hope, because the community survives and evolves. Everyone leaves children and friends and fond memories behind, and the life of the town carries on an inch at a time, founded on these deep-seated bonds and feelings. Leo understands his mother's suffering, or her enthusiasm when she recounts a journey with aunts and friends and describes the cabins on the ferryboat as if Leo had never seen such a thing, or the lounges of some Grand Hotel, as if he had never set foot inside such a place. He understands but he does not feel either anguish or happiness. It is all part of a life that is not his, a life in which he will never find a foothold. All he can do is listen, smile and feel melancholy. In his body he can never feel the state of good or evil in the life of the people of his town. He enjoys watching his mother. He enjoys her stories which make him laugh until he cries. But it is all just at some slight remove from him. It is as if he is a witness to life in a town apart.

When his thoughts revert to his own tragedy, he feels horror and despair once again. Because he knows that it is a drama that belongs to him, and to him alone. He knows that, in the years to come, no one will remember his lost love, no one will rest a hand on his shoulder to tell him it will all pass. He will not show his mourning on the main street of his own home town. He will not see other people's eyes reflecting the pain that fills his. He will not shake hands or embrace anyone else. And no one will accompany Thomas's body to the cemetery, not even he. He realizes that this, too, is part of a separate town. A different world, in fact, which lives and suffers and rejoices parallel to the other one. He knows that the hardest thing for people is to achieve some contact with the world of other people. Going out and meeting other people with sincerity. Leo tries to blend these two remote and different worlds. But it seems impossible. He does everything possible knowing that it will be quite useless. It is just possible that things might change in the future, but many years hence. People will be born who will try other ways of combining the different worlds in which people go on living. Eventually, someone will come along for whom the memory of "Leo-and-Thomas" will be accepted and guarded as something life-giving and hopeful. But only in years to come. Maybe not for centuries. In some ways the room which was his for twenty years is no longer the same. It is still a bedroom, with the same old bed, the same white writing-table and the same shelves fixed to the walls full of paperbacks and schoolbooks and university textbooks. But it is still not the same. It does not have him, Leo, between these four walls. All that remains now is wistful reminders or meaningless vestiges of the past, all lifeless now.

It is like reading manuscripts in the showcases of a museum. Publicity posters for sneakers, Levi jeans, pirate radio stations like Central City Radio and Anti-Radio Rock Station and World Radio are still stuck to the door, along with signs saying "Marijuana Right On" and "Nuclear Power No Thanks," the blue-green emblem of the Superski season-ticket in the Dolomites, the yellow mouse of "Aktiv gegen Berufsverbote!," the WWF panda. The blow-up of a black-and-white photo of him still hangs above the stereo, where his old albums of Leonard Cohen, Nina Simone, Tim Buckley, Cat Stevens, and Neil Young are all mixed up with his mother's records of Edith Piaf and Luciano Pavarotti. A piece of dark wooden furniture in a corner contains a sewing machine. A large ironing-board leans up against the wardrobe. And beneath the desk there is a vacuum cleaner.

His room has been invaded by household gadgets. And it has changed. Every time he has come back home he has noticed his things differently arranged, until they finally vanish altogether. His large film posters of *Cabaret* and *Straw Dogs* are no longer around, probably thrown into the wastepaper basket. The photos of the Italian Film Festival of 1973 have gone, and so have the photos of his friends. The photos of Claes Oldenburg and Yves Klein, once pinned to a cork board behind the bed, have also gone. The walls have changed colour as well. They used to be a very light, almost a transparent green. Now they are bright yellow.

His room has turned into a sort of boxroom. It is in this room, which looks more and more like a broom closet, he wrote his first words, his diaries, the essays for his degree, and his very first book.

While he wrote, he stared out from that balcony at the town lights twinkling beneath the distant peaks of the Apennines. Out there, that was where life was really happening, and in the wretchedness of his boyhood, here up on the eighth floor, all he could do was dream about it and describe it. Imagine it like a maelstrom of people dancing from one bar to the next, and from parties to discos. Describe it like a city of night where dreams sparkle and where everyone is merry and dressed to the nines and beguiling in their cars speeding across the plain. He sits down now at the table, where he always used to sit. He has to move the steam iron and a bottle of distilled water to see out through the window. But he cannot see anything. He tries to lift up the heavy wooden shutter, but to no avail. It gets stuck halfway, askew like a guillotine blade.

The books he left behind last time are still on the bedside table. He only ever manages to read them here in this room. Books by Antonio Delfini and Silvio D'Arzo. From the balcony of his room he can see where they were born, just a few miles away. It is only in their books that he finds those particular types of madness, boredom and melancholy that are not normally associated with the people from his native land. But he is tired of descriptions of a lively, open, jovial and sensual people. What interests him now is the hidden side of this character, the dark side that causes suicides, creates rifts, and makes village idiots. It is only in these two writers, in their different ways, that he finds descriptions of that particular impenetrability of the Emilian character, that particular offhandedness, that eccentric, mad melancholy that he has known in his father and now sees in himself. He undresses and slips into bed. He opens one of Delfini's books and starts to read: "If we had ever had the gift of lamentation and ill-will, despair and dogged hope, the expectation of bitterness and the impossible relinquishment of love dispersed, in the midst of the world's disasters and the remorseless march of time or the march of man; we would say . . . "

It occurs to him that, once again, he has gone to bed early, as he had done for a long time.

Translated by Simon Pleasance

PART IV

Views from Afar

The Sea Voyage of Baron Mandralisca

Vincenzo Consolo

SICILIAN WRITER Vincenzo Consolo's *The Smile of the Unknown Mariner* (*Il sorriso dell'ignoto marinaio*) introduces us to a new type of historical narrative. In the excerpt that follows, historical memory is above all a visual sort of memory, and "the sea voyage of Enrico Pirajno, Baron of Mandralisca, from Lipari to Cefalù, bearing the canvas with the portrait of an unknown man by Antonello da Messina" is the first panel of a fascinating historical fresco. Published in 1976, two years after Morante's *Storia*, Consolo's novel is more an exercise in the art of *staging* history than a linear reconstruction and representation of events. Described by the critic and translator Joseph Farrell as "a complex, multi-layered piece of work, with constantly shifting focus," the *Unknown Mariner* can be considered a sort of anti-*Leopard* (Giuseppe Tomasi di Lampedusa's 1958 classic historical narrative also set at the time of Garibaldi's expedition), closer in inspiration to Leonardo Sciascia's historical-judicial mysteries (*The Counsel of Egypt, The Death of the Inquisitor, Open Doors*).[1] Consolo was born in 1931, in the Sicilian village of Sant'Agata Militello, "halfway between the provinces of Messina and Palermo," that is, between the "Greek" east and the Norman and Arabic west of Sicily, as he himself writes. Consolo explains how he then chose the west (Palermo) where, compared with the rest of the island, the sense of history is more marked, and became what he calls a "vertical" writer: "Vertical writers are people like us [Sicilians], like the Neapolitans or the South Americans . . . the greater the social unhappiness of a country the more its writers are made 'vertical,' by a need to explain their own pain and to understand its origins."[2] Consolo's page is a sophisticated composition of many voices, lost to our ears and eyes: the political rhetoric of the nineteenth-century Risorgimento, the dialect songs of fishermen and mariners, the epistolary style of a nobleman, the baroque style of a seventeenth-century treatise, all give form to a work that challenges our simplistic sense of what is the past and awakens us to the perception of its secret links with our present.

NOTES

1. Joseph Farrell, "Vincenzo Consolo: Metaphors and False History," in *The New Italian Novel*, ed. Zygmunt G. Baranski and Lino Pertile (Edinburgh: Edinburgh University Press, 1993), 65. Consolo's novel (Farrell writes) "is imbued with a deeper sense of history than Lampedusa's work, and is free from all suggestion that there exists an eternal, mythical Sicily outside history and impervious to change."

2. This interview can be found in the proceedings of an international conference, "Rinnovamento del codice narrativo in Italia dal 1945 al 1992," held in

Belgium May 3–8, 1993: *I tempi del rinnovamento*, ed. Serge Vanvolsem, Franco Musarra, and Bart Van den Bossche (Rome: Bulzoni, 1995), vol. 1, 542–43. Another extensive interview (one of several in Italian) is available online at: http://www.italialibri.net/interviste/consolo/consolo11.html. Books by Vincenzo Consolo (in addition to *The Smile of the Unknown Mariner,* the only one so far translated into English) include: *La ferita dell'aprile (The Wound of April,* 1963), *Lunaria* (1985), *Retablo* (1987), *Le pietre di Pantalica (The Stones of Pantalica,* 1989), *Nottetempo, casa per casa (At Night, House by House,* 1992), *L'olivo e l'olivastro (The Olive and the Oleaster,* 1994), *Lo spasimo di Palermo* (1999, *The Pang of Palermo*).

The Sea Voyage of Baron Mandralisca

by Vincenzo Consolo

THE SEA voyage of Enrico Pirajno, Baron of Mandralisca, from Lipari to Cefalù, bearing the canvas with the portrait of an unknown man by Antonello da Messina. The painting, recovered from an inset panel in a cabinet on the premises of the apothecary, Carnevale, is slightly disfigured by two crossed scratches on the forward part of the sitter's smiling lips. According to the people of Lipari, the apothecary's daughter, Catena, still unmarried at the ripe age of twenty-five, enraged (there was, they report, a particularly oppressive sirocco blowing that day) by the man's intolerable smile, inflicted on him two blows with the agave spine she used for punching holes in the linen pulled taut over her embroidery frame. This was believed to be why the apothecary Carnevale sold the work to Baron Mandralisca; he had the good of his daughter at heart, and wished to see her back behind the counter serenely engaged on her embroidery, picking out the patterns for which she had such a knack (in a trice she could do you a set of initials, produce the most elaborate flourishes, arabesques, frills, run up lines or strings of dots and stops . . .). In a shaft of light falling from the lunette in the side wall, between the counter and the shelves loaded with flasks, jars, ointment pots, cruets, boxes, crucibles, she herself remained barely visible to the darting glances of the young men passing backwards and forwards on the Strada San Bartolomeo (the beautiful, unattainable Catena remained a mystery; was she concealing some unconfessable love of her own or merely taking delight in playing havoc with the suppressed passions of others?).

And now the great island came into view. The lamps on the towers along the coast were red and green, they swayed and fell from view to reappear as bright as before. Once it entered the waters of the gulf, the vessel ceased rolling. In the channel between Tindari and Vulcano, the waves whipped up by the sirocco had battered it from every side. Throughout the night Mandralisca, standing near the forward railing, had heard nothing but the roar of the waters, the creak and snap of the sails, and a rattling sound that approached and receded with the wind. And now that the vessel advanced, silent and stately, within the bay, on a calmer, more slow-running sea, he clearly heard behind him the same rattle, drawn out and unchanging. The sound of breathing which, with choking noises and rasping coughs, came painfully from rigid, contracted lungs, forcing its way along the windpipe and issuing, with a low groan, from a mouth that he imagined open as wide as possible. In the lantern's faint light, Mandralisca made out a brightness which might have been the gleam of eyes in the darkness.

He turned his gaze back to the skies and the stars, to the great island ahead, to the lamps on the towers. Keeps built of sandstone and mortar displayed their high, crenellated finery on the sheer rock that takes the force of the sea winds and waves—the towers of Calava and Calanovella, of Lauro and Gioisa, of Brolo . . .

Out on the balcony of the castle of Lancia stands Lady Bianca, feeling sick. She sighs and vomits, peering at the distant horizon. The wind of Swabia tears her apart. The Emperor Frederick of Swabia confides to his falcon:

> O God, what madness was in me
> When you made me depart
> From where I had great dignity;
> I pay a bitter price,
> Like snow I melt away . . .

Behind the lamps, in the centre of the bay stood cities once, under the olive groves: Abacena and Agatirno, Alunzio and Calacte, Alesa . . . cities in which Mandralisca would have knelt down to claw at the soil with his bare hands, had he been sure of finding a vase, a lantern or even just a coin. Now those cities are no more than names, sounds, dreams full of yearning. And he clasped to his chest the painting wrapped in waxed canvas he'd brought from Lipari; he tested with his fingers its solidity and hardness, relished the subtle aromas of camphor and mustard with which it was impregnated after so many years in the apothecary's shop.

But these scents were suddenly overwhelmed by others, wafting from the land, stronger than the sirocco, heavy and powerful with garlic, fennel, oregano, bay leaf and calamint. With them came the cries and beating wings of the seagulls. A great fan-like brightness rose up from the depths of the sea; the stars disappeared, the lights from the towers grew faint.

The rattling sound had changed into a dry, stubborn cough. Then Mandralisca saw, in the dawn's sharp light, a naked man bent over backwards, dark and desiccated as an olive tree, his outstretched arms clinging to the foreyard, his head thrown back as he struggled to open his throat and release some clot gnawing at his chest. A woman was drying his forehead and neck. She became aware of the gentleman, removed her shawl and wrapped it round the sick man's thighs. He was racked by a last, terrible fit of coughing and immediately ran to the rail. He turned pale, his eyes dilated and staring, and he pressed a cloth over his mouth. His wife helped him lie down on the deck, among the ship's tackle.

"Stone disease," said a voice which seemed to come from inside the Baron's ear. Mandralisca found himself face to face with a man, who smiled strangely—the ironic, caustic, bitter smile of one who has seen much and knows much, who is aware of the present and senses the future, who strives to defend himself from the pain of knowledge and the continual temptation of compassion. His eyes were small and sharp under arched eyebrows. Two deep wrinkles scored his hard face at the mouth's corners, as though to mark and emphasise that smile. The man was dressed as a sailor, with cloth bonnet, jacket and flared trousers. On closer examination, however, he turned out to be an unusual mariner: he lacked the somnolent detachment and dull alienation characteristic of someone who had spent his life at sea, but had the alertness of a landsman who has lived in the midst of men and their affairs. An observer might have noted in him an aristocratic bearing.

"Stone disease," continued the mariner. "He's a pumice quarry-man from Lipari. There are hundreds like him on this island. They're lucky if they reach forty. The doctors have no idea what to do with them, so they come here to implore the Black Madonna of Tindari for a miracle. Apothecaries and herbalists treat them with poultices and infusions and make a fat profit. These same doctors slice them open once they're dead, to study those whitened lungs which have turned as hard as the stone they sharpen their little knives on. What is there to look for? It's the stone, the pumice dust. They'll never understand that everything depends on not swallowing the stuff."

And here, noting a mixture of pain and surprise in the Baron's expression, he smiled his bitter, ironic smile. The Baron, still intent on the mariner's speech, had been trying to remember where and when he'd seen him before. He was so certain of this that he would willingly have wagered his estate at Colombo or the *Tuna Vendor* vase from his collection. But *where* had he seen him?

Under the man's piercing glance, however, his thoughts returned to the quarryman. Beyond Canneto, towards the west, a dazzling white mountain called Pelato rises from the sea. There a vast army of men, a black swarm of tarantulas and beetles, labours under a sun as fierce as that of Morocco, cutting into the porous rock with their pickaxes. Bent double under their baskets, they emerge from holes, caves, galleries in the rock; they slither and slide along narrow planks, bridges stretching into the sea, towards the boats. As these images arose, Mandralisca strove to repress others which were just then, by some unexplained association or counterpoint, forcing their way to the surface (flocks of birds migrating towards Africa under a stormy sky; green snails leaving silvery trails on the rock;

high swaying palm trees offering a fleeting glimpse of the vulva of the spathes with their Easter-white inflorescences . . .). And then, to the Baron's acute dismay, before this man, who was both investigator and judge, his own various studies presented themselves. Arranged volume by volume, each with its title, publisher and year of publication; these were the monographs which—in ordinary circumstances—gave the Baron quiet delight, pride and a certain satisfaction: his *Catalogue of the Birds Native to or in Passage in the Aeolian Islands*, *Catalogue of the Terrestrial and Fluvial Molluscs of the Madonie Mountains and Parts Adjacent Thereto*, *Catalogue and Fecundation of Palm Trees*.

The mariner read, and smiled, with ironical commiseration.

From the stern came the noise of shouting and of the anchor chains being unwound and lowered into the water. The ship had arrived at Oliveri, under the rock of Tindari. The mariner left the Baron and walked off, with a sprightly step, towards the foremast.

The sun's rays above the horizon lit up the massive rock with its ancient theatre, gymnasium and sanctuary perched on top, the whole form rising sheer out of the great wastes of land and water. The beach was an embroidered pattern of golds and enamels. In sinuous tongues, circles, zigzags, the yellow sand formed basins, canals, lakes, inlets. The waters contained every shade of blue and green. Reeds, rushes, mosses, slimy filaments grew all around; fat fish swam and slow seagulls and lazy herons waded in those waters. The mother-of-pearl of mussels and shellfish, and the white of limed starfish glistened on the sand. Small boats with sails still furled on the mast floated motionless on the still waters among the dunes, like the flotsam and jetsam of tides. A heavy, humid air hung over the beach, with a dormant sirocco visible in some low, frayed twists of cloud.

What cosmic event, what earthquake had cast into the sea the highest peaks of the rock together with the ancient city that once nestled there? What lost treasures lay under those green waters, those sands! Wholly unknown herbs, unimagined vegetation, encrustations covering the shoulders, arms, thighs of Venuses and Dioscuri!

So Adelasia, carved alabaster queen, the lace frills rigid over her sleeves, waited impassively for the convent to disintegrate. "Who is there, in the name of God?"—the centuries-old, solitary Abbess's question echoed round the cloister, until it lost itself in the cells, the huge chambers, the deserted passageways. "Did His Grace the Archbishop send you?" And outside all was emptiness, a whirlwind of days and suns and waters, gusts of spiralling winds, crumbling sandstone walls, tumbling dunes, hills, falls of stone, waste. The thistle emerges, wrenches round, offers at last its trembling, diaphanous flower to the white donkey's hollow eye. A light that burns, bites, smoothes sides, angles, points, lightens shades and stains, abolishes colour—it welds together wisps of grass, whitens stray branches and, beyond the moving plain of fish-scales and horizons, dissolves and reshapes the massive forms.

Now, above the rock, on the cliff's edge, the little sanctuary sheltered the *nigra Bizantina*, the Virgin Most Gracious, encased in the veil's perfect triangle, resplendent with garnets, pearls and aquamarines, unsuffering Queen, silent Sibyl, Libyan ebony, with the unchanging gesture of the hand clasping the stem of the three-lilied silver sceptre.

"Mind your own damn business," Mandralisca ordered Rosario.

The servant had only just appeared, his head still enveloped in veils of sleep, to beg his master to go and rest.

"Your Excellency, is this how Christian folk behave—you stay outside all night long, on your feet, with that bit of wood stuck to your breast as though you were giving suck?"

"Rosario, I know what I've got here. If you want to carry on snoring, snore away! Like the beast you are."

"Sleep, Excellency! I haven't so much as closed an eye, God strike me dead if I tell a lie. Every last one of those lobster claws I was sucking away at yesterday evening ended up in the sea."

"Yes, together with every last piece of flesh inside the shell those four claws once carried along the sea-floor, Rosario, not to mention the caper sauce they were so nicely soused in."

"Yes, Excellency. Exquisite. What a shame!"

"To say nothing of what washed it all down."

"Yes, Excellency. Julep wine. But I was saying . . . "

"Rosario, I understand. Go back to sleep."

"Yes, Your Excellency."

The unknown mariner, standing upright in the crow's nest, blew the triton shell three times, and the sound, echoing from the rocks, returned three times to the sailing ship. A flock of coots and seagulls rose up from the beach, while crows and ravens swooped down from the cliffs. A four-oared boat set out from the Oliveri shoreline. From every corner of the decks and up from the holds, groups of pilgrims appeared. There were dishevelled women travelling barefoot in fulfilment of a vow, old women with baskets and bags as well as children in their arms, men laden with sacks, barrels and demijohns. They were bringing wine from Pianoconte, malvasia from Canneto, ricotta cheeses from Vulcano, wheat from Salina, capers from Acquacalda and Quattropani. And each one carried, high aloft, pink or flesh-coloured limbs made of wax—heads, legs, breasts or secret organs—painted blue or black in various spots to mark the disfiguring growths, swellings, scars and other ills. The pumice-stone quarryman now wore a hooded goatswool cloak and carried a candle as tall as himself. Two complete, pear-shaped *caciocavallo* cheeses, shining with the oil smeared over their surface, hung over his wife's breast, attached to a cord that cut into her neck. The rowing-boat touched the wooden side of the sailing ship, and the pilgrims, calling to each other and shouting, crowded on the gangway to disembark.

A long boat with a cargo of clay pots, vases, amphoras, jugs, plates and pitchers, all from the factories of Marina di Patti, put out from the shore. It was carrying, lined up on deck at the prow, four white marble statues of toga-clad consuls, leaning forward like captains, one with a head and three without, each reflected upside down in the water. Behind these, other dismembered marbles, and, still further behind, miniature trees from the nurseries of Mazzara— orange, lemon, bergamot, mandarin, cedar and lime—were lined up in their plant pots. These bushes, which adorned the stairwells, winter gardens, galleries and pavilions of palaces and courts in Palermo, Naples and Caserta, Versailles and Venice, grew luxuriantly in Mazzara on account of the heat and humours of this land which resembled a quarry, hollow, ditch, groin, female organ (Baron?!). The long boat glided slowly, silently below the sailing ship where Mandralisca stood, giving him the opportunity to observe at leisure.

The marbles behind the statues represented *the most elegant Greek workmanship, depicting two feet with legs up to the thighs of a youthful male nude, with a skilfully decorated altar in white alabaster marble, to the left. A further two large items of marble statuary together form the colossal torso of a man: in one of these items the decorated, bas-relief armour is clearly visible, and among the features one can observe the breastplate with crest of matted hair, such as can be found on many medallions.*

A highly worked strap hangs from the right shoulder over the chest. On the left shoulder the pallium intended as cover for both shoulders is elegantly picked out. Over the belly, two hippogryphs appear. The other piece of marble was the remainder of the armour, i.e., the fibulae and the breast plate, reaching down to the loin-cloth over the thighs, which themselves present divers incisions. The breast plates depicted small heads of various animals and some humans. The existence of these fragments in the Tindari area has caused some to conjecture that they formed part of a statue of the Dioscuri, described by the poets in military attire. Ah God! what beauty! But where was that thieving long boat bound for? For white, thalassic, rocky Syracuse, or for red, sultanic, palmy Palermo? A pirate; the Baron would have loved to play the pirate and attack that boat at the head of some rascally band. He'd haul it off to his own beloved port of the Vascio at Cefalù, nestling beneath the rocks, teeming with shoals of mullet, on salt waters made fresh by currents from the springs and founts of Arethusa. And then he'd have shown Biscari, Asmundo Zappalà, Canon Alessi, perhaps even the Cardinal, as well as Pepoli, Bellomo and even Landolina!

The procession of the other pilgrims, who had come from the countryside and towns of Val Demone to Tindari for the September feast, snaked along high up in the rocks, following the winding road that led from Oliveri to the shrine. As they climbed they chanted incomprehensible songs, which ricocheted from the front to the rear of the group, criss-crossing in the middle to create a tangle of sound, but then, after countless endeavours and detours, seeming to fuse, to become one strong, clear chant which grew under its own force and swelled as the procession proceeded towards the shrine.

A beautiful girl with raven-black hair and green, flashing eyes, seated in the long boat with the others, rose to her feet when the song's echo reached her and, swaying softly, struck up a chant of her own: a vile, obscene chant which the prisoners over there in Lipari, clinging to the iron bars of the castle, intoned in the evening. Her mother, in the attempt to prevent her and stop her mouth with her hand, dropped a votive wax head into the water, where it floated a moment, its pure, white forehead still visible, before sinking from sight.

Translated by Joseph Farrell

Melodrama

Pier Maria Pasinetti

OUR FICTIONAL itinerary would not be complete without an opera stage, and we find two in this final section. The first, Pier Maria Pasinetti's prelude to his 1993 novel, aptly entitled *Melodramma*, raises the curtain on a gallery of effervescent historical cross-references, a perfectly orchestrated choral performance (with a couple of dizzying solos as well). Pasinetti's highly mobile narrative world stretches between the new and the old continent, between Venice and California, "mutually opposed places and vast, mutually opposed distances [that] can generate sparks of energy that pique our ever-expanding curiosity and ever more active imagination." Born in Venice in 1913, Pasinetti had, in addition to his long career as a writer (he had been writing pieces for magazines and newspapers in Italy since the age of eighteen), a parallel career as a professor of comparative literature at UCLA (with a stint as an academic and diplomat in Sweden, where he spent most of the war years).[1] His first published fiction appeared in the *Southern Review*. In 1949 he arrived in Los Angeles, and in 1964 he was appointed to the Institute for Creative Arts at UCLA (he was also the recipient of the Fiction Award of the National Institute of Arts and Letters). "Why shouldn't the first serious bilingual novels about the international high life of post-war Italy be written by a Venetian aristocrat teaching comparative literature at UCLA?" wrote R. W. Flint in the *New York Review of Books* in 1965, reviewing Pasinetti's novel *The Smile on the Face of the Lion*.[2] As Gore Vidal has written, Pasinetti's world is no less complex than those of Proust, Joyce, or Mann, although his passions are as different as Venice is from Paris, Dublin, or Lubeck. (In Pasinetti's past there is also a thesis on James Joyce, completed at Oxford in 1934.) Oscillating between the large canvases of history and memory, with Mitteleuropean flare and a Venetian musicality balanced between opera and operetta, Pasinetti's virtuoso *partitura* perfectly embodies at least two of the qualities so praised by Calvino, lightness and quickness (not to mention multiplicity).

NOTES

1. In addition to *Melodramma*, Pasinetti's books include: *Rosso Veneziano* (1959, trans. as *Venetian Red* [New York: Random House, 1960]), *La confusione* (1964, trans. as *The Smile on the Face of the Lion* [New York: Random House, 1965]), *Il ponte dell'Accademia* (1968, trans. as *From the Academy Bridge* [New York: Random House, 1970]), *Il centro* (*The Center*, 1979), *Dorsoduro* (1983), *Piccole veneziane complicate* (*Little, Complicated Venetian Girls*, 1996).
2. The review is readable online at:
http://www.nybooks.com/articles/article-preview?article_id=12930

Melodrama

by Pier Maria Pasinetti

Prelude

Spento il rio civil furore

Amedeo Passina—a man in his eighties, ailing yet spry—has more than once shown me a small painting hanging in his house. It depicts a youth of modest build wearing a nineteenth-century officer's uniform replete with shoulder strap, arm-band, and sword. Amedeo believes this young warrior in oils to be his great-grandfather and claims he can situate the picture in time.

"Count Gregorio Passina. Captain. Civic Guard. 22 March 1848 . . . 2 April 1849 . . . And so on, *usque ad finem.*" At this point Amedeo stares you in the eye and translates. "*To the very end.* Until another 22nd. The surrender of Venice to the Austrians. 22 August 1849, at about midnight . . . 'We have always been on the side of revolution and the Republic,' he concludes rapidly and in a hoarse whisper. 'As a matter of course.'"

It was never officially called a republic, my cousin, Bianca Angelone, remarks. It was unusual, unique. Yet she was willing to bet that for most people the dates were no more than street names: in the case of 22 March the Calle Larga Ventidue Marzo from Calle delle Ostreghe to the Ponte San Moisè on the way to the Piazza, and in the case of 2 April the Due Aprile from San Salvador to San Bartolomeo. Besides, she points out, the key scenes in the drama of the Venice Revolution of 1848–49 are the liberation and the siege and the resistance—to the very end, as you put it—and the main characters—Daniele Manin, the lawyer, on one side, and Field Marshal Count Radetzky on the other.

And suddenly our minds are overrun with words, scraps of phrases, shards of images, like frames of comic-strips or notes taken in a far-off schoolroom amidst preoccupations and ironies, but also like bars of melodies or arias . . .

22 March 1848

The Austrian government surrenders its civil and military power on both land and sea

Hail to our Civil Guard

Fellow Venetians
I ask you to behave like men
worthy of freedom
your friend
(Manin)

2 April 1849

Venice will resist Austria at all costs

The first aerial bombardment in history

Welch Schauspiel! Aber ach . . .
(Goethe, *Faust*)

A thousand cannonades a day

22 August 1849
Hey, you in the gondola! What news?
The epidemic rages
We've no bread
(the poet-soldier Arnaldo Fusinato)

An olive branch in one hand
A sword in the other
(Field Marshal Count Radetzky)

A white flag
flutters on the bridge
(Fusinato, *idem*)

End of the 1848–49 European revolutions
Venice last to fall

Pace—Onore—Fede—Amore
Regni—Splenda—Ogn'alma accenda
Spento il rio civil furore
(Rossini, *Tancredi*)

The Field Marshal Count Radetzky in San Marco

Te Deum

The Field Marshal Radetzky! A walking legend. Eighty-three, hoary-headed, and sprightly. Landed 30 August 1849 in Piazzetta San Marco in the midst of a sirocco and flights of malnourished pigeons;

intent blue eyes; short, straight nose over a bush of a mustache; armor-like chest and dazzling white tunic with a jeweler's shop of crosses, ribbons, and medals strewn across it. The man himself, though, is simple, sober, in his past, in his deeds, "distinguished" as well, and affable, in his greeting to the dignitaries, to the Patriarch Monico, to the Podestà Correr. One of them takes the symbolic gold keys to the city from a pillow handed him by a subordinate— they lie on it like an infant's corpse—and proffers them to the venerable gentleman. Quadrilateral walls of men in uniform, bayonets at the ready, and, discernible perhaps beneath the porticoes of the Ducal Palace, stumpy little cannons aimed at the ghosts of stay-at-home crowds.

Which is to say, in my cousin Bianca's choicest didactic words, Venice had returned to the fold of the Austrian Empire after being besieged, blockaded, and bombarded—but independent—for seventeen of the twenty-four months comprising the fatal years of 1848– 49. The Austrians re-enter the most coveted city in the Empire. The Kingdom of Lombardy-Veneto, my cousin goes on, was the richest and most civilized component of the Empire if only for its splendid combination of capitals, Milan and Venice. It was perfectly natural, my cousin the teacher adds hastily, not wishing to overstate the obvious, that the imperial and royal government in Vienna and the white-tunicked officials and the noblemen and bureaucrats and civil servants, in short, the privileged subjects of Franz Joseph, a radiant twenty-year-old newly ascended to the throne, Emperor of Austria, King of Hungary, Bohemia, Lombardy, Venice, and so on—it was perfectly natural that they should do everything in their power to keep the Italian jewels in their crown, to administer, to serve such matchless property.

And I confess, Bianca confesses, that the Gregorio Passina of the miniature oil portrait, great-grandfather of our friend Amedeo, played his part in the military and civilian activities of the short-lived Republic, though when all is said and done he was not among the exiled, forty in number, or the voluntary exiles; indeed, he was soon permitted to move about, go where he pleased, leave the city and re-enter it without police interference, as a result of favorable action upon the request for a passport made on his behalf by his father, Count Benedetto Passina, and forwarded to the authorities by the Director General of the Public Order, the well-known and highly learned Doctor Martello, who approved and warmly supported Count Benedetto's petition *given that the father is a long-time servant of the state and that his young and unseasoned son, having given no one reason to impugn either his conduct or political principles previous to the calamitous revolution of 22 March 1848, had merely succumbed to illusions which in those unfortunate times invaded the minds of men more advanced in age and more endowed with experience than he . . .*

Amedeo, Bianca, and I—we all feel that the most important journey made by Venetian citizen Captain Gregorio Passina after returning to civilian life as a subject of the Empire was a journey he made to Milan, with a stop at Padua, late in 1850, because it was in Milan that he met a childhood friend, Maffeo Partibon, who was on his way home from London and Paris and who happens to be *my* great-grandfather.

Bianca has been to America more often than I and has traveled the length and breadth of the place, and she tells me that her feelings about these things took on a more definite, vivid, but also agonizing slant—in short, she was bowled over by them—while in Death Valley one day treading the same rocky, moon-like paths followed by the prospectors, who believed they had discovered a short cut to the Pacific, whereas what they had in fact discovered was the face of death.

Forty-Niners those adventurers were called, because the Gold Rush took place in 1849. And it was while contemplating the two numbers—1849 and 1849, identical, yet separated by a yawning abyss—that Bianca came to realize how radically differing events taking place more or less contemporaneously can give radically different colorations and implications to the number dating them, how disparate incidents occurring at substantially the same time and at mutually opposed places and vast, mutually opposed distances can generate sparks of energy that pique our ever expanding curiosity and ever more active imagination.

Who, for example, was Maffeo Partibon, my great-grandfather? Remote as he is in time, I almost feel I can reach out and touch him when I think he was the father of my grandfather Taddeo, whom I can remember (it seems like only yesterday, though it is actually some sixty years now) painting his meticulous still lifes or, every bit as fastidious, flicking the cylindrical ash from his cigar into a silver ashtray. To say nothing of his wife, my grandmother Elisabetta, daughter-in-law of Maffeo the wanderer, of whom she must have been able to garner at least a fleeting idea, which she would then most assuredly have passed on in her typically authoritative yet rather vague tone, which could as well be deprecatory as laudatory . . . He was a man of the theatre, a man of the stage, but he would seem to have done a bit of everything . . . There are certain enigmas, even mysteries . . . He appears to have had acquaintances everywhere, another family as well, actually . . . We shall never know the whole story . . .

So here we are again: three voices, echoes in time, melodies and arias and certain recurrent fragments and themes, fragments and themes giving rise to the notion that begetting my grandfather was more or less an ancillary, accidental operation burdened with the shadows of a complex and probably theatrical relationship of the type that must also have existed between Maffeo and Gregorio, the two of them having come together after many years, Maffeo from foreign parts and Gregorio from a "fallen" Venice . . . Had they remained friends? Had they ever been friends? And why did Maffeo return to Italy in 1850? Why did the two meet in Milan?

We have letters from Maffeo's father. In one, dating from that year, he has visions of Maffeo braving the winds in open sleighs across the ice fields of northern Europe or flinging himself onto a straw pallet in alien cities, and therefore calls out to him, *Come back, my blessed Maffeo* . . .

In another of the letters to his blessed Maffeo we are drawn to, no, galvanized by an allusion, a name he prefixes with a possessive: *your Ifigenia*. Amedeo Passina's trembling index finger points to those words in the brief letter and states in no uncertain terms and one of his hoarse whispers, "Ifigenia. Therein lies the heart of the matter."

It must be age; age whets the emotions. When I think of those phantoms, I too am "bowled over," I too am in Death Valley. I feel torn between curiosity, anguish, and the joy of discovery. They deserve more attention than we have paid them, closer observation; they need to take center stage, have voices given them, life breathed into them. We shall see what happens.

Translated by Michael Henry Heim

From the Diary of Baron Scarpia

Paola Capriolo

A FAMOUS stage persona is the protagonist of Paola Capriolo's novel *Vissi d'amore* (translated into English by Liz Heron as *Floria Tosca*). The Italian title is, of course, taken from one of Puccini's most famous arias ("Vissi d'arte, vissi d'amore"), which Tosca sings in the second act of the opera that bears her name. Capriolo's novel, however, is not a readaptation of the libretto (based in turn on a historical melodrama by Victorien Sardou), but is based instead on a fictional document: the diary of Baron Scarpia, the chief of police who investigates and arrests Tosca's lover, the painter and "subversive" Mario Cavaradossi. Born in 1962 in Milan, Paola Capriolo made her first mark on the literary scene in 1988 with a collection of stories entitled *La Grande Eulalia* (*The Great Eulalia*).[1] A "magic" fascination with mirrored images is the leitmotif of the title story of this book. In Capriolo's fiction, inspired by such classic models as Musil, Kafka, and Dostoyevsky, we find an avowed tendency to theatricalization. In *Vissi d'amore*, Tosca is first revealed to us through Baron Scarpia's eyes, in the semidarkness of a church, her features sacrilegiously mirrored in those of the Virgin Mary, as painted by Cavaradossi, crushing the head of Satan (the serpent) with her foot. Tosca thus becomes the baron's "obscure object of desire" and an object of torturous speculation on the holy-unholy mirroring of sin and power (Scarpia calls his torture chamber "Paradise"): "The diary unfolds as a Gothic thriller, by turns brooding and suspenseful, in which tyranny rapidly descends into sadistic obsession."[2]

NOTES

1. In addition to *La grande Eulalia* and *Vissi d'amore* (1992), Capriolo's books include: *Il nocchiero* (*The Helmsman*, 1989); *Il doppio regno* (*The Double Kingdom*, 1991); *La ragazza dalla stella d'oro* (*The Girl by the Golden Star*, 1991); *La spettatrice* (1995; *The Woman Watching*, trans. Liz Heron [London: Serpent's Tail, 1998]); *Un uomo di carattere* (1996; *A Man of Character*, trans. Liz Heron [London: Serpent's Tail, 2000]); *Con i miei mille occhi* (*With My Thousand Eyes*, 1997); *Barbara* (1998); *Il sogno dell'agnello* (*The Dream of the Lamb*, 1999); and *Una di loro* (*One of Them*, 2001).
2. Lawrence Venuti, "The Villain's-Eye View," *New York Times*, August 24, 1997.

From the Diary of Baron Scarpia

by Paola Capriolo

OF HER THERE is no need to speak, but this cavaliere Cavaradossi seems to me now to have lost all restraint. His opinions, his suspect friendships, and now in addition this blasphemous gesture . . . I fear, alas, that the day is not far off on which it will be my thankless task to accompany the distinguished Cavaliere to the threshold of Paradise. In speaking of the other, the singer, there is nothing to be gained; doubtless she has nothing to do with political intrigues; yes, she is an accomplice of the Cavaliere, but in sins of a different nature.

Already the fact that a man of his rank should devote himself in all seriousness to the craft of the painter, publicly exhibiting his own works, is in itself a violation of the natural order, and therefore unseemly. Were he at least to refrain from dealing with religious subjects, but no, he has wished to install his lover in the house of the Lord, placing her upon an altar, and what is more showing an utter lack of regard for the very traditions of his art. Indeed, I wonder, wherever has anyone seen a painting in which the Holy Virgin is represented with those overweening features, those coal-black eyes worthy of Lucifer, or rather, since such a comparison would do over-much honour to the model, some lesser fallen angel? If the intention is to be reproached upon religious and moral grounds, the result, it pains me to say, is also repugnant aesthetically, as always occurs when the image contrasts with the idea which it should offer to our senses instead of supporting it. In this the good Cavaradossi has revealed himself to be a painter of oxymorons, a creator of artistic contradictions, as if enough of these did not exist in this world of ours without the need for devising new ones.

But all this is irrelevant, for I went to that church without even knowing that the picture was already on display; I sought out Cavaradossi for other reasons, and it was seriously negligent of me to have forgotten this and to have left that place without any further thought to find him. For it is my office to prosecute the guilty with implacable zeal, and those who might be surmised to be so with a similarly implacable zeal, and likewise those who might be surmised to become so, since guilt spreads like a contagion, like a cancer, and in order to prevent its further transmission it is often necessary to isolate the area of infection with drastic measures. Nonetheless, the uncontrollable sense of outrage with which I was assailed before that desecration might well excuse my neglect of duty.

The church was dark, there was no one at prayer in the naves or before the main altar, where the few lighted candles pierced the darkness with sombrely gleaming points of gold. Anyone else would certainly have concluded that no living soul was in that place, which would have been most likely besides, since this was a church that was little frequented. The main door was of a magnificence ill-befitting the alleyway on to which it opened, this being too narrow to admit the passing of carriages, while on every side this temple is hemmed in by the crumbling walls of houses such that as I entered I had wondered whether the eye of God might notice it, whether He himself might be ignorant of its existence or have forgotten it. It was moreover the early afternoon and long hot hours lay ahead before the celebration of the Vespers, hours in which only policemen and conspirators would venture out on the scorched cobbled streets, beneath a sky that the sun's rays corroded. But I am a hunter of men, from habit and, I dare to say, from vocation; I can discern the presence of my fellows, especially when they hide, with the same unerring sense with which a good dog scents the trail of game, and therefore I knew at once that, despite appearances, the church was not empty.

I set about scanning all the aisles, peering through the gratings of the closed chapels, scouring the pews to see whether anyone had left behind some object, a handkerchief, a fan, or perhaps a painter's brush; in other words I carried out the customary procedures to confirm what I already knew for certain within myself, that the cavaliere Cavaradossi, the famous painter and notorious miscreant, was hidden within those walls or had only just fled, startled by the sound of my footsteps. Indeed when the sinner himself has departed there still remains for some time that metaphysical odour thanks to which I have already consigned so many sinners' bodies to justice and entrusted their souls to divine mercy, and what I now perceived was without a doubt the odour of Cavaradossi, or of something which belonged to him so intimately as to be by now permeated with it. Of this, in fact, I had confirmation almost at once.

I had found open the gate of one of the first chapels on the left nave, and, taking care lest it creak, I had entered; from there, through the gratings which separated one from the other, I had been able, unobserved, to observe the whole line of chapels. I was untroubled by the darkness, for my nature, though it has a side akin to the bloodhound, has another which resembles the more cunning ways of the cat, and of felines in general, and so that I might better carry out my earthly task, God has given me eyes able to make out shapes and movements even in the dark. But scarcely had I crossed the gate when I realised that I would have no need of recourse to such faculties: in the adjacent chapel a long row of candles was lit before the altar, and kneeling at the first pew, her face almost touched by the flames, was she, Floria Tosca, the singer. Perhaps Cavaradossi had left her behind instead of the brush, a handkerchief or some other object of his. I deemed it a fortunate chance, since a trace endowed with speech is without doubt more useful, if properly made use of, than a mute trace.

I had seen her before, in the street or at receptions in certain patrician houses where she had made use of her vocal talents to insinuate herself, but I had never spoken to her, nor had I joined the crowd of those infatuated persons who rushed to the theatre to applaud her every time her name should appear on some playbill. Now however I would have to approach her and question her. Duty imposed it. Besides, the thought of this did not worry me, certain as I was that I would know how to resist the allure of that voice, triumph over it, bend it with the subtle art of persuasion to reveal to me all that it would wish to keep silent.

Even less was I troubled by the seductions of her appearance;

these had always left me indifferent, and against the prevailing opinion, I instead take it upon myself even to deny their existence. Female beauty is harmony, a limpid mirror of the harmony of creation, but Tosca is all dissonance and unresolved contrasts. An impression due above all to that mass of black hair which crowns the palest of faces, a black so deep as to provoke a certain disgust in those who look upon it, an impression augmented by those ardent eyes of hers, as if she were at all times intent on singing duets of unbridled passion with some invisible companion. All of this appears designed to be in keeping with the tastes of our times: the people have a surfeit, it would seem, of the simple grace of virtue, which is scorned as something cloying, and instead seek out morbid attractions which reflect vice, excess and an inner deformity.

And yet at that moment, seeing her rapt in prayer, I could not stop myself from contemplating Tosca with different eyes. I had approached the grating on tiptoe, lest she notice my presence. Her form melted into the darkness, from which there issued only her joined hands and her face, with the reddish light of the candles gathered upon it, and it seemed to me to find there an expression which was singularly sweet, of serene beatitude.

I had heard talk that Tosca, for all the dissolute life she led, was a pious person who frequented churches with scrupulous regularity, yet in this conduct I had always suspected a pose, an affectation. By parading, between her acts of wantonness, contrition and fear of God, perhaps she deceived herself that she could swindle the Father Eternal, or perhaps she hoped only to increase her own charms by adding a new contrast to those that were already in her nature, to pursue by artificial means the enterprise embarked upon, doubtless distractedly, by her Creator, when He gave her eyes and hair so black and skin so white. Now instead I recognised in her the spark of a real faith and it came to my mind that her piety would procure for her forgiveness for many sins, so that one day, should He whose irrevocable sentence I await judge me worthy to contemplate His glory, I would find Floria Tosca, the singer, the lover of Cavaradossi, seated, by virtue of that pure spark, in the circle of the blessed souls.

I started towards her, resolved now to speak to her in tones quite different from those I had at first meant to employ: not as the judge who addresses the reprobate to wrench from him the confession of his misdeeds, but as the doctor addresses the patient, or the brother a sister who has fallen but who remains very dear. I made up my mind not to disturb her at prayer, and to wait respectfully in the nave until she herself should come towards me.

When I stood before the chapel where I had noticed her I stopped to observe its interior. Tosca was still on her knees, engaged in reciting a quiet litany. Beneath her veil I glimpsed the outline of her shoulders and her head held high, lifted towards the altar where the reflection of the candles shone upon the cornice of a painting. She raised her voice a little at one point in the prayer, stressing the words with clarity, "*Benedicta tu in mulieribus,*" she said in that voice of hers with its warm, deep timbre, which for the first time succeeded in moving me. Obviously the unfortunate woman's prayer was addressed to the image of the Holy Virgin, and indeed, as I looked with greater attention, I discerned on the canvas above the altar a female figure dressed in a tunic of gold. I took a few steps forward the better to see it.

Perhaps Tosca heard me; I had the impression that she moved, but I took no notice, nor was I troubled by the thought of having broken into her prayer. I stared at the picture with incredulity and anger, with my blood running cold, wondering how Cavaradossi could have dared to give to the Mother of God the features of the woman who was his companion in illicit pleasures, and how that same woman could have dared to kneel at prayer in front of her own portrait. Because the image up above the altar, taking in vain the holy name of Maria, was in truth the image of Tosca reproduced with absolute fidelity, down to the long flowing raven-black hair, whose tresses fell uncovered by any veil around the pale white face and on the cloak of an indigo hue so dark as to appear black. In the ecstatic expression with which the painter had given life to the features of the Virgin I recognised the self-same one which I had perceived just before when spying upon Tosca, but only now did that ecstasy reveal its nature as in no way virginal. Each detail displayed exultation, voluptuousness and infinite self-regard: the fleshy lips, painted with exaggerated realism, seemed about to open in an ambiguous smile, and the eyelids were half closed over the glittering eyes. It was not hard for me to guess in what circumstances, in the course of what licentious congress the painter had seen that expression on the face of his model.

"*Benedicta tu in mulieribus,*" I whispered indignantly, and Tosca must have heard me, for she hurriedly made the sign of the cross and rose. Inexplicably I was unable to bear the thought of finding myself face to face with her and, quite forgetting the reason that had brought me to that church, I moved towards the entrance, almost running. When I reached the great wooden doors I stopped; all at once I saw I could not leave without meeting Tosca, without holding her eyes for a moment at least. My self-respect, my dignity as a man, made it imperative to remain and wait for her. I positioned myself next to the holy water font, thus compelling her to pass by me on her way out.

I kept my eyes on her as she came down the aisle. Just then I saw her falter, and I realised that she had recognised me; she too apparently possessed eyes able to make out shapes in the dark, like cats, like nocturnal animals. From the dark dress she wore and from the raven-black abundance of hair to be discerned beneath her veil, she seemed even darker than the darkness of the church, as if it were she who irradiated that shadow in the same way as the stars irradiate light.

Deliberately, I left the entrance door ajar to let in a ray of sunlight that would illuminate the face of Tosca. I saw her lift an arm to shade her eyes; then she continued walking, but more slowly. Perhaps she was frightened, yet her bearing remained proud, almost disdainful. She would not turn back, I was sure of it, she would not look for some side door, she would come right up to me, overcoming apprehension, out of some feeling not dissimilar from the one that kept me there. Determination endowed her demeanour with an aura of majesty, and as I watched her I found it hard to see in that haughty creature the woman who was ready to surrender so easily to Cavaradossi and his predecessors. I should rather have imagined her as practising that brand of virtue or rather that simulacrum of it whose innermost spring is a boundless arrogance.

When she arrived beside me Tosca pretended not to see me and made as if to proceed, but I was quick to block her way. I dipped my hand in the holy water font and held it out to her in an act of offering, so that she was compelled to reach hers towards me to accept the holy water. She did not withdraw her palm from mine immediately, she did not lower her eyes as I stared at her; she remained motionless, yet I felt a slight tremor in her hand. At last she removed it abruptly, and without crossing herself left the church.

Translated by Liz Heron

The Day of Thanksgiving

Paolo Valesio

THIS SECTION concludes with a more meditative piece, an adagio of sorts. Paolo Valesio's "The Day of Thanksgiving" is a fine example of this writer's ability to evoke a subdued yet intense atmosphere in what he, a poet and also an admired critic, would perhaps define as "poetic prosing."[1] Born in 1939 in Bologna, Valesio (like Pasinetti) is an expatriate Italian scholar, and in his distinguished career in the United States he has taught at Harvard, Yale, and Columbia Universities.[2] He is the founder and editor of the journal *Yale Italian Poetry*. Writing "in between" his two literary and existential homelands is the stylistic key to his work: "The dominant subtext of my works, both in prose and poetry, is neither America nor Italy but the interplay between the two worlds," Valesio has said in an interview. "'Interplay' is the necessary term here, because it evokes the ludic element in this constant back-and-forth between two countries; an element to be sure, that—like all ludic phenomena—is also deadly serious."[3] In the story included here, the other world (and the element of "interplay") is Canada (Edmonton), but it is also (as in a Japanese puzzle box) the image of a Buddhist temple on the slopes of Mount Fuji, captured in a photograph, framed and hanging on the wall of a North American house turned into a suburban shrine. Thus a tale of displacement, both geographic and emotional, turns into a tale of spiritual quest. As a faithful witness to this time of dislocation, Valesio is currently engaged in writing a sort of cultural diary (being published in the art magazine *Anfione Zeto*), composed of five parallel journals, a literary pentagram in five voices.

NOTES

1. The reference is to *Prose in poesia* (Milan: Guanda, 1979).
2. His narrative works include two novels, *L'ospedale di Manhattan* (*Manhattan Hospital*, 1978) and *Il regno doloroso* (*The Painful Kingdom*, 1983), and a number of short stories and poetic prosing published in various literary journals. Most notably: *Dialogo del falco e dell'avvoltoio* (*Dialogue of the Falcon and the Vulture*, 1987), *La campagna dell'Ottantasette: Poesie e prose-in-poesia* (*The Campaign of Eighty-seven: Poems and Poetic Prosing*, 1990). In addition to his fictional output, Valesio is also an accomplished poet. Available in English are: *Nightchant: Selected Poems* (Edmonton: Snowapple Press, 1995) and *Every Afternoon Can Make the World Stand Still: Thirty Sonnets, 1987-2000*, bilingual ed., trans. Michael Palma, intro. John Hollander (Stony Brook, N.Y.: Gradiva, 2002).
3. The interview can be read in "New Italian Fiction," ed. Francesco Guardiani, special issue of *Review of Contemporary Fiction* 12, no. 3 (fall 1992): 151.

The Day of Thanksgiving

by Paolo Valesio

1. IT WAS the first time in I don't know how many years that I had not spent Thanksgiving in the United States: in fact, during that tail end of November, I found myself in Edmonton (the last real city in the northwest of Canada, just before the expanse of pine and fir woods, and, beyond that, the tundra). As you know, Thanksgiving Day in Canada is celebrated in October rather than November. Therefore, on that day—a freezing November 22—a whole lot of nothing would be celebrated in Edmonton, while everyone in the States would be sitting round the Thanksgiving dinner table.

Call me sentimental, go ahead and say that I have been Americanized (actually, please don't say it, because it isn't true); but I had become attached to the afternoon ritual of the Thanksgiving meal (which, in the United States, is consumed even more religiously than Christmas dinner); and I felt much lonelier than I had expected.

I had gone there to close a business deal: the exclusive distribution rights in Canada of my computer program for writing personalized booklets about children. Not generic books *for* children, but specific books *about* children: there's my whole idea—small, granted, but quite successful in the United States. The whole concept hinges on one simple but basic phenomenon: nothing fascinates a child more—or rather, to be precise, nothing bores him less—than a very simple story where he or she is at the center (a story that "places him in the role of the main character," as I state in my advertising brochure).

I ask the parents or the grandparents of a child who has just begun to read to furnish me with some background information: first and last name, naturally, and then place of birth, name of the doctor that brought him into this world, weight at birth, and so on. I insert this data in the program I designed, and print a nice small book (with a more or less fancy cover, depending on the price they are willing to pay), that the child in question will never tire of reading and rereading with the help of grandparents or parents, making giant strides in his reading ability.

After a stopover in Toronto, with a flight from New York, I had landed in Edmonton, as I was saying, to sign the papers that would have given me the exclusive rights in Canada for this program which was already reaping benefits in the United States. Everything seemed ready, but then suddenly they asked for another forty-eight hours before the final signing. And so, besides worrying that they might go back on their word, I had to spend a Thanksgiving Day in sub-zero weather without any celebration.

I had just left the elevator and was walking through the hallway of the guesthouse near the university (my trip was on the company's account), when a woman, on her way to the elevator, ran into me. I noticed her in that moment with a clarity to which later conversations added nothing: she was minute and taut, as if distilled inside her own features (her face, too long to be beautiful). Everything about her proclaimed she was a nice and proper (married?) woman. She was wearing one of those sleeping-bag coats that enclose people in a kind of large tube; dark blue and puffy all over. She was carrying a very small patent-leather purse hanging from a thin chain. What struck me (in every sense) was the harshness of the contact: she hit my body with the force of a tall and large man, rather than that of the small, tiny woman she was. Stunned, I turned around. I saw her migrate towards the two elevator doors with a tilting motion that steadily became ever more askew. Was she drunk? That seemed very strange to me: such a prim-looking young lady, and at nine-thirty in the morning.

But in the next instant her drift became a careening
(and I felt it reverberating in my guts as if it were happening to me: the nucleus, pearled and minuscule, inside the shell of the nightmare)
    and she began to kneel softly,
(I saw lotus flowers—I guess I woke up poetic that morning—you know, the ones that grow in ponds and no sooner have they bloomed and begun floating, than they begin to bend their heads)
    onto the purplish wall-to-wall carpet under the row of arm chairs, unable to make it to the elevators.

Leaping forward I reached and took hold of her just before her body hit the ground
(meanwhile the purse had slipped, dark, small and shiny, onto the floor, and here again I thought of a flower, but the chain kept it tied to the wrist of the swooning one.)

You always forget how heavy the body becomes when it is abandoned. That young woman, *petite* (as the saleswomen say over here) had suddenly become large and looming, and I felt as if I were holding a dolphin (a strange coincidence: I was going to see dolphins a few hours later—which I did not at all expect to find up here—in a vast aquarium right in the middle of the largest mall in the world, the pride of the city of Edmonton), or the capital of a pillar.

Incidents such as this one reveal how petty we are in our normal and instinctive state. As I was trying to hold her up, I was not actually thinking of her but, more selfishly, of myself. I felt awkward in that position, and particularly embarrassed by the fact that I was showing (whom?) that I was not strong enough to hold her up.

I sensed, nonetheless, that the best I could do was to protect her from a violent crash (an "impact," as I say when I explain the effect of the products I sell). Thus, holding her by the waist, I was able to transform her fall into a gentle settling down. Meanwhile, "This woman is ill," I was saying loudly (in a baritone, the calm voice of a person keeping the situation under control), looking at the back of her head, but actually addressing the receptionist who was at the counter around the corner, beyond the row of chairs.

"No, no thank you, it's not necessary," uttered the young woman (who had already leaned her right hand on the ground to support herself), with a thin thread of a voice, yet clear and firm. I felt a little foolish—I must have come off as one of those people who, in the presence of a crippled or handicapped person (a "scartellato" as they say where I come from), speak of that person to others around him as though that human being were a thing, a log.

"But—are you feeling ill?" I said, with my hand on her shoulder. "No, thanks, now I feel better—it was a temporary loss of senses,"

(yet that is not how she said it; she said *blackout,* a word that for me was filled with violence, renewing the brutal impression she made when she ran against me)

"I'm only nauseous, I must go to the bathroom." In the meantime, the receptionist had arrived—a robust and cheerful girl—and I entrusted her with the semifaint woman, whom she led to the bathroom at the end of the hallway, where she stood guard, outside, in case of an emergency. At this point I was clearly useless, so I left.

(I went to visit the famous shopping mall with eight hundred and fifty different stores, where I saw the dolphins, and lost myself in thought, watching them as they played around with so much humanity—what if one of them were to suddenly faint in the water, what would they do, how would they hold the dolphin up?)

But I soon got bored at the mall, and a couple of hours later I was already back at the guesthouse, sitting at the coffee shop on the corner that was trying to look like a New York café. I had just put down the menu when in she walked, the no-longer-swooning lady. She approached me with a slight, timid smile, and thanked me. I asked her to sit down, and after that, the invitation to lunch felt like a natural thing to do.

Don't misunderstand: this was not an attempt to pick her up. My intentions, in fact, were even less honorable. Once, *less than honorable intentions* would have meant "the intention of getting into her bed," but such an intention is not at all dishonorable for the one who is entertaining the thought, nor for the one who is its object. What I was thinking about was not very honorable in the sense that it was a bit too selfish, too judging, too grossly astute. It was not at all dishonest, and certainly not unreasonable; it was a real feeling, and at least plausible, but not particularly honorable (in the basic sense of *honorable*, which shuns common sense and has more to do with fervor and valor).

I mean: what I was thinking about was to steer clear of her. This was not at all dishonest or unreasonable, although judgmental and, perhaps, too grossly astute. First of all, as I already said, the young miss, or Ms. (whose name was Manuela, if it is of any interest), was not particularly beautiful, although not bad looking, not bad looking at all. There was that certain slight asymmetry of excessively long faces, the kind that makes one look again and again, as if to verify that it truly is as it seems; as if a more attentive glance could be an eraser on a pencil-drawn sketch, correcting one minor flaw.

In the second place (and above all), there had been that fogging over—and who knows what lurked behind that sort of a blackout, that darkening? It could have been nothing more than a bad case of indigestion, but it also could be epilepsy, or some other similar serious disease. I would have never allowed myself to seek an intimate relationship with a person who turned out to be sick or sickly— whose reactions would be, therefore, not very predictable and could actually turn out to be embarrassing. I had promptly transformed a small accident, a moment in the life of that girl, branding her forever in a rather negative fashion. I considered her a lamb that one looks at with tender sympathy, while, at the same time, worrying about catching scabies (there you have it: the flaw in my honor).

But then why was I having lunch with her, and why was I ready to linger a while in her company? Not only because I was isolated in Edmonton, but also because I practically have no friends. Generally speaking, the people with whom I come into contact fall into two categories: those who are impressed by the complexity and sophistication of my work, and those who look down upon it. I tend to scorn the former and resent the latter. Those who regard me with condescension are not aware of the commitment required when you are a small businessman and inventor such as I am; always dangling from a tenuous thread of creativity. I'll give you an example: the deal before last—before this one on computerized children's biographies— was the manufacturing of T-shirts, which I undertook with a partner. In this case also, there was an original idea: we had found a way to print traces of cats' paws on the shirts. People came with their cats and ordered the T-shirts. We took their pets' paw prints and made them appear in three or four different colors, all lined up diagonally on the shirts like footsteps on a little path. Thus the T-shirt was personalized in a very special way, and if you think that this is not an interesting concept, then you haven't an idea what stuff New York cat owners are made of.

But the ones who think that I am doing a great job—well, they are embarrassing. I mean it: they seem sort of pathetic to me. So, it often happens that I find myself alone, and have therefore learned to enjoy the company of whoever happens my way, accepting what they can offer me in their fugitiveness.

Manuela, then: she was married three months ago (she described her husband a little: a great guy, a polyglot, six foot two, blue eyes and blonde hair; when she spoke about him, a light broke through and shed beauty across her face), and she was torn between the need to accept the position that had just opened up for her, right here in Edmonton (or losing the job), and the danger—beginning the moment she crossed the Canadian border—of being separated for more than a year from her husband in the United States. They both had Italian passports and serious problems with their American visas. (I made sure not to ask—given my situation, the less I speak about American visas, the better.)

A few months ago, Manuela decided to take the leap: she entered Canada, and was waiting to hear if her husband would be able to rejoin her or not. I confess that at a certain point I became distracted: I nodded as I listened, but her words had become a hum in the background . . . then suddenly I started: I heard some exotic word (*daimoku? gohonzon?*) . . .

"Excuse me, would you repeat that?"

"Well yes, of course. I spent a month doing little more than cry for hours every day, locked up in my room. Then my brother-in-law (my husband doesn't believe in these things) told me flat out: 'Are you seriously determined to get what you want? Well then, you have to get to work: pray!' That is how I began."

"And how long do your prayers last?"

"A little less than two hours each day (fifty minutes or so in the morning, fifty in the evening). Each of us in our own home, in front of our scroll; but once a week we get together and pray as a group. It just so happens that today is a meeting day. You seem interested: would you like to come with me?"

2. And so, late that same afternoon, at the time when, south of the Canadian border, the Thanksgiving feast is sluggishly and warmly coming to a close (it was nearing seven in the evening), Manuela and I leave her car and enter an ordinary little house in the suburbs of Edmonton.

At the entrance (no one comes to meet us, and the door is not locked), Manuela removes her shoes. At first, I think that this is the casual Canadian custom (quite justified by the contrast between the cold outside—about twenty degrees below zero Celsius—and the luxurious warmth of the indoors), of taking off one's shoes.

But in a flash, as I look at Manuela's light pink socks, I realize that this baring of one's feet must be a gesture of respect, a sign that we are about to walk across a holy threshold. (On the other hand—I think, as I take my shoes off, and as what I already knew somewhere inside of myself floats to the surface of my consciousness: there is a hole in one of my socks—who knows exactly what happens in these situations; is it a Buddhist act or simply a Japanese custom like that of taking off one's shoes before sitting on the raised floor of a restaurant? In short, in all these things—these rituals—what is the religious part and what is merely etiquette?)

The lady of the house (about thirty, sweet face, dressed in a shirt and blue jeans) greets us at the foot of the stairs. We enter a bare room (the carpet on the floor reveals the tracks of recent and careful vacuuming): aside from a few chairs and, hanging on one of the walls (otherwise empty), a framed, large, color photograph

(a large temple, as Manuela will explain tomorrow—which, she will add with a dreamy look, she hopes to visit one of these years—along the slopes of Mount Fuji, a temple that is the headquarters of her group)

and a small altar against the wall (the room is rectangular), which we now face: a long, low, shiny wooden table with a fruit bowl and small plant. Underneath a shelf, some books are sitting on the floor, and next to these, a few large framed pictures lean against the wall. In front of the small table is what appears to be a vase in the shape of a cone, black and in glossy enamel

(but it will turn out to be a gonglike bell, and the small white stick at its side will serve as a hammer).

231

On the wall above the small table is the second and most important component of the altar: a sort of wooden tabernacle, three feet
tall. Its two shutters are open and inside at the back there is a rectangular piece of cloth hanging, embroidered with Chinese characters. Under the cloth, two small round brass pieces rest on the edge
of the tabernacle: etched in the center of each is the profile of a bird
that looks like a pelican.

I confess, this detail disturbs me; that is, it disturbs the desire I
had of entering into a completely different and exotic environment.
I don't understand what it's doing there, this image that I've seen
described as a symbol of the Messiah. (Maybe it's only a coincidence—
but here we go again: in an environment such as the one I just entered, how can I distinguish between casual coincidences and carefully calculated correspondences? It would take months.)

And yet, man is really a funny creature: when the chanting begins
(Manuela had already explained in the car that the weekly religious
service of this group consists of a series of prayers recited and sung
together for a whole hour)

my reaction becomes the opposite. I mean, for a while I resist, re-
jecting everything that is happening around me. Don't get me wrong:
I have been baptized, but for years I have not been inside a church. I
am a free thinker (now, huddled up on the floor, and covering the tip
of my foot, I repeat it mentally to myself, "free-thinker," and it
sounds odd: but I can't get stuck on this, otherwise I will lose my
train of thought). Yet I never realized how completely absorbed I
was in that stuff—I don't know exactly what to call it: faith? a collection of tics?

Of the seven people present (three young men and, including
Manuela, four young women; and I, a little older than they, am the

eighth), some are seated, but most are kneeling on the ground in a way that, to me

(the only one to sit cross-legged on the ground, not for any religious reason or particular homage to the Buddha, but because I am comfortable this way, and, besides, I can cover the hole in my sock with one hand)

looks like a cross between east and west, because their knees are resting on the ground, yes, but the weight of their bodies lies on their heels (sort of partly kneeling and partly cuddled up). There are also a couple of tiny stools or stands made of two laths nailed together in the shape of a T, but nobody is using them.

Many years ago (when I was courting a woman in New York who later married a financier of Rumanian origin—but that is another story), I sometimes attended the Anglican services she was going to, and what had been most attractive to me was the chanting done by the celebrant reading the Epistle and the Gospel of the day: which is a way of slowing down, dreamily, the recitation.

Here instead the rhythm is the opposite: very fast, like a rhythmic race. They recite in Japanese (a language which none of them know, except for Manuela who has begun to study it): and the impression of nasality that these sounds create is enhanced by certain gestures. For example, once in a while, some of the chanters raise their hands (which everyone holds together) and bring them very close to their mouths, so that they become a filter for the sounds escaping, bestowing a slightly metallic vibration to them. In addition, almost all the chanters pray/recite holding tightly in their hands a sort of rosary or small garland of colored glass pearls (the ones they call "worry beads") between their fingers. At times they quickly rub the beads against one another, producing a low shrilling sound.

After about fifteen minutes of this rapid buzzing chant, I have the feeling (here is the rejection I mentioned before) that something diabolical is agitating the air—like gigantic insects flying to and fro, back and forth, invisible and with silver elytra (and who is making me think of something like that—who is now making me feel like I am submerged in a chorus of bronze cicadas—who makes me think in these terms if not they, the little demonic presences evoked by this non-Christian congregation?).

All around me, the prayer swiftly continues; swiftly, not hurriedly. There is no impatience here towards the form of the ritual (and how could there be, in people so solemnly committed?). It appears to me that they have reached a good balance between order and exuberance—a depth of participation. (There is an agreement here, a harmony between these young kneeling chanters—yet two have decided on chairs—as they sit with their backsides leaning on their heels and their socks standing out dimly on the greenish carpet: a harmony for which, at this point, about halfway through the service, I confess to feeling a pinch of envy.)

Why does this sound, which at first repelled me, now attract me? I am drawn to it for the same combination of things that first held me at a distance: a metallic stream like that of a gong (which, above all, must be the effect of these syllables foreign to me), a nasal vibration (those hands joined in front of the lips like trembling wings), an intermittent buzzing of cicadas (the rosary beads at times rubbed together so quickly against one another).

Yet there is a rhythm that is not only made of sounds—there is, how shall I say?—a scanning, a succession of different moments. First they were reciting by heart; now they are each holding a tiny book (almost everyone keeps the "rosary" and the tiny book inside a hand-

bag, a purse, or a pocketbook, made of leather or printed cloth—
this religion definitely has something chic about it)

so small, it fits inside a closed hand, and from this, they read.
Manuela, who is kneeling at my side, realizes that I am straining to
see, and, in a kind gesture, slides softly towards me, extending the
tiny thing, always keeping her eyes on the book, which we read together while I hold down one page and she the other. It seems that
the book is more like a musical score: there is no translation. The
minute pages are printed in Chinese characters, with an interlinear
version in Latin characters

(the next day, Manuela will offer some explanations, but in an un-
clear way, so that I will not really understand if the language represented by those characters is a form of ancient Japanese or Chinese;
in any case, it is an archaic language that is no longer used)

and the transition from one phrase of the recitation to the next is
marked by a brief tapping of the bell-vase. The lady of the house
taps them out; she is kneeling at the front, very close to the altarpiece, and generally appears to serve

(Manuela will explain to me later that this woman is a ballet teacher,
who has already visited the founding temple on the slopes of Mount
Fuji two or three times, and has been practicing this form of Buddhism for sixteen years)

as the leader of the group.

Even in the restricted quarters of that room (or maybe due to exactly that), the small black gong that resembles an upside-down
flower vase almost sounds dramatic. Once the booklet is read, it is
closed, but the recitation continues and, by now, I begin to recognize the repeated phrase—the one which accentuates the greater
part of this hour of prayer:

Nam-Myoho-renge-kyo

(As far as I glean from Manuela's explanation, this phrase contains the group's philosophy in a nutshell and is also a cosmic symbol; but this explanation will seem too vague and inadequate, so later I go to the public library to gather some information; the translation of *Nam-Myoho-renge-kyo*, to the extent that one is possible, seems to go something like this: "Long live the Lotus Sutra!" which is one of the most famous among the various sutras or short aphoristic treatises officially attributed to the Buddha—a part of this sutra becomes the core of the doctrine elaborated by the Buddhist holyman Nichiren in Japan, at the end of the thirteenth century, a doctrine which, through the work of his disciples, spreads and is institutionalized in many different religious sects within Buddhism—whew, what an effort of synthesis! I wonder why I'm working so hard at this thing.)

Nam-Myoho-renge-kyo

continues to resound in my ears, and I feel the ever-growing desire to become part of the chorus; if I fight it, it's because I am afraid of what was instilled in me as a small child and ruined a good part of my life: going off-key.

What is this phrase anyway? A prayer, an invocation of help, a magical formula, the agent of enlightenment or "the buddhahood"— a word which, to me, appears compromised by its funny sound— the fulfillment of the fundamental law and rhythm of the universe? The easiest solution—that of the faithful, such as Manuela, and of the encyclopedists, such as the one I will look up in the library—is to assert that it is a mixture of all of these things. But then how does one explain briefly what this phrase is all about? Listening to Manuela speak, I will learn the trick: define it with a foreign word. Manuela will tell me that this phrase is the *daimoku,* and I will think, "But, in this way, one incomprehensible formula is defined by another," and I believe I will be right to think so. But this substitution of terms works in any case, because, in the end, thanks to it, a bit of knowledge—or familiarity—is acquired.

Nam-Myoho-renge-kyo

some have arrived late, a little less than fifteen minutes left: no one turns around, and I certainly don't (turning to look at the latecomer in such circumstances has always seemed to me to be a rather petty act). But I sense that the newcomer is a woman (a certain reserve in the rustle of her settling down into a chair, a certain way of whispering), and with her a child, who sometimes huffs and snorts, and sounds like compressed energy on the verge of popping a valve.

Nam-Myoho-renge-kyo

Nichiren, the founder, had this phrase written on a scroll, which became famous. What we are looking at is a copy of it: the scroll constitutes the distinctive trait of the sect, and as Manuela, who naturally also has a reproduction of it in her house, will explain—is owned by every follower of the sect (along with the nice wooden reliquary and its altarpiece); the scroll which contains the power of all the Buddhas and all the Bodhisattvas, that is, those who have achieved the highest spiritual degree, so that each one may, in their next reincarnation, become a Buddha; the scroll which represents a center of sacred energy and which, in the terminology of the group, is called—with another unfortunate-sounding word—the *gohonzon.*

Nam-Myoho-renge-kyo

the child is now puffing more and more—he sounds like a small but robust wild animal (a puma cub, maybe): he knocks over something—it must be one of the tiny T-shaped stools—you can sense the woman busying herself to control him. I imagine a husky, tough boy, with curly hair perhaps, bubbling with energy; and it seems a rather bad idea to bring him to this meeting of sung prayer— a meeting which has a name (Manuela will inform me) that sounds like a gong, but even funnier, the *gongyo* (a name that the child behind me should really like).

Having decided that it would be inappropriate to turn around, I indirectly satisfy my (inevitably growing) curiosity by shooting a quick glance towards those prayer-mates whom I manage to see without changing position. I see only the back (quite broad, for a ballet teacher) of the group leader, and Manuela's profile. As for the others: there is a tall and pale young man, close to me, who has, I don't know why (maybe because of the rough leather purse with a brass buckle in which he keeps his "rosary" and booklet? or perhaps because of the tuft of hair tied behind his head?) something of the romantic about him, an air or aura of the sixties (later he will tell me—before I even open my mouth—that, before beginning this experience, he was a Catholic); there is another one a little further up, a pudgy man with beady eyes, who will turn out to be the spouse of the group leader (and who will continue to ask me if I found the meeting too heavy); there is a blonde, thin young girl who is seated instead of kneeling (she will turn out to be a college student whose main problem was her boyfriend: "What does the Buddha say," she will ask the ballet teacher later, who will offer a brief, wisely generic answer, "if you have a boyfriend who is really a jerk?") . . .

Nam-Myoho-renge-kyo

recapitulating now: the invocation—*daimoku*—which offers homage to the Lotus Sutra; the altarpiece, which contains the icon of this invocation, the *gohonzon;* and (I forgot it before, sorry), the pace of instruction—the *kaidan,* where the chanting recitation of this invocation and of other passages of the above-mentioned sutra take place. There you have it (she will explain), the so-called three great secret laws that characterize as such this particular current inside the great river of Buddhism.

Nam-Myoho-renge-kyo

the child has rolled, dragging himself on his knees at high speed— and, so self-convincing had my imagination been (with the stubbornness of all the fantastic and arbitrary turnings of the spirit), that I barely held back the jolt with which my surprise would like to express itself: that is not right, this absolutely cannot be the sort of child that should be present at a meeting such as this; he is not the kind of kid that should attend the culmination of this ceremony.

For an instant I am reminded of fairy tales where so many troubles and misadventures occur because of a changeling. But fairy tales have really nothing to do with what is happening here; what I feel overwhelmingly is—I don't know how to define it—like a nightmare of reality. For a few moments,

(but they are so intense that, on a certain dimension and in a certain sense, they last for the rest of the evening, they continue to flow in a parallel manner alongside the other different moments that actually succeed one another)

I erase that real figure (like a dissatisfied photographer who changes his model)—I don't want it: I push it aside, I throw it away, I obliterate it—and I replace it with the ruddy boy, all curly and full of the explosive animal energy I had so powerfully imagined behind my back.

Yet the small figure remains, because it is a real child: one of those whose face is all wrong. Not the healthy animal face of certain primitive characters you can find in the streets of even the most refined metropolis and which, in the end, create a necessary contrast to the monotony we cause by our own hypercivilized snouts. No, this small face is even too human—but it is stretched, strained, ill-formed and ill-framed. A little like a kid who is wearing a stocking on his face to rob a bank. He almost has no forehead, no chin, no neck; he has eyes like tiny furry buttons, cut in almond shape (these are the only Japanese-looking—actually, mongoloid—eyes in this entire congregation of Japan-lovers).

In retrospect, then, all that agitation from before (in the case of these children they speak of "Down syndrome"—to me his seems more like an "Up" syndrome, since he is so high spirited), proved something altogether different from a burst of springtime energy. What disappointment—it is something surly and sickly.

But now the little being has calmed down: he is kneeling next to Manuela, and evidently he has studied her very closely out of the corner of his eye, because he has assumed her exact position; now that the participants have taken up their booklets again, he holds it with her, on each of their palms has fallen the infinitesimal weight of a very small page.

And he has even taken up the chant! I am stunned at his ability (the diabolical impression returns) to pick up the rhythm of the chanting and its buzzing-metallic-nasal effect; he reproduces it perfectly, in measured and continuous unison. It seemed like he has had a lot of practice—and, come to think of it, why shouldn't he? In my imagination of a moment ago, I had seen, with my mind's eye, a small child suddenly introduced into an environment strange to him; but at this point, after the total reversal of this image, I begin to doubt all of my pre-visions.

For example: how do I know that the one who brought him into the room is his mother? (I certainly cannot trust the game of matching features, in the case of this crazy seed.) In fact, now that I have seen him sitting, so well behaved and quiet next to Manuela, I begin to ask myself "what if . . . " When she had spoken to me about her recent marriage with the strapping blond man, and of the pain and suffering the two felt when apart, I had imagined them as two whining thoroughbreds who in a year or two would start to generate a brood of impeccable pedigree.

But who assures me (here they come again, the not-so-honorable thoughts—since honor is naïve) that Manuela has given it to me straight? Who knows how many other marriages or commitments or relationships lurk behind her or him, who knows if this "he" really exists . . .

Two or three light and vibrant rings—longer than the others—of the little bell conclude the meeting. As we rise slowly (it is always rather difficult to untangle oneself from these positions), I can't help tracing a quick mental balance of this Thanksgiving Day of mine, which had begun in the most disappointing inertia and emptiness, and was then transformed into the most unusual occasion

(usually my Thanksgiving Days have a gleam of purplish luminosity: the red of flowers and table ornaments, and strong wine, and the color of roast meats, and sometimes flames in the fireplace; this time, instead, the day had become oddly blue and metallic)

which promised to endure and prolong itself with a certain solemnity into the time of my remembrances, but instead is warded off with a sudden swerving towards an apparition that has provoked that slight sense of freezing in the groin, which happens to me as an aftermath of seeing wounds or deformities or degenerations (the various sorts of "scartellati").

And anyway, why should I not admit it? In that first moment of anticlimax at the end of the prayerful chanting, that appearance made me feel almost—and I would not really know how to explain why—as if I had been

(but the next day, when, among other things, I will receive the news that the contract for the Canadian concession had been postponed indefinitely, and as I think over all of this, I realize that that sordid and subquotidian moment, that moment of quasi-grotesque disappointment, was the only point in the entire prayerful meeting in which there emerged a glimmer of what the Enlightened One, if we know how to listen to him even when he is silently pointing out with his finger)

swindled.

Translated by Graziella Sidoli and Stefania Stewart

EPILOGUE

Leave-taking

Franco Ferrucci

LEAVING THE last word to the Tuscan-New York writer Franco Ferrucci (b. Pisa, 1936, both a novelist and a prominent essayist and scholar) provides an apt epilogue to this collection: his is the literal word of God, taken from his novel *The Life of God (As Told by Himself)*.[1] In this fictive autobiography of the Creator, a novel-essay and a memoir to end all memoirs, Ferrucci depicts a God who is almost as clueless as His creatures (and perhaps even more so) as to the meaning of it all: "For long stretches at a time I forget that I am God. But then memory isn't my strong suit. It comes and goes with a will of its own. The last time it came back to me I was sunk in one of those late-winter depressions. Then one night I switched on the television set, and a firestorm of events burst before my eyes. . . . Life caught me again in a hypnotic net. . . . I suddenly remembered that I created all this."[2] God's last attempt at making sense of his own creation provides the compelling series of metamorphoses

which compose the tapestry of Ferrucci's narrative. In the end, God
is off to a new beginning. Yet, waving good-bye to it all, even Ferrucci's Creator (the ultimate traveler and exile) cannot help feeling
some nostalgia for the bits and bobs, the buzz and hums of subplan-
etary stories, all the unpredictable narratives for a millennium still
to come.

NOTES

1. The original Italian title (*Il mondo creato* [Milan: Mondadori, 1986]) contained a direct reference to the seventeenth-century biblical epic poem by
Torquato Tasso, *Il mondo creato* (1609, *Creation of the World*, trans. Joseph Tu-
siani [Binghamton: Center for Medieval and Early Renaissance Studies,
1982]). In addition to *The Life of God*, Ferrucci's novels include: *L'anatra nel
cortile* (*The Duck in the Courtyard*, 1971); *Il cappello di Panama* (*The Panama
Hat*, 1973); *A sud di Santa Barbara* (*South of Santa Barbara*, 1976); *I satelliti di
Saturno* (*The Satellites of Saturn*, 1989); *Fuochi* (*Fires*, 1993); and *Lontano da
casa* (*Far from Home*, 1996).
2. Franco Ferrucci, *The Life of God (As Told by Himself)* (Chicago: University of
Chicago Press, 1996), 5.

Leave-taking

by Franco Ferrucci

I DESCENDED along the small peninsula as it celebrated the victory of one army over the other, and reached the Tyrrhenian coast, at the mouth of the Arno, on a warm summer afternoon. As I wandered through that landscape that was so dear to me, memories swarmed through my mind. More than a hundred years earlier, on that same beach, I had recognized the body of Shelley cast ashore after a storm. I remembered my sorrow at that now distant event. I spoke with him across time, and my words mingled with the wind, confused among the cries of the gulls, beneath clouds shaped like roses. Not many miles away, another poet was now imprisoned for treason. I watched him from a distance, while he wrote his poems among the prisoners of that camp by the ocean. Perhaps it would be better if poets did not try to change the world, I said to myself.

Pursued by my memories and regrets, I had gone all the way to the pine groves that lay beyond Marina di Pisa. I was tired of my peregrinations and needed some rest. From the distance I heard the waves shatter against the rocks. The nearby village was plunged in meridian silence, and the sun reached me in fragments through the century-old pine trees. I would have liked at that moment to become a pine tree or a grain of sand or a thorny bush or a bird asleep on a branch. I was overcome by an invincible weakness and stretched out on the pine-grove sand. That is when I made the mistake for which I was to pay dearly. Right beside me I saw a lizard dozing on the sand. It seemed so trusting that in the end I fell asleep in it. I sank into my lizard-sleep as into a childhood bath. It was a dreamless sleep, fraught with oblivion, the true slumber of an animal.

When I awoke I was in the hand of a boy who stared at me closely with eyes that were immense and cruel. He was the leader of a gang roaming the grove in search of pine nuts and of animals to torture. Now I was aloft, suspended, kicking furiously. The eyes of the boy who gripped me vibrated, brown and greenish, beneath thick lashes.

I squirmed in the air and still hoped that the gang would let me go. I sensed their uncertainty. The executioner vacillated! That instant might have been the turning point for the world, but the boys did not release their prey. Everything was ready for the game in which I was to be the victim.

Suddenly the gang leader laid me out on the ground and began to cut me into strips with a sharply honed knife. What a curious sensation. Violent pain, then only a soft prickling as the blade entered my body and severed it into many fragments, like railroad cars detaching themselves from a train. The head was noticing everything. You see that I say "the head" instead of "I"; and indeed what was an "I" divided into so many pieces? In that interregnum I was separate and yet whole, held together only by the fingers that pinned me down. I still saw everything, in a strange and hallucinatory way. One of the boys had moved away from the group and had gone to vomit behind a bush.

Now that I was all cut up, the second part of the game began. After a pause, the fingers let go of the prey, and my body exploded like a firework. The pieces flew off across the sand, blindly bouncing about; only I (I mean, my head) did not move, but lingered to watch. So that was the amusement I had not been able to avoid at the end. I looked at my persecutors. I, a dwarfed and toothless crocodile who fed on grass, caterpillars, and insects, observed the giants above me with their keen and pensive eyes. I watched them as the fly watches the spider, already captured in the aerial and multiform net. I was a point in the trajectory of evil, something between a fly and a child in the interminable scale of violence, there under the pine trees and under the sky, between sea and countryside, in the ardent noon, in the twentieth century, millions of miles from the sun.

In the last shiver of my life as a lizard, I summoned the sinews of my body, like a defeated and dispersed army, and leaped into the pale animals with the cruel eyes. A piece of me ended up inside each one of them, and I walked through the labyrinth of their souls. The torturers of lizards were invaded by God. One shook me off. One carried me with him on a journey of which I have lost all traces, but which I will recall again when my story is written by a hundred hands. Still another deposited me in a drawer of his soul and forgot me for so long that when he reopened it he was faced with a memory that seemed to belong to someone else.

Through the pine wood wafted a breath of hope that someone would find a bit of me in a corner of the world, so that I would be able to recognize myself again after my innumerable oblivions.

*

One part of me remained hidden in that pine grove, close to the site of the sacrifice, within the soul of a poor man meditating in a secluded hermitage.

I go and see this man from time to time, and pray with him. God while praying is something to see. I pray to become better than I am, while my solitary believer prays for me to have mercy on him. Mercy on him! I should be grateful to him, to the deep probity showing through his face. "Have mercy on me, if you ever know me," I whisper to him; "and do not ask me too many questions! I wouldn't know the answers." At that moment he feels that God is near, closes his eyes, lowers his head in humility. "He is so unassuming," I think to myself. "Goodness is so bashful. That's why he seldom ventures out."

Another part of me wanders across the earth with an army of refugees and returning veterans. Some of them are escaping hunger, some are fleeing from the cruelty of their leaders, some others are simply running away from the enigmas of existence.

I leave the usual signs behind me: winter and summer, springtime and autumn, assorted missives that every so often reach their destination. Many of those letters remain unopened and pile up in life's basements. One day they will be burned, together with all the unanswered mail; and so the sheets of paper, the envelopes, the stamps, the postmarks, the fingerprints of the clerk, the dust of the cellars, the match that has lit the fire—all will return to ashes.

Occasionally I take a cab and wander for hours in some city. I do it in Lyons, in San Francisco, in Moscow, in Hong Kong. I look at people as attentively as I can. I go to the factories and look at workers, I go to the offices and look at business people. I notice the ways people think of me, usually without realizing that they are thinking of me. They glance at their watches, and they do not know that they are thinking of me. They caress their lovers, and they do not know that they are thinking of me. They wake up after a dream they have already forgotten about, and that is the moment when they are closest to me. People should not run to those places where divinity is celebrated! I am less likely to be found there than between trains and appointments.

Often I concentrate in order to become aware of myself. I do it in various ways. The simplest trick is to become an object: a mountain, an armchair in some hotel room, a house on the seashore, a drop of water from a faucet. But whenever I am at rest, something strange happens to me. I become agitated and feel an impelling force inside me like a buried fire, or like ice on the verge of melting.

I think of when I exploded over Japan, liberating the energy of my every particle, a bomb not much larger than a cake. As I rose again in the form of a mushroom cloud, I rushed away from Earth so as not to hear my laments and sorrows down there, in the suffering inferno that was also myself. I caught up with the pilot who dropped me, like the unknown father who in the time of times abandoned me in space to create my universe. I wanted to speak to him but did not succeed. I returned to Earth with the crew, listening to their banter from a corner of the military plane, looking at the clouds through which we passed like hurrying archangels.

I know the reason why the memory of myself came back to me while I was in front of the television set. It is because I also nest there, in the space between the programs, like a spider in a hole in the wall or an astral signal at the crossroads of galaxies. Television and the atomic bomb are different signs of my existence, and both show how difficult it is to grasp my entireness; as that bomb, I was to explode above another part of myself. Every time I see the mushroom cloud on the small screen, I see myself arising on the stage of life, like the dawn of a day when everything begins all over again. When I mirror myself in that way, I would rather be a flower on a pond—so calm and green and suffused with azure light—or the flavor of ice cream in the mouth of a child heading home after school.

I hide in the laboratories where the devices of nature are being manipulated, and I entertain the idea of an animal that can reproduce beauty and knowledge as organs of its own body. Then I remember that beauty and knowledge were supposed to be remedies against the pain of existence. What would they do in a world that does not suffer? I am now and forever the artificer of the world's imperfections.

I go to the hospitals to watch people die. Some take a long time, some do it in a second. Death walks busily through the corridors, in and out of the rooms. She wears blue jeans and a cotton sweater. She wears dark glasses and I cannot look into her eyes. I move to the maternity wing and watch the birth of children. What a fight to come into the world! Life is always here, and she is as busy as her sister down the hall, but her eyes are not hidden and I gaze into them. From time to time Death comes and takes a child or a mother away, or both of them. When that happens, the two sisters do not even look at each other. They do what has to be done.

If I am more curious than ever about what happens in the world, it is because I have decided that the time for my departure is almost at hand. By now everything is almost squared away. I feel nostalgic already. But I have no doubts about my resolution. Light will be my means of transportation, and I am entitled to an open ticket good all the way to the borders of the universe. It is a one-way ticket to the unborn world where I want to rest in the late ripeness of my years. I am not afraid of the cold anymore.

Nostalgia for love affects me especially. Lovers sitting on park benches, lying together in bed, missing one another when apart, have always had me at their side, and they've guessed as much. I look at children, lost in the dream of play, walking on the verge of creation, knocking at my door. I sit on the grass, and I am unseen, but I am felt by all of them.

Of all my intentions, at least my departure should not fail. In order to make reliable plans I use a computer, the most recent gift from the active and disorderly human race. It takes up no more space than an attaché case, so the baggage problem is solved. Still, I find myself ogling more recent models, the notebooks that contain more and more memory, entire centuries in a small disk. What would one human have to do to amass even a small part of such memory? If I put this question to the computer, it flashes and blinks, then stops, because my question has no answer. I have never seen anything less vain. It could become my best friend if not for its deep inability to make decisions. What if I found myself in need of counseling?

I go back and forth, make the rounds, close the doors, turn off the lights. My anxiety about watering the plants before I leave has made me overflow more than one region. My moving the furniture and my emptying the drawers has caused some recent earthquakes that could have been avoided with more caution on my part. I feel sorry about that.

I put away books, I switch off the music, I turn the pictures to the wall. Obedient to the signal, humanity has almost stopped creating, and feeds on the past. Scraps of discarded music and leftover pictures decorate the departure lounge that the world has become. The malls and the supermarkets stock preserved images of creation— endless warehouses of the useless and forgotten.

The New York skyscrapers rise ever higher, like the control towers of an airport. I often find myself on their peaks, taking my bearings, charting my course. I lose myself in fantastic conjectures. What would have happened if I had created two thinking animals? Perhaps things would have turned out better. I imagine, for instance, man and dog walking together and talking about the existence of God or some equally compelling matter, trying to overcome their deeply hostile feelings toward one another. The world would become accustomed to every manner of doggy development, including canine architecture and a running debate on whether or not foxes and jackals belong to the same race. Maybe the dogs would think of me as a great Saint Bernard type or as a mountain wolf.

The news of my departure is spreading around, although I have not talked much about it. Some react to it by pushing and shoving, as if they imagine they also could leave and are afraid of not finding room on board. Some think that poverty will make it difficult for them to find a place at my side and do their best to accumulate wealth. Some travel frenetically during their summers, possibly training for the greatest journey of them all.

I have decided on the date of my departure. The idea came to me as I was watching an athletic competition. Halfway between a hurricane in China and a migration of Canadian ducks toward the Gulf of Mexico, I took a rest, stopping in the stadium at Barcelona to watch my favorite athletic events: pole vaulting and the hundred meter run. They were both exceedingly beautiful, and in the pole vault a world record was achieved. As the pole vaulter ran around the track amid the applause, I resolved to depart on the day when the last record in that event is set—and that day will come for all competitions. I open the newspaper to the sports pages and check my travelers' advisory. The record is at five meters ninety, six meters twelve, six meters twenty! I vibrate with expectation, like the transverse pole grazed by the vaulter.

A majestic feeling pervades me. It is summer. I am flying from Colorado to Alaska over water, forests, and glaciers. The sun penetrates the clefts in the clouds. I peer through the white cotton, and all around me the interminable blue opens up. It won't be easy to abandon such beauty.

Confused prayers reach me, intersected by electrical signals. I can barely make out the words.

Translated by Raymond Rosenthal and Franco Ferrucci

Credits

Serpent's Tail. From *Camere Separate*, published in Italy by Bompiani, Milan, 1989.

Paolo Valesio, "The Day of Thanksgiving," trans. Graziella Sidoli and Stefania Stewart. Copyright © 2004 Paolo Valesio, Graziella Sidoli, and Stefania Stewart.

Sebastiano Vassalli, "Zardino," from *The Chimera*, by Sebastiano Vassalli, trans. Patrick Creagh, published by the Harvill Press. Used by permission of the Random House Group Limited and of Scribner, an imprint of Simon and Schuster Adult Publishing Group. Copyright © 1990 Giulio Einaudi Editore s.p.a., Turin. English translation copyright © 1993 by HarperCollins. From *La Chimera*, published in Italy by Giulio Einaudi Editore s.p.a., Turin, 1990.